THE BOSS

ALEX ROSE

BLOODHOUND
— BOOKS —

www.bloodhoundbooks.com

Print ISBN: 978-1-916978-54-6

CONTENTS

PART 1

ONE

The punter's face was hidden behind a £20 note held against the driver's side window. Kenna gave him a thumbs-up. The punter wound down his window, but not until he'd hidden the cash. A guy who'd been burned by prostitutes before?

'Full naked and I get to call you a bitch,' he said, grinning. 'A bit coarse, I know, but it's my thing.' He was skinny, middle-aged, with little hair and glasses too big for his thin face. If not for that slimy grin, she might have felt sorry for him. On the passenger seat she saw a red jacket with a name badge that clearly said *Don Jones Team Member*.

'I know your partner, Mr Jones. I'll be letting her know you sleep with women for money.'

The guy immediately fumbled to put his car in gear and escape. She watched him race away as if he'd just heard his wife was in labour. Once the vehicle had vanished around a corner, Kenna turned towards one of many grim, dark alleyways that separated old four-storey Victorian residential buildings and new commercial edifices. A big man emerged from the darkness, laughing. He said, 'How did you know his name?'

Kenna explained, which got another laugh. Ray said, 'He must be freaking out about now. Will you feel bad if he quits work out of fear that everyone knows he likes prostitutes?'

'I'll never find out.' She hooked her arm through his. 'Enough of this crap. Let's just get home.'

The quickest route home from the pub they'd just left was only a mile, but it meant walking down Western Road, a notorious red light area. Her husband had worried that they'd be mistaken for pimp and prostitute, but Kenna had found the prospect amusing. Barely a hundred metres into the trek, Ray had darted into an alley to piss, and then the inevitable had happened. A man on foot had approached Kenna and outright asked what she charged for anal.

'Normally twenty,' had been her reply. 'But I'm doing discounts at the moment because I've got syphilis.'

'You dirty fu–' The guy froze mid-word as Ray came out of the alley at speed. A second later, he was double-timing away. When Ray asked if she was okay, Kenna laughed.

'That was fun. Let's do it again.'

Ray wasn't as drunk as her, and wasn't game. But he reluctantly agreed and hid in an alley the next time a car – Mr Don Jones's – cruised down the empty road.

Now, as they walked home, three separate cars cruised slowly by, their lone male occupants giving her the eye. All in the time it took them to stride a hundred metres. Ray was surprised. 'It's amazing how many guys come round here.'

'I bet these girls make a pretty dollar,' she said.

'Thinking of a career change?'

'Maybe, with you as my protector.'

Ray rubbed his nose, which was a sign she knew well. His headache was back. She stroked his cheek. 'Poor baby. You need to get to bed.'

'With you.'

'For twenty pounds, sure.'

They both laughed. A short while later, when in sight of the junction denoting the end of the red light area, a small black hatchback with tinted windows came towards them. It slowed as it cruised by, like the previous vehicles. Kenna was bored of the game. If this driver accosted her, he'd get both barrels.

The car drove past, but she heard a change in its engine and looked back. The hatchback had slowed about five metres back and was turning in the road. Ignoring it thereafter was impossible – because it started to trail them.

'Maybe he's waiting for you to finish with me,' Ray joked. But she didn't find this funny anymore. Clearly no girl could walk down here without a demand for sex, and that just wasn't on.

She stopped, turned, and stared. The car immediately halted.

'What you doing?' Ray asked. 'Come on, let's just go home.'

She could see four men inside. She walked to the passenger side of the car since it was kerbside. The window came down. The man sitting within was as big as Ray, but he oozed a menace her boyfriend didn't. No gentle giant, this.

'Your kids know you do this?' she snapped. She saw he had something in Chinese tattooed under his left eye. 'Or your wife? Parents? They know you shag girls for money?'

His hand lashed out and clamped onto her shirt. She tried to pull back, and to slap those meaty fingers away, but his grip was like a bear trap.

'Oi, you damn dickhead,' Ray yelled. He ran to her aid, but the goon let her go. She overbalanced and fell, landing hard on her butt.

In the next moment, all four cars doors blew open, and three men were suddenly on the street.

Kenna and Ray had been standing by the end of a gravel lane between a tall house and a closed MOT service station. A wire-mesh gate barred access about four car lengths down and high hedges swallowed all illumination from the streetlamps. The gate was rusted and padlocked and clearly long out of use.

After being dragged down the lane, Kenna and Ray were pushed against that gate. The driver turned his vehicle into the lane, so that its headlights washed over them. The three brutes stepped back, alongside the car, so that only their outlines were visible beyond the bright lights.

Now free to fight, Ray got up to attack, but Kenna grabbed his arm. 'No,' she pleaded. 'They want to talk to us.'

She knew it from the way the men had moved back; it was confirmed by a voice: 'Listen to your missus. Now take a seat.'

She pegged the speaker as the smaller of the four men, the one who'd driven the car. When she and Ray had been bundled into the vehicle, this man had not laid a hand on them. Even then he'd appeared to be the man in charge. Now she knew it. They were boxed-in and the only way out of this mess was with his permission. So she sat and tried to drag Ray down with her.

'What do you want from us?' she asked.

The speaker stepped forward. He sat on the bonnet of the car, between the headlights. Enough light coated him to expose an ironed shirt, neat trousers, and a clean-shaven face. He looked more like middle-management than a gang leader. He appeared to be about thirty, like her.

'You want to fight, big guy?' he said. He pointed at a dark form beside the car. 'I can arrange that. I've got a man here who brawls in cages. But he's a dirty cheat. Likes to bite and eye gouge. You want to fight? Or you want to listen?'

Ray was still seething. He was a former rugby player, used to violence and not eager to back down. Kenna yelled at him: 'Ray! Just sit down.'

He calmed a little. Aided by a yank from her, he dropped into a squat. But with clenched teeth and fisted hands, he was still a coiled spring.

'That's better,' the leader said. 'This is my area. No girls do business in my area unless I say so. Eli's girls have black nail polish.'

Now she understood. This wasn't a guy who'd come seeking a girl and had brought heavies for protection. He ran all the women who worked the street. Her assessment of him as management was right, but his business was selling sex. She had been spotted talking to punters. 'I'm not a prostitute. I'm sorry. I wasn't trying to get business here. I don't sell sex. It was all a joke. Please, we don't want trouble.'

'Why are you here this late?'

'We were at a pub on Fulham Palace Road. My husband's mother's fifty-seventh birthday. We don't see her often. This was the quickest way to walk home. We knew this was a red light area. We just had a silly idea to pretend I was a sex worker and wind a few men up. We're both drunk. That's it. Just a joke. No harm done.'

'Except to my bottom line,' Eli said. 'I watched you mess with two people. Two paying customers. That's my money you threw away for your little jest.'

Kenna hauled her purse from her handbag. 'I'll pay. One guy showed me a £20 note. So is that the price for a girl? Two men, so that's forty pounds, right? I'll pay.'

As she was fumbling for cash, one of the shadows moved into the light. It was the bruiser with the Chinese tattoo. The same hand that had violently snatched her shirt now carefully

7

plucked the purse from her fingers. As he returned to the shadows, he handed it to Eli. Eli extracted something from within. But it wasn't money.

'It doesn't work like that, Mrs Barker,' he said, holding up her driver's licence. 'Those two men have been burned and won't ever be back to this area. Eli's girls are real good at what they do and men always come back. Week after week, month after month. Over the next twenty years, how much will that cost me?'

'I don't know. I'm sorry.'

'Not only that, but those two men will talk. Week after week, month after month. They'll tell friends to stay clear. Friends will tell friends. One day a friend of a friend might decide on some payback and hurt my girls. Or call the police so my girls can't work that night. Or scare off other clients. I'm not sure it's possible to put a price on what you've cost me.'

Kenna said nothing. It was obvious that this pimp didn't want to let her off easily.

'I have an idea. Perhaps you work for me for free for a year. I see you've got captivating eyes. They're grey, right?'

The coiled spring released its compressed energy. Ray jumped to his feet and pulled Kenna to hers. 'Listen, dude, she said it was a mistake and we're sorry. You're playing some game of your own with all this talk. We've been reprimanded, and we're guilt-ridden, so why don't you all now piss off?'

Eli laughed. He still sat casually against the car, seemingly not caring that Ray could have closed the ten feet between them in a second. His heavies hadn't moved an inch. Kenna grabbed Ray's arm in both hands, now fearful that Eli's lack of worry was because of an unseen weapon.

'I have your address,' the pimp said, holding up her driver's licence. 'You've been warned. You never again put shoe leather on this street. What are you going to tell the police?'

'Nothing,' Kenna said. 'Nothing at all. We're not hurt. We deserve the warning. You've been reasonable, given that we cost you money. We won't come back here. I promise. We just want to get home, that's all.'

He tossed her purse back to her – minus the driver's licence. 'Then go. But just you for the moment. Go wait on the street.'

She looked at Ray, then back to Eli. 'What do you mean? Are you saying my husband can't go?'

'This lark with the headlights and the licence, all for show. A fear tactic to convince you it's unwise to fuck with me. You seem adequately subdued. The big guy here doesn't. He needs further encouragement.'

'No,' she snapped. 'You can't hurt him.'

'Don't worry. No weapons and nothing too serious. My man will be on his best behaviour. No biting or eye gouging.'

'No, he has brain damage. You can't hit him. It could kill him.'

Ray said, 'I'll be fine, Kenna. Just get out of here. Wait on the street. My further encouragement will only take a minute.'

He was coiled again. Ray's rugby days had made him tough and fearless. But his anger clouded his judgement. He was outnumbered and these men were probably skilled at street fighting. She also doubted they'd be sportsmanlike if he damaged one of them.

She got in front of him. 'Please, Eli. Ray's learned his lesson. We both have. He's just drunk. You can't hurt him. It could do irreparable damage.'

'Don't throw stones if you live in a glass house,' was the response. 'Stay and take a share if you like. But it's happening.'

She stood firm. 'Then I'll stay. Beat us both up.'

Eli's eyes lifted from her to Ray, who stood a head taller. 'You've got a good one here. Keep hold, pal.' And back to Kenna.

'I'll promise his junk won't be damaged. You can still fuck each other tonight. But he won't be going down on you.'

He made a gesture and the three shadows moved into the light. At the same time, Ray lithely stepped around Kenna and leaped forward to collide with the enemy.

TWO

Kenna used her phone to light Ray's face. The damage wasn't as bad as she'd feared, at least visibly. As she used tissues to wipe blood from a gash above his eye and where his lip was split, she said, 'How's your head?'

'Fine. And the junk. They kept their promise.' He tried to laugh, but it opened his lip again and more blood trickled down his chin.

'Stop joking,' she said. 'Have you got the headache again?'

'It never went away. Look, I'm okay. Let's just go before they come back.'

A fine idea, she agreed. The men had left in their car half a minute earlier. She had heard the engine recede and now all was dark and silent, but that didn't mean the thugs wouldn't attack again.

She got to her feet and tried to help Ray to his. But he was stubborn and ignored her hand. Once upright, he was wobbly. He was much bigger and heavier, but she held him upright.

'We need a taxi if you can't walk,' she told him.

He started walking. 'I'm fine, babe. There's a supermarket

on the junction. Let's just get some plasters. You know, I could have beat that guy with the tattoo.'

'I know.'

'The other two held me for him.'

'I saw. Come on, let's walk.'

'If it was one on one...'

'I know. Forget it.'

They started walking and within a few steps Ray didn't need help. But she needed comfort and kept hold of him. They said nothing until the junction, at which point the lights and noise relieved her. She asked if he was okay and scrutinised his eyes to check for dilated pupils to try to determine a head injury. Yet again.

Ray noticed. 'I'm good. Fine. Outstanding.'

To prove it, he took her hand and led her across the road, and into the supermarket. This late, the twenty-four-hour store was virtually empty of customers and staff were out in force to stock shelves. The medicine aisle was free of souls so Kenna chose to tend to Ray's injuries right there. She ripped open a box of plasters for his split lip and the thin laceration above his left eye. There were various other tiny scratches, which she used antiseptic liquid on. To finish, she dragged him to the cosmetics aisle to apply concealer on a shiner forming under his eye.

'I've had bruises before,' Ray moaned. 'I don't want make-up.'

'True, but right now it's late on Friday night and you look like a wild boar. This is just for the trip home. Did you see the looks the staff gave us when we came in?'

'I did. But that's because of this.'

He tugged at her shirt and she looked down, then almost shrieked. Back in the dark lane, she'd used her fingers to clean away most of his blood and must have wiped her hands on her shirt. It was stained red. 'My God, they probably think we've been in a car crash.'

'Or we're another Fred and Rose West and we just killed someone. My turn to help you.'

He led her to the clothing section, where he selected a cheap rain cagoule. She put it on and zipped it up to hide her bloodied shirt. Job done, it was time to leave. The used items and the tag for the coat were run through a self-checkout, although the scale had no clothing to weigh and called for assistance from a staff member. A bored-looking teenager authorised the sale without a word or eye contact and they were on their way.

The remainder of the walk home used lit, populated areas, which was a comfort. Neither of them mentioned the attack.

Once safe in their own house, Kenna put the TV on for comforting sound and Ray targeted an old bottle of vodka in a cupboard. It was for guests because neither of them liked to drink in the house, but he announced tonight as a special occasion. Kenna agreed. Ray added blackcurrant cordial to his but Kenna drank the spirit neat.

They watched TV for only a moment or so before Ray said, 'Forget about it or call the police?'

She looked at him. 'I don't know. That man, the one called Eli, he took my licence. He knows where we live. If we call the police, who knows what will happen.'

'You'd rather just chalk this down to a bad experience and move on?'

'I don't know. I just want it all to be over. Do you want to call the police?'

'If we've already seen the end of it, no. To be honest, all I'm thinking about is punting that fat bastard's head off his shoulders. But I'm worried that something could happen. Those sods are pimps. They're involved in crime. They must have enemies. There must be punters that are pissed off with the prostitutes.'

Kenna understood. It was something she hadn't considered. 'You mean someone could do something and Eli might blame us? So you're saying the police are the best bet?'

He sipped. Shook his head. 'I'm just saying I won't relax for a while.'

'But if those men have many enemies, maybe they'll blame them.'

'Maybe.'

He didn't sound convinced and that worried her. Ray was certainly no criminal, but in his rugby days he'd known a lot of men and not all of them had abided by the law. He'd heard tales, some of which he'd shared with her. Neither of them was an expert in the ways of the world's bad people, but she was far more naïve. If he worried, so would she.

She didn't push the subject and they lapsed into silence. Decision made, it seemed. No police. They would see what the future brought.

Around an hour later, they were buzzing from the alcohol. Ray had flavoured his with blackcurrant cordial and it had allowed him to drink far more than her. When she announced that she was going to bed, he gave her a look she knew well.

'Surely not, Ray? Could you really?'

'I could. Couldn't you?'

Actually, she could, but only for Ray. She'd lost her driver's licence, but Ray had suffered far worse tonight. She felt he deserved sex, even if only to take his mind off the pain. It would help her to avoid wallowing and worrying, too. Hell, if they did something wild in the bedroom, perhaps that would give their memories of the evening a soft hue in years to come.

'Okay,' she said. 'But are you sure? You said your ribs were hurting.'

'They are, but we have to do what we're told. And that man said I could still fuck you tonight. Sounds like an order to me.'

She grinned and took his hand. 'You're right. And we don't want to piss him off.'

Ray didn't always do what he was told. Six years ago he'd been introduced to cannabis by a rugby teammate and had gotten fixated. Another colleague had let this information slip to his wife, who had a big mouth and knew Kenna. Ray had gotten slayed by his wife. He had promised to quit, but instead had begun a campaign of secrecy. An hour after Kenna had fallen asleep, he sneaked out to the shed and lifted a floorboard to expose his stash. Kenna was always moaning at him to clean the shed, but the chaos of junk and scattered tools kept her at bay.

Hidden amongst his stash was also a newspaper cutting that delved into the science of marijuana's painkilling qualities. Just in case Kenna found out. It was no trick, for dope truly helped his headaches and worries about brain damage.

He rolled a joint, sat on an upturned bottle crate, and took a deep drag. By the time the joint was finished, his headache was gone. Unfortunately, dope got him thinking deeply and tonight's events became his focus.

Kenna's driving licence was in the hands of a criminal, but why had he taken it? Ray doubted the bastard wanted it as security against a criminal complaint. Those men had attacked a couple in the middle of the street, so they didn't fear the police.

No, the man – what had he said his name was? – had other plans for the licence.

Bad plans. Ray had seen enough crime shows to know the kind of activity criminals got up to with stolen identities. The licence might be cut open and used to create a fake one in another name. Someone closely resembling Kenna could use it to buy products or sign up to organisations, all of which she would be liable for.

Worse, they also had the address. The gang could order items to be delivered and send men to collect them. They could try to use the house as a safe place for fugitives. Ray had also heard of something called cuckooing, which involved criminals commandeering a property for use as a drugs depot or brothel.

Ray laughed at himself. That was the dope talking. Maybe the guy with the licence had taken it for the reason stated after all – a threat against going to the cops. More than likely nothing would come of it. Only time would tell that tale.

However, sitting and doing nothing wasn't worth the risk. Kenna's computer had digital security software that could check if her details had been used online. Tomorrow he would do a search and–

His thoughts were cut as, though the grimy shed window, he saw the bathroom light in the house flick on. He turned off the shed light in case Kenna realised he was out here. For sure she'd come out and then she'd smell the dope, and being sucked into a criminal underworld would be the least of his concerns.

A serious need for the toilet woke Kenna. As she walked to the bathroom in the dark, light coming through the blinds caught her attention. She peeked out and saw the light on in the shed.

Ray. She continued into the bathroom and sat to pee. She was upset.

Ray thought he had her fooled, but she knew full well that he had a secret stash of weed in the shed. The place reeked of cannabis. When she'd learned he'd taken up the habit, she'd done the moral thing and warned him against it. However, she had voiced her concerns just once, then left him to it. She knew weed was good for his headaches. She had even found his stash and noted that he had a newspaper article detailing the psychotherapeutic properties of cannabinoids.

Unfortunately, he had tunnel vision. The article hadn't *promoted* the use of weed and had even mentioned that recreational cannabis could have detrimental effects on those with brain injury.

Once an intelligent, calm individual, Ray now had memory issues and was prone to bouts of anger and anxiety. So far these problems weren't really negatively affecting his life or his work as a builder, but they'd progressed over the years and would continue to do so. Ray continued to joke about his memory, especially when he didn't do a house chore and claimed he'd forgotten, but more recently he did so with less humour.

Cannabis seemed to chill him out for hours after he'd smoked, so she wouldn't dream of forcing him to quit. The drug itself wasn't her worry, but rather his reasons for smoking it. Painkiller or not, it would do nothing to relieve his other symptoms and would certainly not fix him. Nothing would. He had been diagnosed with early-onset dementia and probable (only a post-mortem could diagnose it) chronic traumatic encephalopathy, or CTE. There was no cure. And he would only get worse, and worse. Cognitive problems, slurred speech, motor skill difficulties – all lay ahead.

After peeing, she returned to the bedroom. The shed light was off, but she hadn't heard Ray re-enter the house and knew he'd realised she'd gotten up. He was hiding out in the shed. She lay in bed, stared at a sliver of moonlight on a wall, and considered the coming days. In the silence and the dark, it was impossible not to worry about what the man called Eli would do with her information.

There probably wasn't much he could do with the licence itself, although she had to admit she wasn't data or tech savvy. No, her concern was that he knew their address. He could come for something, and she was scared of what that would be. He had said her grey eyes were captivating. What if he tried to recruit her? Was he right now making plans to force her to become a sex worker?

Worrying right now, in the grim dead hours, wouldn't help. She had no idea if Eli planned anything at all. For all she knew he'd simply made a threat so there would be no police, hadn't even looked at the address, and right now the licence lay dumped in the dirt. Only time would tell that tale.

THREE

'Identify yourself.'

'You first.'

Alfie laughed. 'I'm not required by a code of practice to do that. You are. Just like you're supposed to tell me when you're filming me on bodycam.'

The woman now laughed. 'You're filming me. So we're filming each other. So why are you–'

'Identify yourself, or this conversation is over. Three forms of ID. I'll take the uniform as one. Shoulder number and name.'

The police officer jerked her shoulder at him. Alfie read the number aloud for his phone camera. She then said, 'I'm based at this station right here. That makes three forms of ID. The very station you're outside filming. So why are you doing that?'

Alfie said, 'My business. I'm not required by law to answer you. And I'm not in the station. This is a publicly accessible car park. Close the gates if you don't want people coming in.'

For the first time since the two uniformed constables had come out to talk to him, the male spoke. He gave his number, flashed his warrant card, and said, 'You know your legislation. Google lawyer. So you know about implied right of access?

We're now revoking it. So can you leave the car park, please? It's Saturday morning: can't you find something better to do?'

Alfie aimed his phone at the male. 'Trespass? A civil matter, unless it's aggravated.'

'You're aggravating us,' the female jumped in said. 'Why are you filming private police vehicles? I want to see your ID.'

'You're not getting my name. And why I'm filming is my business.' Alfie had had many conversations like this one, and he knew how it would play out, the route it would inevitably take. Sure enough, she turned down the 'current climate' path, and he couldn't help but groan.

'What's so funny?' she said. 'Don't you realise that police—'

'Yeah, yeah, police officers are targets of terrorists. I could be doing "hostile reconnaissance". You have a duty to protect this station, your colleagues, the public, and all of that crap. You said I looked suspicious. The straggly beard, the dreadlocks, the surgical mask: that makes me a terrorist, does it? Sounds like profiling to me.'

That got her. She suddenly turned defensive. 'No, no, I'm just saying it's a bit weird that you're filming a police station and won't tell us who you are. You've got a hand stuck in your pocket constantly. We've seen you video the private cars of the police. You would tell us who you are if this was all kosher.'

'Who says I've videoed anyone's cars? That's an assumption. And I don't have to tell you anything. Right to privacy. Your codes of practice say you shouldn't infer anything negative from that.'

The male officer decided his partner needing rescuing. 'We have powers to demand your name, you know? And to search you. If it comes to that.'

Alfie watched the woman take blue surgical gloves from a pocket. The bitch was really going to try to detain him. 'I hope you're not thinking of searching me, missus. Under what legislation? Section 43 of the Terrorism Act. What crime do you think I've committed or am about to commit?'

'I don't need a crime. I have reasonable suspicion that you're here for hostile reconnaissance. Under section 43 of the Terror–'

'A guy standing in a publicly accessible place, doing the perfectly legal activity of photography? You'll get sued for illegal detainment and search. You fools used to abuse section 44 and that got taken away like you'd take a toy from a naughty kid. You'll lose 43 as well. Go for it. In fact, I dare you to detain me.'

That got her back up. She took a step forward, and Alfie was sure she would have grabbed his arm and cuffed him. If not for her wiser colleague.

'Enough's enough,' the male said, putting a hand out to block his partner. 'Look, are you an auditor?'

An auditor? Alfie asked whatever could he mean.

The male laughed. 'I think you know. Bloggers, YouTubers. People who go round police stations to get a rise out of officers for likes and subscribers. The jobless people with nothing better to do.'

Alfie snapped his fingers. 'Yeah, you got me. But it ain't for likes. The police are public servants and the public needs to know they're doing their jobs properly. Not abusing powers with illegal searches and arrests. Like section 43, which you guys throw around like confetti. It's great for a civil claim, you know. I could do with a few grand courtesy of the Metropolitan Police.'

He turned his attention to the female. 'What else would you like to try? Section 1 because you think I have inappropriate items in my pocket. Some bullshit about a call from a member of the public who's feeling alarm, harassment and distress, so you can do me for public order under section 5? You're itching to get hands-on. But your colleague here is wiser. So avoid getting yourself a complaint and a court case and just leave me to film, okay?'

'Terrorists can pretend to be auditors,' the woman said. 'I wouldn't be doing my job if I just let—'

The male called her aside for a chat, but she made the mistake of telling Alfie to wait where he was. 'Whoa, what do you mean, wait? You don't tell me what to do. Unless you're detaining me? That what's happening?'

'No, sir,' the male said. 'You may continue your audit. I hope we pass.'

Said with sarcasm. Alfie had to strike back. 'It's a bloody fail big time. Now I'll go photograph some private cop registrations.' Alfie did just that. While the officers discussed the pros and cons of executing their powers, he was walking around the marked and private cars in the small car park, aiming his camera here and there and making a show of getting up close to registration plates.

Decision made. 'Have a good day, sir,' the male called over. The two officers started walking away.

'Don't tell me what to do,' Alfie yelled back. 'Until a crime has been committed, you have no authority. Next time I come, I'm bringing the pregnant missus and she's going to piss in your hat.'

The pair retreated back into their station. Alfie continued to film. One of the cars he captured was a red Fiat. Five minutes later, and watched by at least eight faces at windows, he vacated the car park. His parting gift to his audience was a big wave.

'Red Fiat Tipo. Here's the registration.'

Alfie held out a slip of paper with the vehicle's details. He was in the back office of the garage, a grimy, littered shitpit that was partly in such a condition so as to portray the image of a respectable, legitimate workplace. The man at the desk, watching yet another history documentary on his phone, was the boss, but he was no mechanic. His oily coveralls were, like the business, a front.

Eli took the slip of paper without looking up from his phone. 'Get stopped?'

'Always. No name given.'

'Upload the video this afternoon. Make sure the Fiat is visible.'

'Will do. Anything else?'

Eli turned off his documentary and called a number on the mobile. To wait, Alfie sat on a worn two-seater sofa against one wall. He had to move a car battery to find space for his skinny ass.

While he waited for Eli to finish his call, he fiddled through items in a clear plastic storage box on a table in front of the chair. It was property left behind by customers: coins, a lipstick, an empty wallet, all sorts. But not all. Alfie was surprised to find a driver's licence. And more surprised to find it belonged to a pretty girl. Kenna Barker from neighbouring Fulham was thirty and had short blond hair, and a face he could stare at all day.

He held the picture up. 'Who's this? Anyone we're interested in?'

Eli glanced over. He had to think for a second. 'No, just some woman. Her and her bloke were hanging around one of my zones. I was waiting to see if they snitched, but I think we're good. Just bin it. I've got the address if anything happens down the line.'

That explained why the licence was in the lost property box. If the police raided the place and found it, the explanation would be: some customer left it after we worked on her car.

After the call, Eli scribbled on a sheet of notepaper and held it out for Alfie. It contained a name, address, and a rank. So, the copper who owned the Fiat was an inspector.

'Tonight?' Alfie said.

'Tonight, so keep your phone handy and free. I've got a meeting so I won't be coming along on this one. On you go now. I'll get someone to call you back later to go over the details.'

Alfie didn't ask who was being met or why. Some gang leaders like to sit back on their thrones while others did the dirty work, but Eli loved to be hands-on. Especially if the job involved giving some cheeky bugger a lesson. If he was forgoing tonight's revenge mission in favour of a meet, it had to be something mega-important. Alfie had heard rumours that Eli planned to join forces with another London firm, so perhaps it was something to do with that. He was eager to know, but he was just a foot soldier, far below the required pay grade, and knew better than to ask.

He pocketed the notepaper and tossed the licence in the filled bin by Eli's desk. It landed face-up on top of a burger box. After another long stare at it, he left the office. Outside, he pulled out his phone and loaded Facebook. Thirty seconds later, he was looking at a profile.

He flicked through photo after photo, until one hypnotised him. It was a head and shoulders shot against a countryside background. Her blonde hair almost glowed and she smiled for camera with blood-red lips, but it was a colourless feature that entranced him. She had gorgeous grey eyes that sucked him in. He couldn't tear his own from them.

Wow. Kenna Barker was a fine piece of meat. Such a shame she hadn't left her licence here by accident, for he would have loved to personally return it.

In the early afternoon, Alfie phoned a pal to go play snooker. Snooker was only part of the reason however, because the boss of the place was one of many who paid Eli protection money. He'd paid for this week, but a little whispered threat could elicit free time on a table and gratis drinks and food. Plus, the girl behind the counter was cute, although she claimed to have a boyfriend.

His pal, Trevor, a Jamaican guy with dyed blond dreadlocks, had no free time. Eli had tasked him with visiting some of the girls to get their photographs.

Photos? Puzzling. Alfie wanted to know more.

'The boss wants them for someone he's got coming into town,' Trevor said. 'But ask no more, because that's all Dom told me.'

Eli liked to get hands-on, but he didn't have ten to spread around. Dom was one of three underbosses who ran sections of the firm in his stead. And Dom, luckily, was a guy Alfie could call a friend. He'd recruited Alfie right off the street a few years ago. If Dom knew what Eli had planned with the photographs, surely he'd spill the beans. Alfie called him.

'Eli's got The Magpie coming in for a meet sometime next week. He likes to have a girl or two on his trips, so Eli's arranging it. The Magpie's got a man coming to check the photos and pick a few. But you didn't hear that from me.'

If there was one aspect of organised crime Alfie found a little pathetic, it was crime bosses giving themselves cheesy nicknames. The Magpie – real name of Alan Marshall – was as silly as any he'd heard, but fool be the man who said that to his face.

Marshall ran The Marshalls, London's biggest criminal empire. Eli's 'Boys Firm' was in second place, but the chasm was vast. Eli had smart men, but they occupied the top tiers and the masses below were brash, lunatic. They were out in the open, in your face, feared by proximity, like roaming packs of wild dogs. They liked to flaunt who they were. Conversely, The Marshalls operated in the shadows, like the Grim Reaper. They were educated men, former soldiers and government operatives, mostly unseen. Publicity wasn't their thing.

Eli had near misses with the police all the time and various charges against him got dropped at the last minute because of evidence or witness failure. Scotland Yard was always letting it be known they were a half-step behind and gaining.

The Magpie, on the other hand, had been branded by the same police force as too big to chop down. Even if they could pin something on him, he was far from the public figure Eli was. Eli haunted the garage most days so he'd have an alibi for whatever timeframes, but it also meant the people with cuffs knew where to nab him. Marshall gave his orders from a secret location in France and no copper had photographed him in years.

All this considered, Alfie was a little perturbed by the idea of a meeting between the two men. Figuring Trevor might know a morsel or two about what the hell was going on, he asked to accompany his friend on the photograph mission. He asked no questions until Trevor picked him up and they'd been riding for a few minutes.

'Hey, I just remembered. I heard Eli is having some meeting with The Magpie. What's going on there?'

Trevor, driving, shrugged. 'I heard that as well. Not sure. They might have a deal, or be arranging a ceasefire.'

Ceasefire? Eli's remit was whores, drugs, blackmail, violence-for-hire, and robbery, all the heavy, in-your-face stuff. The Magpie was more cerebral, with a portfolio concerning identity theft, counterfeiting, fraud. Each guy dipped his toes into a little bit of everything, but there wasn't enough of an overlap to cause any tension. The two empires co-existed and mostly ignored each other and Alfie couldn't think of a single time when a guy from one gang had killed or hurt someone from the other.

'Nah, it's gotta be a deal,' Alfie said as the car drew up at a kerb. They were on a pretty notorious street – a given since thirteen of Eli's whores lived and worked here – but it was daytime and surprisingly serene. 'That's not good for us. Not if Eli's going to be giving up some of his pie.'

'Why? The Marshalls are bigger. If we join forces, we control a bigger slice of the pie. More pie all around.'

They got out of the car. 'I don't buy that, Trev. I say more people at the table means less pie for everyone. When one business takes over another, staff get lost.'

The two men walked up to a front door. It was always unlocked, so they waltzed straight in. Trevor said, 'I see where you're going. But in takeovers it's the higher-ups that get canned. Because bosses can cancel job roles, can't they? They can say they don't need assistant managers and kick out all those guys. Then they bring their own people in for the jobs and call them something else, like assistant controllers. The low-levels tend to get left alone. The bosses can't just say they don't need guys on the street like us.'

'I don't know, Trev. You can have too many plebs.'

The flat room they needed was on the first floor, so they started up the stairs. 'Don't fret, Alfie. We'd only get canned if The Marshalls were taking us over. I doubt that's it. Eli's hardly the retiring type. I reckon it's a caper. Some job that needs both teams. Something big. But we won't know shit until Eli tells us.'

'So why hasn't he?'

'Same reason my missus hasn't told anyone she's pregnant. We're waiting for the end of the first trimester. That's what some women do. So we know if it'll survive or not. Maybe this job could still fall through and Eli doesn't want people getting their hopes up.'

Alfie thought about this. 'Maybe. I guess we'll see.'

Trevor stopped him. 'Dude, did you miss my hint there? The missus is pregnant. I'm gonna be a dad.'

Alfie never found other people's good news worth knowing. So what if Trevor was having a kid? It wouldn't change Alfie's life, except that he might see his pal less. But he knew he was supposed to show surprise and joy, so he shook Trevor's hand and said well done.

They moved on, and thank God Sherrie's door was first on the landing because it gave Trevor less time to warble on about whether or not he and the missus were going to wait for the birth to learn their kid's sex. The door, like the one downstairs, was always to be kept unlocked, so again they just walked right in.

She was servicing an Asian guy in the bedroom. As two strange men walked in, the client threw her off him and scrambled for his clothing. If not for the way Sherrie giggled at his panic, Alfie might have smacked the bastard for manhandling her.

'Calm down, pal,' Trevor told the client. 'Just wait here. You can have an extra half hour for free. Just give us a sec. We apologise for the interruption.'

Alfie tried to get to Sherrie before she could grab her dressing gown, but she was too quick. At least he'd gotten a look at her pussy. He led her out of the room, with Trevor following. In the hallway, Trevor took a close-up photo of her face with phone. Sherrie just stood there, a little scared but without enquiry. Alfie got her fear. The whores sometimes never knew they'd fucked up until a post-beating explanation.

'You might get the chance of a lifetime in a few days,' Alfie said, just to calm her. Sherrie was a tiny little thing, almost a foot shorter than his own five-six, and he had a soft spot for her. She was the only girl who treated him nicely. Before he knew he was doing it, he had slapped open her dressing down and latched a hand onto her breast. She didn't resist.

'Dude, stop that,' Trevor said.

'She doesn't mind.'

Trevor clucked his tongue. 'Where these slags have been, I wouldn't touch them without a hazmat suit.'

Trevor checked his photo for quality. All good. He told Sherrie to get back to work and to give the punter an extra half hour. Alfie tried to slide his hand down to her groin, but she turned away and scuttled to her room. Alfie wanted to slap Trevor just for his presence here, because Sherrie would surely have let him have a slice of her if they'd been alone.

Job done, they headed to the next flat on the landing, where another girl lived. She was out, which was annoying. Downstairs were two more flats, one of which was empty. The occupied residence was home to a girl called Sharon. She was in, but last night she'd been beaten by a client who'd scarpered before Eli could send a man to sort him out. Sharon's face was bruised and unfit for a photograph.

Trevor and Alfie returned to the car and drove it just three houses down, to where another pair of girls resided. This time, when they just walked in the house and again found the girls with a client – both servicing the same man – the reception wasn't as cool. The black lady, Luiza, got her gob off the guy's dick and yelled insults. Even the guy started bellowing. Trevor and Alfie had to wait in another room until the work was done. Luiza came to them first. Even though she was naked, she told Alfie to get his nasty eyes off her. But both men were looking.

'Why just me?' he said.

'Because you're the cretin. Now what the hell do you two want?'

'Listen, you bitch, we can have you shipped off back to Honduras or wherever the fuck you're from for attitude like that.'

She laughed. 'Piss off. I make more money than you. There's only about twenty of us girls. You low-level bozos are ten a penny. Now why are you interrupting us?'

Once she knew there was a chance for a rich client on Saturday, she was all smiles. She posed for a face-shot and even offered to spread her legs for another. Alfie was game, but Trevor ruined it with his morals. The other girl, Michie, was also happy to be involved. Bizarrely, as Trevor and Alfie headed out afterwards, they heard the pair of women arguing about who should get the rich client.

The next house was four along. When they parked outside, Alfie said, 'What did that whore mean about me being the cretin?'

Trevor laughed. 'Sorry, dude. Nickname that the girls call you. You have to admit you're a bit slimy with them. Touching and leering. You do that a lot. You need to get yourself a girlfriend.'

'Fucking bitches. I don't want the hassle.'

'It's not hassle if you get the right one. She'll become part of you. I've got that with mine.'

'The controlling part of me, you mean. That's what your lass does. Controls you.'

'I let her. It's love, mate. Try it sometime. You might be pleasantly surprised.'

Alfie doubted it. But maybe he should give it a shot.

Inside the house, alone, was a girl called Leodora. Like Sherrie from the first place, she was petite and sweet and never gave anyone attitude. Alfie wanted to be nice, but he was pissed because of the cretin remark and knew she'd be a docile target. After her photo was taken, he asked her questions.

When she gave no answers that riled him up, he got abusive. He insulted her. He touched her. When she tried to get away, he held her, and at this point Trevor said they had no time for shenanigans.

Back in the car, though, Trevor got serious. 'That was out of order, Alfie. Why'd you do that to her? You crossed a line there. If she tells Eli, you could be in the shit.'

Crossed a line? These women fucked men all day, so why couldn't he take a portion? 'Piss off, Trev. I don't tell you what to do.'

'Just saying. That was bad.'

'Leave it. Start driving.'

For the first time ever, there was tension between the two men. The next location was two miles away and they covered it in silence. When they parked outside another whorehouse on another estate, Trevor said, 'You on the cop job with me tonight?'

Alfie knew his pal was trying to make amends. Which meant Trevor knew he'd been wrong to reprimand him. Alfie let his anger subside. 'Yeah. I arranged that bastard, didn't I? Got the copper's reg. So Eli says I get to go into the guy's house first.'

Eli. He would normally jump at a chance to join a mission like the cop smashing. Instead, he'd backed out to have a meeting with one of The Magpie's top boys. Alfie's worries came back. If there was some kind of joining of forces, The Magpie was going to have a big say in the structure of the gangs. Personnel would be cut, and people like Alfie and Trevor were bottom-rung scum with nothing to offer.

The other day, Eli's nineteen-year-old sister had borrowed his Porsche to show off to her friends. The three girls were waiting at traffic lights at a junction when a man in casual clothing got out of the car in front and approached.

Fascinated, she buzzed down her window to speak to him. She expected him to praise the vehicle. He didn't.

The bright sky must have made him unable to see her face through the windscreen, because he was surprised to see who sat behind the wheel. 'Where's your brother? Up to no good, no doubt,' he said.

'And who are you?' she asked.

'Just one of the men who'll be in court when he goes down. Do me a favour and remind him he's an evil lowlife sack of shit, please. I get the impression he's unaware.'

And with that, he went back to his car. She was determined to follow him, see if she couldn't get an address for her brother, but the driver got across the junction in the nick of time, leaving her trapped at another red light. However, she noticed his car take a turn fifty metres up the road. Into a police station.

When she told Eli the news, at first he was angry with her. How many times had he warned her to be careful?

'But I didn't know he was a copper at first,' was her defence.

'Which is worse. The police just want information. Until he was a cop, that man was a stranger. What did I tell you about strangers?'

He was intensely secretive and what she knew about his work came from the grapevine, but one thing he had told her was that he had enemies. The type of people who would target not just him but also his family. He put a lot of work into keeping them safe, and she had taken a massive risk by just sitting at traffic lights, in a car the Boys Firm boss was known to drive, as an unknown man approached. She was lucky he'd been a cop and not someone with vengeance in his blood.

'Well, you shouldn't have lent it to me.'

'Lesson learned. Keep those memories of what the Porsche

felt like.'

She knew her brother couldn't let the matter lie. He would have to save face with a revenge attack. When he demanded to know which police station and what type of car, she refused. He couldn't believe it.

But she stuck to her guns. 'Give me the Porsche for another week, I'll give you the details.'

He tried to hold out, but she was right. He tossed her the keys, and she gave him Goddard Street cop shop and a red Fiat. The next morning he sent Alfie to get the registration plate. Alfie was an auditor and his presence at the station wouldn't be connected to the copper's tragic fate. Once Eli had the name Inspector James Bunyan, who had headed up an investigation into one of Eli's robberies a year ago, finding an address was easy.

Inspector Bunyan's home was nothing special. A bland semi in a standard housing estate. Sweet, though, was that the street curved around one side of a children's playpark, so Eli had his approach method. His people would park on the far side of the park and cross it to reach Bunyan's back yard.

Four guys would do. Three would enter the home and snatch Bunyan, and haul him out to the street as the driver brought the car around. He picked his guys and sat them down to drill the plan. They would meet at midnight to do the job. Alfie couldn't wait. Because he had found Bunyan's registration, he would be the guy who kicked in the door and roused the cop from bed. And he'd have his best mate by his side.

It wasn't to be. Around ten that evening, as Alfie was getting dressed for the midnight meet, Trevor called with bad news.

'I'm off the job, Alfie. Got another one on. Eli just said so.'

'What job?'

'I wasn't told much. Eli's taking the lead on the new job, so you know how it is. Bummer. I wanted to do that copper in.'

Eli was taking command of a different job tonight? Something to do with his meeting with one of The Magpie's men? Sometimes, if Eli was mission lead, he would keep the details to himself and dictate orders on the fly. Whatever it was, it was juicy enough that Eli was willing to miss out on operation cop-smack. He asked how much Trevor knew.

'Just that it's got something to do with a house we have to break into.' Trevor spoke one more sentence, and suddenly Alfie didn't care about some copper. He hung up on Trevor and called Dom, Eli's main right-hand man. Dom answered with, 'You on your way to the meet? Don't say there's a fucking problem.'

'No, but I just heard about another mission tonight. I want on that one instead.'

'Too late, Alfie. We've got our team. And we don't go changing roles around at the last minute. This ain't Asda, you know.'

'Trevor's on the job. Swap him out for me. He knows the details of the copper job. Trevor wants the copper and I want this one. You've got two guys who want what the other's got.'

Dom wasn't happy about a pair of guys moaning over who did what job, but he agreed to ask Eli. Twenty minutes later, the answer came back. A big, fat yes, which put a smile on Alfie's face. Dom told him where and when and hung up.

Some slapper whose driver's licence was lying around in Eli's office, Trevor had said. He'd had no idea what that meant, but Alfie knew. Surely the driver's licence in question was the one he'd seen earlier at the garage. The sweet, grey-eyed girl. She must have snitched to the police or told someone else, and now she was due a serious heaping of trouble. It would be a shame to ruin that pretty face, but she had been warned.

It was good news for Alfie, though. He'd hoped to meet her one day, and tonight he'd get that chance.

FOUR

Earthquake. That was Ray's first waking thought, until his brain got on track and he realised Kenna was shaking him. He stared up at her face, barely visible in the dark.

'I left my phone at theirs,' she said.

Groggy, he croaked, 'We'll get it tomorrow. At whose house?'

'No, downstairs,' she said. He realised he'd misheard. Her voice had been a whisper, but full of tension. 'Someone's downstairs!'

That woke him fully, as effective as a bucket of water. He sat up fast. Someone downstairs? He cocked an ear. 'I can't hear anything–'

–and then he did. A creak that he knew was the door to the kitchen opening. Ray got out of bed, and cursed as the floor made a creak of its own. If someone was downstairs, now they knew the residents were awake. He grabbed his phone off the floor and immediately noticed the screen said NO NETWORK.

'What do we do?' Kenna said. Wait them out? Shall we block the door?'

'I need to check. It might be nothing. Maybe a window is open and letting in a draught.' He couldn't remember if he'd shut all the windows. Didn't matter. Someone was in the house, and there wasn't a chance in hell he'd hide up here and let some scumbag help himself to their belongings.

He went to the bedroom door and opened it. The hallway was dark, the other three rooms closed-off. He moved to the top of the stairs and stared into the blackness below.

Nothing. He started down the stairs, nice and slow. His phone was still in his hand, but still it hadn't connected to a network. He had 999 already on the screen, ready to hit the call button in a flash. Sometimes burglars operated in groups. If it was a lone guy down there, there would be no rush. Ray would need a little time to teach the scum the error of his ways.

At the bottom of the stairs, he saw the living room door was open. The room appeared to be dark and empty. He looked up the stairs and saw Kenna at the top, holding her curling tongs as a weapon. He signalled for her to wait.

He approached the door and fed a hand through, to feel on the inner wall for the light switch. He wouldn't step inside until he was certain the room was empty. When he snapped it on, he saw only his own furniture and wallpaper. No scumbag with a swag bag.

That was when hands closed on his own and yanked him into the room.

'Come on down, baby,' Ray called out. 'It's okay. Bring your phone.'

She'd heard the other voices. Sounds of scuffling that clearly painted an image of Ray struggling with someone. A shout of pain that wasn't her husband's. Despite having no signal on her phone, she had tried to call 999, but even that had failed to connect.

She had been buzzing with panic, but now it subsided. It had sounded like more than one burglar down there, but Ray had fought them off. In her dressing gown, she raced down the stairs, asking if he was okay, and fully expected to enter the living room to find him towering over a pair of subdued drug addicts.

She barged open the door – and froze. She saw four men in black clothing and balaclavas. Two stood, one seemed to be perusing the contents of their bookcase, and the fourth sat comfortably in an armchair. He had a small gun pointed at Ray, who was on the sofa. He didn't look hurt. The scene, while terrifying, was easy to diagnose in that first shocking second: checkmate. Without prompt, she walked to the sofa and sat by her husband.

'I had to call you or they'd have gone up,' he said. She took his hand to show him she understood.

One of the men approached and squatted before her, his hand held out. The way his balaclava was lumpen in the face and head, she knew he was bearded and had a lot of hair, She also knew he wanted the phone. He got it.

'Thank you,' he said. 'I love your eyes, by the way.' He stepped away and handed the phone to the gunman, who was obviously the leader of this gang. The man put her device next to Ray's on the arm of the chair. Then he lifted a small black device and pressed a button. She figured it must be a signal jammer, which pinpointed these men as professionals. Which might mean they could be reasoned with.

'What do you want?' she said. 'Take it. We won't try to stop you.'

The gunman showed her a card before tossing it on the floor. 'We don't want this. You can have this back.'

It was her driving licence on the floor, but this information wasn't what told her who this man was. He had a voice she would never forget. Her panic rose again, and beside her she felt the same worry from Ray. 'We didn't call the police on you, I promise.'

'I know. Actually, I don't. They wouldn't come after me for something so small. But well done. No, I'm here for something else. That pretty face of yours. Those grey eyes, actually.'

'It's a lack of melanin,' said the bearded thug, who hadn't taken his own bloodshot eyes off her. 'Less than three per cent of the world has grey eyes. She's rare.'

The guy looking at books laughed. The other three men gave beardy a strange look.

'See? My comrade here is clearly fascinated, too,' Eli said. 'By "too" you can figure that there's a second admirer. You beat all my girls.'

Her breath was coming in short gasps. She had hoped these men wouldn't hurt her or Ray, but this was so much worse. They wanted her sexually. Instinctively, she squeezed her knees harder together.

'None of you bastards better touch her,' Ray snapped. He didn't seem about to launch himself at anyone, but to be safe she anchored him with a tighter grip on his hand.

'Calm down,' Eli said. He pulled off his balaclava. 'There will be no forced sex. But I do need you for a sexual reason. Want to hear what I need from you?'

'No,' Ray said. 'Just take the fucking chinaware or something and get lost.'

Eli stood. 'If that's your answer, then we'll move to the execution stage.' He raised and pointed the gun.

Kenna pulled away from Ray and got to her feet. 'No! Tell me! I want to know. Please. There's no need for anyone to get hurt. My husband is just upset, but he won't do anything.'

None of the thugs had moved when she burst to her feet. Clearly they weren't threatened by her. Eli sat again and told her to do the same.

'There's a man coming into the country on Saturday, Mrs Barker. Let's call him Mr X. He is very important and it's my job as host to make his time here comfortable. Give him what he wants. And what he always wants on business trips is a girl for the night–'

'You're a pimp, so you've got girls,' Ray said. 'That's what started this whole shitshow. Give him a couple of those.'

Kenna's heart jumped, but Eli didn't seem annoyed by Ray's confrontational attitude. He had that gun. 'They were on the table, Raymond. Mr X sent an envoy ahead to speak with me and arrange the details of his trip. I provided photographs of fifteen girls, laid out nicely on a table. The envoy didn't even get that far. I'd actually binned your driver's licence, Mrs Barker, but the envoy saw it sitting there. A gem atop of pile of rubbish. He knows what his boss likes, it seems.'

'And he wants me? Why? I'm no beauty, especially not on a driver's licence photo. I'm sure you have prettier girls.'

Eli nodded. 'I don't rate you. And I did ask the same question of the envoy. Apparently, you look like a childhood flame of Mr X's. Decision made. Are we on the same page?'

She wanted the page, the book, the whole damn library to be a bad dream. 'You want me to sleep with this man on Saturday. That's your plan. You want me to become a prostitute.'

'Don't look so defeated. I said nothing about having to sleep with him. He wants a dinner date. He always does. He's rich, so it wouldn't be a greasy spoon. I'm thinking almas caviar and white truffles, while a string quartet plays in the background.'

'Why do I doubt it ends there?'

'Maybe he'll try it on with you. Maybe he'll ask. Maybe he'll offer to pay. I can guarantee you that he's a thief, fraudster, blackmailer, even a multiple murderer, but one title he can't claim is rapist. You'll be fine if you choose to do it.'

'If? Are you saying I have a choice?'

'Of course. But your choice might leave me with none.'

Said with a grin, which she felt spoke volumes about this man. Behind many a handsome face lay a psychopathic mind. 'And how would that play out? If I said no right now.'

Eli's answer was instant. 'I shoot your husband in the balls. While you're screaming, I shoot you in the face. After I finish Raymond here, my men set fire to the house–'

'Point made,' Ray snapped.

'–Unsavoury men I know will tease friends and family at your funerals. The headstones will be stolen and your bodies dug up and dumped in your parents' gardens–'

'Shut the hell up,' Ray said, louder. This time he got a reaction as two men took a step closer.

Kenna jumped up. 'I'll do it. Just stop this, please.'

'Good girl,' Eli said. He got up. 'So, we're done here. I'll be in contact sometime in the next few days to give you the details. And that's that. We've had a nice chat and come to an arrangement. Just how all the best business deals are done. One more thing, though. I hate to become a lowly burglar, but, if you don't mind...'

Eli pointed at the man by the bookcase, who had one of her paperbacks in his hands and was looking at her.

'Take it,' she said. 'Take anything. Just please leave now.'

And they did. Just like that. The four men moved towards the kitchen, which probably meant they'd entered via the rear of the house. Eli was last and he stopped in the doorway.

'A couple more things, Kenna. Mr X specifically said he didn't want you handed out to other men until your date night–'

'Not a problem,' she interrupted, 'since I'm not one of your whores.'

'True. But maybe he meant all men. So, no sleeping with your husband before Saturday. And the final point. Think of me, of my people, as cancer. Remission can become recurrence. Now get some sleep. Don't spoil those grey eyes with bags.'

Upon hearing the back door close, Ray tried to get off the sofa, but Kenna stopped him. 'Wait,' she said. 'Keep quiet.'

Unable to believe the nightmare was over, she half expected the four men to be hiding in the kitchen like kids, ready to surprise them. Ray understood and remained silent and still. They gave it at least five minutes, which were counted down by a loud clock on the fireplace. Eventually, she let go of Ray's arm and he leaped up.

He went to the kitchen, but she opted to peek out the window using a gap in the living room curtains. The street was dark, desolate, as it should be. No masked men backslapping each other as they walked off. No car oozing away with its headlights off.

'Gone,' Ray said as he returned from the kitchen. 'The back door was jimmied. It won't lock again. I'll put the tumble dryer in front of it and sleep down here.'

Kenna sat again. It was over, but with this realisation was an adrenaline dump. She started to cry. Ray rubbed her shoulders and told her everything would be okay. She very much doubted that. 'What do we do? They will be back.'

Ray had already decided, it seemed. He got his phone off the armchair. She was sure he wouldn't call the police, right until the moment he asked an operator for them. She flashed across the room, snatched the phone, killed the call.

'No police, Ray, Jesus.'

He looked surprised. 'What? You plan to do what this fucker says? Don't be silly. Give me that phone.'

'No. You heard what Eli said. That crap about cancer? Didn't you read between the lines? If we call the police–'

'They'll be arrested and jailed. The cops must have whole files on this guy and his cronies.'

'But we don't know how many people he has. That's what he meant about cancer. How do we know the police could get them all? If the police don't arrest everyone, every single thug he knows, then we'd always have to watch our backs. Anyone could come and get us, anytime.'

He flopped onto the armchair. 'I agree, Kenna. He's bound to know some guy who knows some degenerate who'd slit a throat for a packet of fags. But we can get police protection. Maybe even witness relocation.'

'Dump our lives? Walk away from everything? Start again as Mr and Mrs Smith in some little village where we don't know anyone? No way. That's not an option. Look, Ray, I know you don't like the idea of this thing with the date–'

'It's nothing to do with that,' he cut in. 'Although you were pretty quick to agree. However, I don't think you can fuck your way out of this problem.'

She almost swore at him, but fighting wasn't a solution. 'Eli said that might not happen. I meet a man for a date, he said. That's all. What do you think, I go out there Saturday and get kidnapped?'

'And by Sunday you're on a boat to start a new life in a brothel in Zambia? Of course not. I mean, Eli said it was just a dinner date. I wouldn't dream of accusing a pimp stroke criminal gang leader of fibbing.'

Kenna walked away, planning to head upstairs. She got as far as the doorway before changing her mind and returning to the sofa. 'I only agreed in order to get those men out of the house. I wasn't really thinking straight. But I was doing my best to try to read the situation. They could have killed us, Ray. Right here. Why lie to us if they had something else planned? If, for instance, they wanted to cart me off to Zambia, they could have just taken me away. I felt... I felt they were telling the truth.'

'But, Kenna, you–'

'Wait. Just listen. They seem professional. It's organised crime, isn't it? They have rules for how they do things. They're not wild animals. I don't think they'd lie.'

'I believe it, Kenna. What they said they want is exactly what I think they have planned. But it's stupid to think it ends there. I wouldn't bet for a second against them coming back for more, time and time again.'

Her head had started to throb. 'I don't know. I don't know what lies ahead. My priority was to get them out of the house, and agreeing to help was the only way. Perhaps calling the police is the best thing, but not tonight. Let's discuss it in the morning when we're less shaken-up. Right now I just want to wrap myself in a blanket and pretend this never happened.'

After a thoughtful pause, Ray nodded. 'I'll block that back door and sleep down here, if that's okay?'

'Yes. And I'll join you. We should stay together. I'll fetch blankets.'

And so it was. Ten minutes later, the back door was barred by the tumble dryer and the couple lay on the floor by it, sandwiched in a pair of thick duvets. But neither of them got much sleep for the rest of that night.

FIVE

Kenna was surprised to find she'd managed to drift off for an hour around 5am. When she looked at Ray, he was wide awake and staring at the ceiling. They had said very little while lying together and had avoided the subject of Eli and his gang. But Kenna had thought long and hard about their problem while sleep escaped her. And she'd made a decision.

She sat up. 'No police.'

For a few moments Ray said nothing and continued to stare at the ceiling. Just as she was wondering if he was sleeping with his eyes open, he too sat up. 'I agree. What's your reason?'

'Calling the police will escalate things when we might be dealing with nothing. There's a chance that these people will change their minds. Maybe that Mr X will pick another girl. It's not until Saturday, so we've got six days for this problem to go away all by itself. What about your reason?'

'The same. We could call the police anytime before Saturday. It gives us time to think.'

'Time to not think is what I want. I want to ride out a few days without worry. I hope we can just go about our normal business.'

'Then let's do that.'

Unfortunately, normal business every second Sunday was a trip to Luton to eat dinner with Kenna's mother. No way. Her mum would sense something was up, and the moment she asked, Kenna would break down and tell the tale. Ray agreed. He told Kenna to call now, before her mother was up, so she could leave a voicemail. He believed that a live call would have the same result as a face-to-face meet. Kenna couldn't give her mum such a hefty worry. The message she left was loaded with fake cheer and lies about a busted car.

Ray didn't have the same problem. With the Luton trip out, he opted to visit his parents and continue tarmacking their driveway. After that, he wanted to go watch his old rugby team practice, which was another Sunday tradition. He asked if she wanted to join him so she wouldn't be alone with her thoughts all day. She declined.

'I'd rather you didn't stick around here on your own,' he said.

There, he'd admitted having the same worry as her. 'We can't worry about people coming to the door, Ray. This is our home and we can't live in fear.'

'I know. I'd just rather not take the risk on this first day. Go to a friend's. I promise that I'll chill out soon, when I get used to this. It's all fresh at the moment. Just for today. I can't go out and leave you here.'

She kissed his cheek. 'I'll call Vicky. We were planning a garden centre trip sometime, so this is the perfect chance.'

'Vicky?'

She felt that same goosebumps-like sensation she got every time she was reminded of Ray's failing brain. Holding back emotion, she said, 'From work. My best friend. You last met her a couple of weeks ago.'

He thought, and nodded. She wasn't sure if that was for her

benefit. The only worry worse than what might happen this coming Saturday... was if Ray would remember his own wife a decade from now.

When he was ready to leave to visit his parents, she walked Ray to the door. When she opened it, she stopped in mid-sentence. There was a police car at the kerb.

'Did you call them?' Ray asked.

'No. This can't be about that? Are they even here for us?'

They were. Two thirty-something male officers got out of the car and came up the path. They introduced themselves: PCs Carter and Haydon. Carter was short, thin, while Haydon was a big, bearded man with forearm tattoos. After Kenna had confirmed she and Ray were indeed the Barkers, Carter asked for a word inside.

'Sure.' She was nervous, but Ray looked scared. She wondered if the police had learned about his marijuana stash. Three of the four sat in the living room, while Ray stood beside Kenna's armchair. Haydon wrote in a notebook and let his partner do all the talking.

'We're investigating a report from a firm located on Western Road. They sent us CCTV of a violent attack that occurred on Friday night. Were you two on that road that night, around midnight?'

Ray and Kenna looked at each other. Each knew the other was thinking the same thing: admit or deny? Kenna made the decision. 'How do you know it was—'

Ray was quick: 'Hang on. Sorry, officers. That makes it sound like it was us and we're wondering how you knew. A better question might be: what makes you think it was us?'

Carter couldn't disclose that. He produced a photograph. It

looked like a mug shot, but wasn't. The featured man was none other than Eli.

Again Ray and Kenna shared a question with just their eyes, and this time Ray took command. 'Who's that?'

'We only know his first name. Eli. He runs a gang of pretty ruthless criminals called the Boys Firm. They're into all manner of criminal activities, and they're pretty much untouchable. We've never had anything court-worthy on Eli or his people. Until now. This was grievous bodily harm, judging by your face. If the prosecutor can prove intent to harm, Eli could face life imprisonment. But he would need a positive identification. The first step in that is a yes or no from either of you, here and now. We'll let you have a moment. Take the photograph and go into the kitchen for a chat. We'll wait. No pressure.'

Kenna got up quickly, before Ray could make this decision for them. She took him into the kitchen and shut the door. 'What do you think?'

'I don't buy it. Eli seems to have money and clout. He could get a good solicitor and get a plea deal to have the charges lessened. A guy I knew from rugby got done for GBH and he only got two years, and served half.'

'I agree. Eli might even beat the charge and walk free. And we'd have to give evidence, so he would absolutely know it was us. Or he could be out on bail if the trial is months away.'

'And he might want to stop us giving that evidence. In prison or not, he knows people. They're a cancer, like you said.'

'A slit throat for a packet of fags. Like you said. So it's a no?'

Ray shook his head. 'If things go bad for us with this dinner date crap, we can always change our minds. Until then, we don't recognise dickhead here.'

The words 'dickhead here' were highlighted by Ray's hand slapping the photo of Eli right out of Kenna's fingers.

Decided, then. They returned to the officers. Kenna sat. Ray stood. She handed back the photo. Ray said that he, 'Got a good look at the people who jumped me. This guy wasn't one of them. It was a bunch of young kids.'

Carter put the photo of Eli away. 'Are you sure? This man causes havoc and pain. We've been after him for years. This would be a favour to society. Do the great city of London a favour.'

'Sorry. It's not him. We've never seen him before.'

'We can arrange it so you never need to step into court. Nor even make an official statement. No one will know you told us anything. In fact, you don't even need to say a word. Just one little nod, and we'll leave, and we'll get this guy. You want to nod?'

'No,' Kenna said. 'It wasn't him or his gang. We've never met him. It was just kids. Sorry.'

The two officers looked at each other and stood. Carter grinned. 'Very good. Eli will be in touch, as promised.'

Kenna was quicker than Ray. While he looked puzzled, she leaped to her feet. 'What? What does that mean?'

'It means continue to keep your mouth shut and you'll come out of this fine and dandy at the other end, as promised.'

Now Ray got it. He almost snarled. 'Wait a damn minute. Eli sent you here? You're on his side?'

'Have a good day, Mr and Mrs Barker. We'll see ourselves out.'

Neither Ray nor Kenna could have escorted them to the door anyway. They were locked in place by disbelief. Once four had become two, they moved to the window to watch the officers enter their car and depart. A real police car, bearing two men with real uniforms and real warrant cards. This was surely a bad dream. Eli had police on his payroll, which meant things had just got a whole lot worse.

Kenna returned to her armchair and just about collapsed

into it. Ray said, 'Was that to scare us? Or prove his power? Was it a test?'

'All three. Can you imagine if we'd told them it was Eli who'd attacked us?'

'I'm trying not to.'

SIX

U sually when Kenna was driving, her biggest worry was whether her little Nissan would survive the journey. Today she was more fearful of a wandering mind causing a lethal crash.

Her friend, Vicky, had lost her right arm in a car accident when she was nineteen. She'd learned to embrace it over the following ten years and even used it as a weapon with which to embarrass other people. She also didn't mind having the mickey taken. When she came out of her house to meet Kenna, she wore a jumper with the redundant left arm tied in a knot. Kenna raised her left hand for a high five. Vicky gave her the finger and they both laughed.

They drove to the garden centre in separate cars so Vicky could head out to the gym afterwards. After looking around garden water features, they hit the café. They chatted about who was secretly dating who at work, until a waitress brought condiments and cutlery. A knife and fork was laid before Vicky, who glared at the woman and said, 'Are you taking the piss?'

The woman noticed the missing arm and her jaw dropped.

She profusely apologised. When that got Vicky giggling, the waitress vanished in a huff.

'That's guaranteed spit in my beans,' Vicky said. She then noted that Kenna hadn't laughed along with her. 'Ray and the devil's weed again?' Vicky knew about Ray's secret dope habit.

'Not this time. Something happened. Something you have to swear not to tell anyone. Anyone. But I don't want to talk about it here. Let's just eat and we'll see about it afterwards.'

No argument from Vicky, who was so hungry that she ate tomato ketchup from a knife as they waited for their meals.

After a pair of empty plates sat before them, the women headed out and grabbed a bench at the quiet end of a children's playpark. 'So, tell me,' Vicky said.

Kenna wondered how the hell she would begin her wild story. She started with the walk home from the pub on Friday night. Once the ball was rolling, it gained momentum. Kenna told it all in quiet, fast sentences.

She ended with a question: *what would you do?*

Vicky took some time to digest the outrageous tale, and as long again to consider her answer to Kenna's query. 'It depends on what's going to happen. Do you think this is real? Or are they up to something else?'

'Like I told Ray, I think what I was told is the truth. I think I'm being treated as some kind of escort or call girl and there really is a man who wants a date for a night. These people don't mess about. They broke into my house in the middle of the night, and one had a gun. If they wanted to force me to do something, they could have carted me away.'

'True. No offence, but who the hell are you? Nobody important. You don't have money. You don't know anyone special that they could be trying to get to. You don't hold the keys to a bank vault or prison or Buckingham Palace.'

'Exactly. So this seems real. Let's say it is. What do I do? What would you do?'

'Probably be grateful some guy isn't disgusted by me. And then do some research and demand some answers.'

'What do you mean?'

'You need to know who this mystery man is. Find out where you're supposed to meet him. Get a full plan of action. If it turns out you have to get in a van and be driven a hundred miles, and they let you go in your casual clothing, and it's at three in the morning, then run as fast as you can to the nearest police station and take your chances.'

Kenna remembered her crack to Ray about being trafficked to a Zambian brothel. The joke didn't seem so silly now that two people had suggested there was a chance her life could be whipped out from under her. 'And if they tell me to dress up fancy and go to an expensive restaurant at 8pm?'

Vicky sighed. 'That's where I fall flat, darling. I'm sorry. If someone had approached you in the street and given this offer, I might have said go for it. Remember I told you about my brother's friend on the beach?'

Kenna did. A man had approached her and offered a modelling job. That young lady was now off earning well in New York. 'Exactly. The whole home invasion thing puts this in a grim spotlight. I'm just too worried about afterwards. Ray thinks these people won't leave us alone. That we'll be on their radar and they'll keep coming back for more.'

Vicky gave this thought. 'Maybe not, though. Let's just play the optimist a minute. You know that this man, Eli, controls sex workers. I've seen a couple of movies where powerful men are offered girls. Your driver's licence was taken, so I don't think it's beyond the realm of possibility that someone saw it and thought, *ooohh*. How many times have guys been drawn to those eyes of yours?'

She was right. Kenna attracted attention just about every time she went out, and to a man they'd mentioned liking her eyes. A girl called Julie from work, who had fashionably fake silver hair, was immensely jealous. The waitress had lingered on them. A guy on another table kept staring. 'You can't see my eyes on a black-and-white driver's licence photo.'

Vicky shrugged. 'Maybe they checked you out on Facebook. I did warn you against that. It's why there's no sexy snaps of me on my profile.'

True on both fronts. Kenna had never intentionally posted 'sexy snaps' of herself, but couldn't deny that she always liked to show off her eyes. 'Are you saying there's a chance they won't be back for more? That they want me just for one date and that's the end of it?'

Vicky shrugged again. 'I really couldn't say. But as you said, they won't be happy if you don't. Ask yourself some questions. One, is calling the police a bad idea?'

'Probably. Eli has cops working for him. People who grass on criminals can end up in serious danger. I agreed to the date, so right now there's no problem. Yet.'

'Okay. Two. Is saying no a bad idea?'

'That I'm not so sure about. Eli made a bad threat, but he doesn't really gain anything from hurting me. But it could be a pride thing. Like he has to send a message to others who might want to go against him. I just don't know.'

'Three. Will they continue to want things from you afterwards?'

'Again, I don't see why. I mean, this man could want to see me again. Hell, he could want to whisk me away and marry me. But not if it really is just a dinner date with some guy who might like a different woman each time.'

The women fell silent as a man came close to collect a ball his kid had kicked near the bench. When he was clear, Vicky said, 'I guess, if you typed those scenarios and answers into a computer, it would probably say the best option is to go ahead with the date thing. Treat it like a one-day job opportunity.'

'So that's what you—'

'Whoa, girl. Never said that. It just seems, technically, statistically, whatever-ally, the safest bet. Just make sure you don't blow the guy's mind. Be a little crap so he doesn't want to see you again.'

The footballing child again booted his ball close to the women, and for a second time they waited for its collection. This time it was the kid himself, and he looked into Kenna's face. 'What's up with your eyes?'

Kenna forced a smile. 'Nothing. That's their colour. Is it nice?'

'It's weird,' the kid said, and scarpered. Kenna watched him talk to his dad and point back at her. She was snapped out of this mild reverie when Vicky spoke.

'Are you worried about going to prison?'

'What? Why would I?'

'Well, they're criminals. Maybe the police are watching them. Surveillance and stuff. And they'll see you.'

'And they might think I'm actually a call girl?' Kenna almost laughed. 'I could get arrested for that?'

'No I meant they might think you're part of the gang. The kingpin, even.'

Kenna's smile died on its feet. 'Jesus, I never thought of that. You think that's possible? Now I don't know what to do.'

'Neither do I. And I can't say I'm jealous. I'd give my right arm to avoid being in your—' She suddenly grabbed Kenna's arm. 'Wait! I just had the mother of all ideas. About the guy falling for you. Listen to this for a plan...'

Ray's old rugby team, the Full Montys RFC, practised at the Camel Lane ground in Hammersmith every Sunday. When Ray left, two years ago, the team had been a tier six outfit attached to London 1 North. Last year they'd been relegated to London 2 North West, and he liked to joke that their downfall was due to his absence.

It truly might have been, he felt, but still he'd never been allowed back. Not since the concussion. He'd performed a dive to take the ball away from a player about to hoof it downfield; he had successfully swatted the ball aside at the last nanosecond, but unfortunately it had left his head in the spot the opponent's boot had been aiming for.

He'd been unconscious for eight minutes. After being roused by smelling salts, he'd been in good spirits, but deep inside his brain some circuitry had begun faltering. It started to show by the next day.

He'd had memory lapses for years, but now there was a new intensity. A common problem was forgetting what he was supposed to buy from the shop, but after the concussion he started to make real daft mistakes. He brought home a smoke alarm, only for Kenna to point out an existing one that he'd purchased just a week prior. He once bought milk, put it in the fridge, and an hour later went out for more. He bought a charger for a Samsung phone he had gotten rid of months ago.

He'd long been one for forgetting passwords, PIN numbers, appointments, names, but now he did this far more often. He used to check windows and doors twice because he'd forget if he'd locked them; now he would sometimes forget thrice.

Then there were anger issues. It was common for him to get enraged by the slightest thing and overreact, but he'd always felt guilty the next day. Now the new dawn would make him forget that he'd been worked up and what had caused it. The guilt would come after Kenna had reminded him what he'd done.

Mostly his memory lapses didn't have major impact and weren't a cause for real concern, until something happened one day. He was painting a house in Doncaster and had headed out to a café for his lunchbreak. After the meal, he went home, job forgotten, and didn't realise until his boss called him.

After that incident, Kenna went from worried to scared, and they consulted a doctor. After half a year of tests and scans and interviews, he got a diagnosis. Official bad news. Your life is going downhill fast, pal. Kenna had cried, but the scary truth hadn't hit Ray until his rugby coach found out and booted him from the team.

Since then, he'd worked on countering his symptoms. Anger management classes had helped control the rages a little and he employed a five-repeat method for memorisation. For instance, when he'd set off today to watch his team practice, he'd said the destination aloud five times. It wasn't a faultless tactic, but today he'd gotten here without once checking the address written on a scrap of paper in his pocket.

Such techniques seemed adequate today and might be tomorrow, but early-onset dementia (the doctor had also mentioned possible CTE, but Ray refused to accept guesswork) was a degenerative disease and he'd only get worse. His manager knew this and Ray had never since been allowed to play. Watching the team was the only way to continue his love with the sport. Sometimes the guys let him kick a ball, but fiery action on the field, his true love, was outlawed. Once an errant ball had smacked him in the ear and the whole team had acted as if they'd kicked it through the Mona Lisa.

He hadn't just come here to watch, though. That wouldn't relieve the tension sitting like a heavy meal in his gut. During a break in practice, Ray approached a man called Liam who was collecting loose balls. The two had been tight since meeting in school year 7. They'd attended the same carpentry course at college and had worked as painter-decorators colleagues for six years. Liam had got new employment as a security guard in a shopping centre last year, which left only rugby Sundays for a meet. They were still real good friends, though, and Ray hoped to capitalise on that today.

For the last three months, Liam had been the team's assistant coach and manager. On day one of his new role, he'd warned Ray never to expect to return to the team, and so far Ray had upheld that and never attempted to manipulate their friendship.

That was about to change. 'I want back on the team,' Ray said.

'Dude, we agreed you wouldn't ask.'

'The missus and me are having problems. Well, we've got one big problem, and I need to get my head off it.'

'You need to keep that head in good nick, Ray. That's the problem.'

'My head is fine. I'm not a blubbering wreck. I drove here and didn't crash.'

Liam gave him a long look. 'I'll do whatever for you, you know that. We go back a long way. But not this. You have to give it up, mate.'

'Easy for others to say. Easy for that one head doctor to say I had brain damage, too. What if another doc said differently?'

'Dude, come on. Hey, that kid there, see?' Liam pointed onto the pitch, where the players sat around. 'New bloke. Asked me the longest kick goal we ever had. It was that game we had against the Pythons in '19. Remember that seventy-metre conversion that Yarwood scored in the final minute to win the game?'

Ray nodded. 'I do. A fine game. I bust my nose. Was that some kind of memory test, Liam? I told you my head is just fine. I remember the bust nose.'

Liam glared at him. 'Longest conversion our team ever had. Made the local papers. And it was your kick.'

Ray didn't believe him at first. But he had a vague memory of... something. The nose didn't really count because the left side was still a little blocked and made for a constant reminder. 'Mate, that's unfair.'

'How old is my son? What's my wife's maiden name? What car have I got? Get all three and I'll put you in for next week.'

'Your wife is Lisa. You drive a Honda with blue–'

'Liz. Ray, it's Liz. And if you look over there, you'll see the motorbike I've been riding for over a year now.'

Ray had no reply. Game over – literally.

Liam said, 'If you and Kenna are having problems, I'm happy to help where I can, Ray. Always. You know that. But where I can. This isn't the way. You want to help with practice, gives the newbies some advice, create some tactics, let's go. Assistant assistant coach, voluntary, no probs. But don't ask about getting back on the team, mate. We agreed. And it's up to Mr Daniels anyway.'

Mr Daniels. The manager. That piece of information was secure and whole. As was Ray's knowledge that Daniels had been the guy to kick him out.

'Anyway, Ray, what's this problem you need help with?' Liam bent down to pick up a ball, but Ray stepped up and punted it. Fast, hard, precise, full of anger. A clean goal from the twenty-two-metre line. A couple of the team, lounging around the pitch, cheered. But Liam wasn't impressed.

Without another word, Ray turned and left.

SEVEN

Alfie woke to find it was midday and he had a missed call from one of Eli's burner numbers. Just the one call, which was standard. Eli would always phone someone within minutes if they missed an appointment, but never a second time. A no-pick-up could mean the cops had nabbed the guy. If the call wasn't answered, Eli would destroy his burner. He had dozens around the city and barely kept them a day anyway, so no problem there. But for making him worry, and for missing a job, Alfie would be in the shit. The depth would be determined by Eli's mood. Guys had gotten a finger wagged at them. Guys had also lost fingers.

He called Trevor, who should have woken him at nine. He woke Trevor up. Who said, 'Shit. The missus wanted some. I was up till six. Spoke to Eli?'

'No. Missed his call.'

'And me. We're big-time late and in deep trouble. I'll pick you up.'

The two men reached the pub half an hour later. The Hungry Fox, in Clapham Town, was owned by one of Eli's old schoolfriends. He wasn't part of the crew, but he kept secrets and his place was for unofficial hire if the money was right. The pub was shut until 4pm on Sundays, but the gate to the rear beer garden was unlocked and through they went.

The pub had had a serious makeover in the '90s, but at the rear of the yard it retained a decrepit, long, single-storey building known as the Games Room. Here patrons could play darts, chess on tables painted with boards, quoits, and it even had a skittles alley. Both men hoped they were in time for the game planned for today.

They weren't. The door was open, but the room was empty of life. Life blood, though, was in abundance at the end of the skittles lane. Alfie cursed.

'You missed it by twenty minutes,' said a voice behind them. They turned to see a guy called Harker, standing there with his arms folded. Mid-twenties and a ladies' man. If Eli needed someone to woo females, Harker got the job. 'I won. Shot right to the nose.'

'No, he was on his way out,' said another voice. A second guy appeared by Harker's side. 'Because of me. Right off the bat, one in the forehead.'

Alfie cursed. For the incident involving his sister, Eli had wanted Inspector Bunyan to suffer. Someone had had the idea of using him in a game of skittles, and a game had been arranged for 9.30 that morning. Given that it was almost 1pm, Bunyan had survived over three hours of men launching four-and-a-half-inch solid wooden balls down the lane at him.

'But you get to join in after all,' Harker said. 'Dom's got all the details.'

Dom was in the lounge, watching the news with two men Alfie didn't know. Nobody else was present but Alfie could hear various voices coming from the public bar next door. The underboss broke off from them when he saw his guests. He sat on a stool at the bar. Alfie apologised for his tardiness and asked if Eli was annoyed.

'Yeah, but you can keep your teeth. He told me to tell you that you got the job of getting rid of the copper. And then you get another job. That couple from last night, the Barkers, they were told not to open their gobs to anyone. They opened them. Take this.'

Dom handed over surgical gloves and a sheet of A5 lined notepaper. It was a map with instructions. 'Call Petey-Man when you've got the copper in the car, and he'll go over the map with you again. Call me when it's done. Car's out back. Brown Mondeo.'

Alfie studied the map. 'Risky, no? What if Eli is tied to this because of his sister?'

'There's no connection. The copper won't have told anyone he spoke to Eli's sister. And they won't find anything on the body. Turn your frown upside down, Trev.'

Trevor looked like a sulking kid. 'Who had the body job before us? Maybe he still wants to do it.'

'Doesn't matter if the guy skipped and sang with joy on the way down here. Eli said you bozos.'

'Where's the cop?' Alfie asked as he admired the room. He thought it would be cool to run a pub.

'Well he's hardly in here, is he? Look, there, we propped him at the bar with a pint.'

'No, I wasn't looking for... I was just looking.'

'The cop is in the grit bin. Memorise all those instructions. And don't leave that bit of paper with the body. Eat it or something. Burn the gloves. Get moving.'

Trevor laughed and left. Alfie hung back until his friend was out of earshot. 'Dom, we're pals. You can't get me out of this?'

'Wish I could. But you'll like part two of today's tasks, so get going.'

The grit bin was in a gated compound around the side of the pub. The stolen brown Mondeo was also here. They gloved up. The body was inside a thick black bin liner with tie handles. As they were heaving it free, the plastic caught and ripped, and a head lolled out. Alfie laughed, but the bloodied, smashed face made Trevor groan and look away. He had to run inside for another bag.

Body in boot, they headed north. Their destination was seventeen minutes away according to Google Maps, but they couldn't risk an accident or getting pulled, so it took twenty-five. They drove into a two-car lock-up garage by a waste ground. Two minutes later they exited in a cloned, stolen car and finished the journey to Goddard Street. The balaclavas Dom had supplied were put on as they approached the police station where Inspector Bunyan had worked.

Trevor stopped the car right outside the heavy-duty mesh gates at the back of the station. People were everywhere but the only coppers around were a scattering deep inside the rear yard. Quickly, both men pulled the bagged body out of the boot and left it where it fell. A filled jerry can got accidentally dragged out with the bag, but Alfie lobbed that back in.

'Oi. No dumping rubbish. Come here, you two.'

Pedestrians knew to mind their business. The voice belonged to a copper who'd materialised at the closed gate.

The auditor in Alfie leaped forth. 'Don't give me directives, officer.'

'You can't dump that there. Come over here.'

It was as if he hadn't even registered their masked faces. As the copper jabbed a button to open the gate, Alfie and Trevor hopped in the car. A wheelspin would have added to the drama, but the tyres had good grip.

As they blew down the road, Alfie adjusted the rear-view mirror so he could watch the copper. He saw the officer approach the bag, tried to lift it, failed, and then bent down to open it.

'Shit.' He'd wanted to see the copper's shock when he realised a colleague lay in the bag. Unfortunately, Trevor took a corner at the vital moment.

He took another corner shortly afterwards, into an alley between two shops. Here they found a Kia blocking their path. While Trevor went to open it with a key hidden inside a wing mirror, Alfie got the jerry can from the boot and started soaking the interior of the clone car. Both men tossed their gloves in. Alfie pulled matches from his pocket.

Trevor put a hand out. 'I'm supposed to do the burning. We agreed.'

Alfie struck a match and lobbed it into the car. Trevor's moan was shrouded by a whump as the interior burst into flames.

'I was supposed to do the burning,' Trevor repeated as they drove out of the alley in the second stolen car.

'I forgot. Sorry, man.'

A third car awaited them half a mile away under an arch bridge. Here they found fresh clothing. They dumped their gear in the Kia, which was driven away by someone who appeared out of the blue. Car three took them to a train station, where they parked neatly. Once in the station, they hopped off the platform, crossed the tracks, and climbed onto the far side. In a quiet corner, unseen, they climbed a fence and dropped into a supermarket car park.

Car four was waiting. Once out of the grounds, they made a handful of turns on various streets, and found Trevor's car exactly where they were told it would be. Someone had driven it around parts of London to get it captured on ANPR and thus create an alibi for the two men.

Now safe, and driving away, Alfie raised a hand for a high five. Trevor ignored it and said, 'I was supposed to do the burning. You owe me for that.'

Alfie apologised again and called Dom, who told him to get a pen and some paper. Trevor had both in the car. 'There's a man called Liam Jones,' Dom said. 'Write down these details about him.'

Dom talked. Alfie wrote. Address, age, workplace. At the end came the order: 'This is the friend that Ray Barker met today. He might have been told everything. He needs convincing that telling others is a bad idea.'

'Fuck him up?'

'No. That creates drama and interest. Just have a word. Give the phone to Trevor.'

Alfie watched as Trevor parked and took details from Dom, which were scribbled on his own sheet of paper. When the call was done, Trevor said, 'We have to split up. I'll drop you back home so you can get your car.'

Alfie noted the name at the top of Trevor's paper. He wanted to swap, badly, but he said nothing and waited.

'You want to swap?' Trevor asked.

'Not really. Why? Who you got?'

'A woman. You owe me for the burning.'

Alfie sighed, said, yeah, he guess he did owe Trev, and they exchanged sheets of paper. Alfie read what Trevor had written.

Vicky Margold, aged thirty-two. Young, hopefully pretty. Trevor might have hated hassling women, but for Alfie any contact with the opposite sex, good or bad, was desirable. He couldn't wait to see her.

As Alfie was pulling up outside Vicky's house, she walked out of the property. It was a nice semi-detached place with ivy on the walls. And she was a pretty thing in a long skirt and a waistless denim jacket.

Trevor called him as he followed Vicky's vehicle. 'I've done my guy. You done?'

'Following her now. What happened?'

'Easy as pie. I knocked on his door. I went for the softly-softly approach. I said I was from the people who spoke to Ray Barker on Friday night. I saw right then he was puzzled. The guy knew nothing. Christ, I almost told him more than I should have. In the end, I got him believing it was mistaken identity so he wouldn't go ask Ray about it. But anyway, Ray didn't tell him. Seems like the Barkers are keeping the secret. So just in case your woman knows nothing, be careful how you approach. Do the mistaken identity thing. Don't freak her out.'

Alfie said he knew what he was doing. The two men chatted about nothing in particular while Vicky led him east a few miles to Mortlake, where she entered the rear car park of a gym near the river. Alfie ended the call.

The car park was large and seemed to serve a number of establishments, but nobody was around. Softly-softly? Fuck that. Quick as a flash, he laid up his car by Vicky's and jumped into the passenger seat. He was shocked to see she had no left arm, so he grabbed her hair to prevent her from leaping out the door.

She had no intention of that. There was no fear amongst her shock. Immediately, she threw a punch that cracked him on the forehead. 'Get the hell out of my car, dickhead.'

She threw another fist and he ducked his head, so it hit the top. It hurt her and she yelped. He pulled out his knife while retaining her arm. 'Just sit still, lass.'

She was breathing heavy, eyes aflame with rage, but the

knife got her compliant. 'Just take what you want and get out.'

Maybe he would. He could smell sweet perfume, and he liked her hair. That missing arm was strangely sexy, too. 'Listen to me carefully. I'm from the people who Kenna Barker met on Friday night. You know what I mean?'

No puzzlement amongst her fear: she knew. 'What do you want from me?'

'To not repeat her mistake. There's dozens of us in the gang. We have guys who like to touch women. Guys who like to burn houses. Hackers who can empty bank accounts and ruin credit. You don't want any of them in your life, do you?'

'No. Look, I won't tell anyone anything.'

'We need Kenna for a job in a week. You know what, right?' She nodded. 'So all you have to do is avoid Kenna for a week. Just call in sick to work, don't answer the door to her, ignore her phone calls. Got it? Oh, and one more thing. Say nothing to anyone for the rest of your life. If you're eighty, and you blab, we'll send someone undercover into the old people's home to whack you.'

'I understand. I won't say anything. Look, Kenna isn't going to do anything silly. She only told me because we're close. She actually told me not to go to the police. I mean, I would have already if I was going to. So that should prove I have no intention of telling anyone else. I promise.'

'Good. Because we'll be watching.' He put his knife away and let go of her hair, to see what she'd do. She didn't fight or run. The long skirt had ridden up to expose two inches of thigh. He was tempted to have her, and he knew she'd be easy to pin down with a missing arm. But for sure she'd run to the cops, so he beat down the urge. 'Best friends, right? You and her? So you know her well. Her and Ray.'

She nodded. 'We've been friends for a long time. So I want

to protect her. That means not telling the police and not trying to stop her doing what you want. I promise.'

'Are they tight? Her and Ray? Loved-up?'

'Yes. Ray's a good man. He won't tell the police, either. He'll do what–'

'Piss off,' Alfie cut in. He got out and slammed the door. Tight? Loved-up? How annoying.

EIGHT

W hen Kenna returned home in the late afternoon, she discovered a small brown envelope on the inner doormat. She felt it before opening it and realised it contained a key. But to what?

The answer was in the kitchen. When she entered to make tea, the back door caught her attention. In place of the busted one was a brand-new uPVC door with a small, double-glazed window. She tried the key and it unlocked. The door was hung professionally. Whoever had done it had also returned the tumble dryer to its alcove.

Whoever? It was obvious that Eli had sent men to make the repair. But why? Guilt, or manipulation? Was he saying sorry, or pretending to? She didn't know whether to be happy or horrified.

Ray chose the latter when he returned in the early evening. Like her, he tested the door. He was immediately suspicious of Eli's motive. 'I don't like this. It must be some kind of trick.'

By now Kenna had had time to think. 'Maybe not. They fixed what they broke. Maybe this is a simple case of keeping us sweet.'

'They've got no reason to do that. They waved a gun in our faces. Maybe they just want us to think they're good people, so we trust them. And now they have a damn key so they can come and go as they want.'

She hadn't thought of that. But she had a solution. 'We can leave this key on the inside and they can't open it.'

'But they plan to, don't they? They don't plan to leave us alone. Now they have a key to the house. We're as good as family, in it for the long haul. What next – they fix your car and then we're in their debt?'

'It doesn't have to be that way. I spoke to Vicky, and she had an idea.'

Ray looked even more horrified than he had upon seeing the door. 'You told someone? What if she goes to the police?'

'She won't. Listen to her idea. When I go on the date–'

'So you've decided that then? You're going to go see this guy? You decided that without me?'

'Ray, we didn't have a choice, did we? Will you just listen?'

He nodded, but he wasn't happy. She said, 'I go on the date. I eat, I speak, that's all. But I make sure this man likes me. He's someone important to Eli and that means Eli will respect and listen to him. The man might not want to see me upset. I could tell him to ask Eli and his people to leave us alone.'

Ray wasn't as impressed by the plan as she was. 'Or this guy could like you so much he decides he wants a regular thing. Now you've suddenly got a husband and a boyfriend. He could have me whacked to get a clear road. Your friend's idea makes no sense.'

'It seems safe, Ray. No option gives us an obvious good ending. But what else can we do? Say no to Eli? Call the police and risk people he's got on the force finding out? Let's hear your plan.'

Ray's shoulders slumped. He didn't like Vicky's proposal but clearly could think of no better one.

They both jumped as someone rapped on the back door. Kenna backed away from it while Ray did the reverse: unlocked and opened it wide. A male outside said, 'Is Kenna about?'

She couldn't see him, but she recognised that voice. One of the men in black from last night. What did he want her for?

Ray made that very same enquiry: 'Why? It's not Saturday.'

'Well, we said we'd be in touch, and there are preparations to make.'

'Like what? A fucking dance routine?' Ray was defiant, not scared, and she hoped he wouldn't overstep a line.

The man laughed. 'Actually, you ain't far wrong. Our man's important, and we don't want to annoy him. Just like when a hotel gets a VIP guest, they check the room, don't they? Check the taps and fridge and stuff. So we have to make sure Kenna is right for him. That's what I've been sent to do.'

'Check she's right for him? What the hell does that mean?'

'Personality-wise. Make sure she's a good date. Able to talk and laugh and eat professionally. That's why I'm here. Eli has ordered me to take her to a pub for a drink.'

Ray snorted with disdain. 'Like a damn test-drive of my wife? Fuck off, pal. I don't care if you're part of some lunatic crew. They're not here. You are, and I could snap you in two.'

He slammed the door. Horrified at the outburst, Kenna rushed over and yanked it open again. Outside stood the man she suspected, but this time sans balaclava. She'd been right about the beard. His eyes, which scanned her, were still bloodshot. The thick hair was in dreadlocks and his skin was pockmarked, which probably the reason for the hairy cheeks. He seemed to have made an effort by wearing jeans and a blue shirt, but both needed ironing and barely diluted his overall yuckiness.

For what she figured was the first ever time he'd heard such words, she said, 'I'll go out with you. The Wired Goose pub is about fifteen minutes from here. I'm sure you can find it. I'll be there in one hour. Please, just go now.'

The man tipped a salute. 'It'll be a pleasure, ma'am. I look forward to it.'

In a slapstick cartoon, she might have vomited right in his face. Before she could make any response at all, Ray pulled her back a step by her blouse and slammed the door. He moved to the window and leaned over the sink to peer out.

'He's going. But not because of me. Because you just sent him to the pub. Care to explain that?'

'Yes. We can't piss these people guys off, Ray. If Eli wants that man to–'

'Come on, Kenna. Did you not see through that bullshit? Ian sent this bozo to test the goods? Really? He was a mess.'

It took her a second to realise who Ian was. 'It's Eli, not Ian, and I don't know. Maybe they sent a dirty man because it's a test. Are you saying I shouldn't go?'

Angry, Ray lifted a knee hard into the cupboard door below the sink. But no words came. She moved closer to him. 'Ray, there's another reason to go. I can find out more. I think that man likes me, so I can question him. I can find out who these people are. I really don't want to, but it can help us. You agree?'

More silence.

'Ray, stop acting like I'm doing something wrong here. You think I fancy this guy or something? Or the man I'm supposed to see on Saturday? I sent him to The Wired Goose because it's miles away and nobody will know who I am. So I'm not recognised with another man. I'm trying to get us through this and buy us some time.'

He deflated. 'Okay, I get it. I suppose it could be a good idea to get more information. But I'm not staying here. I'll follow you. If he tries anything, I'll snap his neck and I don't give a shit what his cronies do about it.'

NINE

Kenna had heard that The Wired Goose hosted karaoke on Sunday evenings, which would mean a big crowd. The bearded man wouldn't be able to try anything untoward. The loud singing would guarantee their conversation wouldn't be intimate.

But talking there would definitely be. She planned to ask a hundred questions about the people he worked for and, hopefully, she'd learn about the mystery man she was to see on Saturday. She also planned to be cold and boring, because maybe, just maybe, beardy would report that and Eli would go pick some other girl for the big night.

Karaoke was at 8pm, another eighty minutes away, and the pub was almost empty. It had four booths against one wall and she'd hoped they'd all be engaged. No such luck. The bearded man was in the one in the corner, the most remote and intimate, and he already had two drinks on the table, so bang went the chance of wasting time at the bar. Sod it. She went straight over. He got up, playing the polite date, and didn't sit until she had. The table they faced each other across wasn't nearly wide enough for her liking.

'You changed,' he said. He seemed happy with this, as if she'd made an effort. In reality she had swapped into baggier jeans and a large pullover in order to hide curves and straights. Her hair was in a tight ponytail so that hardly any was visible from the front. For her meeting with Vicky earlier, she'd worn faint lip gloss and blush to pinken her white, but now it was all gone.

She touched the pint of lager he'd bought for her, but had no intention of putting it in her belly. She didn't trust it. Her plan had been to slowly turn the conversation to the upcoming date, but she wanted to be here as little time as possible. So, straight in for the kill. 'So who is this man I'm supposed to meet on Saturday?'

'I'm Alfie, by the way.' He put out a hand, which she was forced to shake. It was coarse, like a bricklayer's, and he held hers way too long. 'You probs figured I'm a gangster, right?'

Under the table, out of sight, she wiped her hand on the seat cushion. 'Well, you turned up with the gang that broke into my house. Have you all got a name?'

'We're the Boys Firm. Heard of us?'

She had. Where, when, and how eluded her. 'Here and there. And Eli is your boss? Has he got a title? The Don or something? And what's your rank?'

'We don't do shit like that. But I guess I'm a foot soldier. Like I want to be. I'm frontline, all action.'

He seemed eager to promote the image of a hardened criminal, but it didn't gel with the small, unkempt, almost shy man sipping a drink before her. She was intrigued enough to sidestep her mission for a moment. 'And why do you do this? You seem smart. You could get a real job.'

'This pays more. I'm in a crew, I'm cared for and respected. None of that shit in the rat race.' He seemed bitter, as if life had dealt him an unfair hand.

Now intrigue became interest. 'Criminal empire foot soldier isn't something advertised in the job centre. How did you get into this? Broken home?'

He sipped and smiled. 'I sense a bit of scorn there. Lots of people come from broken homes and not all of them become criminals – that's your thinking?'

'I won't doubt it could be a factor. I don't know much about that sort of thing. So I can't judge you.'

'Actually, I was born to well-off parents. Both doctors. We lived in a village called Denway, up in Derbyshire. Quaint little place. All prim and proper, church fetes, largest cucumber competitions, everyone knows everyone and their gossip.'

'Sounds nice.'

He got bitter again. 'Just the sort of place where someone accused of spying on a little girl through her bedroom window wouldn't be welcome.'

To cover her surprise, and disgust, Kenna sipped at the drink she swore she wouldn't touch. 'You spied on a little girl?'

'Accused, I said. Didn't do it. She reckoned I was in a tree, watching her undress. Complete bullshit, but she was a lawyer's daughter, so of course I'm the liar. And yeah, she was a little girl, just twelve, but I was a little boy. Fourteen. My dad died of cancer when I was twelve, so there was only my bitch mum, and she was already worried about what people would think, her being a widow. Having a kid like me was too much. So, soon as I turned sixteen, she booted me out. I came to London because I have an uncle here. But he didn't like me turning up on his doorstep and told me to fuck off. After that, the streets were home.'

This story from a random stranger might have garnered sympathy. Not this guy. 'Right. And you got into crime because there was no other choice?'

Alfie leaned back in his seat. 'Is that more scorn? I can't fault you this time. A guy called Dom found me homeless and offered to help. He introduced me to the right people and they took to me. I needed money and they were there. Now I have my own place, money, soulmates, everything.'

'Right,' she said, because nothing else came to mind.

He seemed to sense this feeling. 'More scorn. I know you've probably seen TV crime programmes. You're thinking big-time criminals recruit teenagers and just use them. It starts like that. But you perform, you show respect, and over the years it changes. Now I'm part of a big family.'

Good for him. So what? She was bored now and returned to important matters. 'So if Eli is the boss, who is the man I'm supposed to meet?'

'Never mind him,' Alfie said, waving the subject away as one would a pesky fly. 'I'm here to learn about you. Eli's done his research, but I don't know anything about you. So tell me about your life and we'll see if it matches up with what he knows. He wants to make sure you're going to be honest about everything.'

That sounded like bullshit. Either Eli was playing a trick to get information, or, worse, this guy had lied to get her to open up. It didn't matter which because she knew she had to play ball. There was nothing in her life that was dangerous to disclose.

She told him she'd been born right here in London, thirty years ago. Her childhood and teenaged years were run-of-the-mill. She lived with her parents until she was twenty, at which time she got a small flat with Ray. She had met him while clubbing one night with friends. Not at a club, though: she'd stumbled across him throwing up in the street as she walked home. He could barely walk and she helped him to a taxi rank, where they swapped phone numbers. They dated, married, got a house all of their own.

'No wild antics to tell me about?'

'No. We're just a boring, normal couple.'

Alfie drained his glass in three gulps. 'Any plans for kids? I'd like one eventually.'

That was a step too far. She didn't want a serious, personal conversation. 'Please. Tell me about the man I'm supposed to meet. He's a big shot, obviously. But not part of your gang?'

'Another gang. The Marshalls. They run the parts of London that we don't. But the boss, The Magpie as he's known, isn't based here. He oversees everything from France.'

'He's French?'

'No. A lot of his people are. He moved there years ago.'

'So how are Eli and this Magpie friends if they run rival gangs?'

'I'm sure the CEO of Tesco knows the CEO of Asda. I wouldn't call Eli and The Magpie friends. All I can tell you is that they're planning to do business. The Magpie is coming to see him. When one guy hosts another, he provides for him.'

'So I'm the gift. Am I supposed to sleep with this man?'

Alfie said he needed another drink. While he was at the bar, she looked at the door. It would have been simple to claim she needed to get back, and do a runner. But she was on the verge of discovering vital information.

Alfie returned and sat another two pints on the table. Her original drink was still untouched. He said, 'Show him a good time, that's all. Get him all happy and stuff the night before the meeting. Which is a shame.'

'What do you mean?'

'The Magpie has his pick of girls. He can have ten a night if he wants. He's picked you. But you'd be wasted on him. It's not right that someone like you should be used like that when girls are just objects to him. He won't see the magnificence in you

77

like I do. It's like using a Ming vase as a money box. You're a Ferrari next to most girls.'

She stood up. She had what she needed. More would have been better, but she couldn't stand any more of this guy's lecherousness. 'I need to leave now. Thanks for your time.'

Alfie looked upset. 'How about a drink at a different pub? It's still early.'

'No. You got what you wanted. You can report to your boss what you think about me. See if I pass his test.'

He missed the sarcasm. 'You will pass. You're very sweet. But I didn't get what *I* wanted.'

Puzzled, she paused as he stood, and she nearly wasn't quick enough to avoid the lips that came at her. But dodge the kiss she did, then stepped out of the booth and aimed for the exit.

The hour that Kenna had waited until leaving for the pub had provided ample time for Ray's mind to play its old tricks. Ten minutes after she left, he grabbed his car keys. He got in his car, started it, and that was when he realised. He roared like a wounded bear and slapped the steering wheel.

Fuck. He couldn't remember which pub Kenna was meeting the slimeball at. He pulled out his phone and asked Google for a list of establishments, but none of the names rang a bell. He recalled that she'd picked a pub that wasn't local, so calling around places was out of the question.

Annoyed, he headed back into the house. His mind threw up images of Kenna and the slimeball laughing over drinks. Sitting close. He wondered if she'd kiss him goodnight, if only to be polite.

When she came home sometime later, he confronted her out on the street. 'What happened? Did he try anything?'

'Not out here. Let me get inside first.'

'Did you cosy up?'

'Cosy up?' She pushed past him. As they walked up the path, he demanded to know every detail of her time with the slimeball. She ignored him until they were in the living room, where she flung her coat and dumped herself in an armchair. Ray paced as he awaited an answer.

'Ray, stop. We can't be fighting like this. We have to work together to get through this. Please. I can't deal with this problem and have you as an enemy, too.'

Ray stopped pacing. He apologised. She got up and they hugged. He said, 'Let's get out of here for a bit. Let's just drive.'

She agreed. Once their car was rolling, she told him everything she'd learned from the man called Alfie. They went to a McDonald's and Ray waited in the car while she bought meals. When she returned, it was to learn that Ray had been busy surfing the internet.

'The Magpie is a guy called Alan Marshall, fifty-eight.'

Kenna almost said that was too old for her, before realising her error. Ray continued.

Marshall's parents were both drug dealers, according to a newspaper feature on him from three years ago. His father, a high-level gangster, introduced him to the crime trade at age six. By nine he was a full-fledged member of the same gang his dad worked for. By eleven he had enough skills, smarts and street clout to realise he wanted to give orders, not take them.

At thirteen, he started his own crew and took a number of people with him, which displeased the top brass. The bosses sought a violent revenge, and they tasked Marshall's own father with carrying it out.

It didn't go as planned and The Magpie found himself on the run, one dead parent left behind. He lived in safe houses and cars, ever on the move, for a couple of years, until one day a man walked into a police station. With minute details of the murder, a confession and the murder weapon. Police suspected he'd been paid to take the rap, but couldn't do anything about it. That guy got a life sentence and Marshall got to show his face on the streets again.

He was free, but aware that the police wouldn't just forget about him. Convinced they'd break rules to knock him off his perch, Marshall fled to France, where he was suspected to reside to this day. Somehow he'd gotten dual citizenship and now had a front as a respected businessman over there. Before the public, he hobnobbed with celebrities and the rich, while behind the scenes he ran a criminal empire. A real modern Al Capone. He was still paranoid, however, and nobody knew where he lived or – apart from when he appeared out of the blue at functions – where he was at any given time. He was suspected of making frequent trips to the UK, to deal with criminal business and to visit his ex-wife, but he always travelled under false names. To aid in this he recruited some of the very best security and counter-intelligence minds available. He was, according to quote a chief constable quote, 'too big to chop down'.

'And this is the guy they want you to dance and dine with,' Ray said.

'Please don't say it like that. You're acting like I won a date with a movie star. This isn't something I want to do. If you can think of a way out of this, I'm all ears.'

Ray suddenly didn't fancy his burger. He wrapped it up again. 'I'm sorry. This is just overwhelming me.'

Remembering what Alfie had said about Marshall, she took Ray's phone, clicked and scrolled, and found what she'd expected. She showed him some pictures. Marshall exiting a flash car at a film premiere, with an elegant woman on his arm. Opening a swimming pool he helped build, with a different woman by his side. In shorts on the deck of a yacht, with bikini-clad beauties all around. He'd been tied to dozens of young women since divorcing his wife three years ago. 'What do these pictures tell you?'

'That crime pays.'

Kenna tutted. 'All these girls. He's got his pick of beautiful women.'

'So why does he want you?'

Kenna knew it wasn't an insult. 'Not the point. Women want him, or at least his money. Or fame. Or notoriety. Whatever. He isn't going begging. And it's all in the public eye.'

'A mask.'

'Yes,' Kenna said, 'but the point is that a man like him isn't going to do me harm. He's not going to kidnap me or rape little old me. See what I'm saying? I'll be safe. For some reason he's taken to a typical woman from a housing estate. But it's just for one night, and then he'll forget about me. I'll be okay.'

'He's rich. What if he wants you to sleep with him?'

'We discussed this. Of course I won't sleep with him. I can't believe you'd think that.'

To her surprise, Ray wasn't finished with his bizarre worry just yet. 'He could pay. What if he offered you ten grand? That's good money and we need it. You might take it.'

'No way. Come on, Ray, serious?'

'You could pretend it's a gift, and I'd never know. Thirty grand. Fifty. Could you turn that down for an hour naked in bed?'

'Yes! In a flash. Are you being serious?'

Ray unwrapped his burger again, but stared at it. 'What if he falls for you? He could buy you cars and a big house. There's a brand-new, elegant lifestyle, ripe for the taking. You'd leave me and go live in the French Riviera. Who wouldn't take a rich businessman over a brain-damaged handyman?'

She grabbed his chin to turn his head and read those eyes for a joke. She couldn't tell. 'You're playing, right? Winding me up?'

He shrugged. 'A bit. Maybe. I don't know.'

She kissed his cheek. 'My poor paranoid baby. Marshall doesn't have the charm you do. I married you, and I'll stay with you.'

He nodded, but was still glum. 'Cheers.'

A joke was a joke, but she couldn't forget that they still faced a real threat. 'I think we'll be okay after this, Ray. I think this Marshall won't do anything to harm me, and with luck he won't let us be harmed afterwards by Eli and his goons. Not if he's been seen with me. Too risky. He's careful. I bet if we look into all these girls he's dated, we won't find one who ended up dead in a ditch. Agree?'

'Yeah. I guess.'

'Come here, you big lug.' She hugged him hard, and he reciprocated. Into his ear, she said, 'Mind you, you just cost us big time. He might have given me ten grand as a gift just to say thanks for a nice dinner date. Can't take it now, can I? Not with your paranoia.'

He laughed. It felt good to hear.

TEN

Halfway through her thirty-minute journey to the office, Kenna became aware that the same car, a Ford Fiesta, had been following her for a couple of miles. It was Monday morning rush hour, so maybe that meant nothing, but she made a number of unnecessary turns to test the theory.

The Ford followed.

At traffic lights, the Ford stopped right behind her. She pretended to check her eyelashes in the rear-view mirror, so she could see the occupants of the car. Two men, both big. Light through the window showed a Chinese tattoo on the face of the passenger, which was absolute proof. These were Eli's men, and they were following her. But why?

She considered calling in sick to work and turning the car around. She didn't want Eli to know her place of employment. But perhaps he already did or didn't care. Maybe the men were on her tail just to make sure she didn't go to the police. She had to act normally or he'd be suspicious, and that might warrant another late-night visit.

At work, she parked and watched as the Ford entered the car park. She thought that was risky of them, but quickly realised the men weren't trying to be secretive. The car parked right behind hers and now she noticed another shape in the back seat: three men. The tattooed bruiser got out. She fought the urge to drive away. Instead, she locked the doors.

He came to her window and knocked gnarly knuckles against it. She buzzed the glass down an inch. 'Give me your keys,' he said. No introduction, so he knew she knew who he worked for.

'Why?'

'Because I want the keys.'

He was hardly going to change his mind. She passed them through the gap in the window. He pocketed them and got back in his car. And there both men waited.

She got out and scuttled to the entrance of her workplace. There was no attempt to follow. Once inside reception, she watched through the glass as the bruiser got out of his car. And into hers. Both vehicles then left the car park. Kenna continued to stare in disbelief.

'Mrs Barker? You okay?'

Kenna turned. The receptionist, Sally, was gawking at her. 'Fine,' Kenna said, then walked to the lift. Her call centre was on the third floor, so she got time to think as the lift rose. Why did Eli want her car? To make sure she couldn't flee at lunchtime? To hold as leverage against her? On her floor, she ran to the toilet and called Ray.

He was on a big decorating job, but according to the banter she could hear from his colleagues, nobody was working too hard. She told him what had happened. He had a far wilder theory than any she had concocted.

'Jesus, they're going to set you up for a crime to make you do the date.'

'What? What do you mean?'

'I don't know, but I've read about this sort of stuff.

Blackmail. They could use the car in a robbery. Or they'll fill it with drugs and leave it somewhere, and send the police to it if you don't do what they say. Shit, we might have to go to the cops after all.'

'Don't call them. Not yet. Let's see what happens. I mean, nobody said anything. I don't understand why they wouldn't just warn us again about the police. Let's talk about it after work. I won't concentrate if I am worrying about it.'

They spoke a little more before hanging up. At her desk, Kenna signed into her computer and put on her game face as best she could.

Vicky had called in sick today. Kenna tried calling her, but it rang off. She'd hoped to use Vicky for a lift home, but two more calls throughout the day also failed. She didn't want to have to lie to another colleague, so at clocking off time she called a taxi. To avoid anyone seeing the taxi and asking questions, she made sure she was first out the door and ran down the stairs.

As soon as she got out of the building, she stopped dead.

Her car was back. It sat in the very spot she'd parked it. She looked around as she walked over, but the Ford was nowhere. The door was unlocked and the keys were in the ignition. She checked the door pockets, glovebox, under the seats, and in the boot. No bags of drugs. No illegal documents. No weapons. No dead body.

She got in and started it up, and that was when she noticed the difference. The engine sounded healthy. And the interior – cleaned. A small crack in the bottom right of the windscreen was gone. She tested the passenger side electric window, busted for months now, and it buzzed down. A giggle escaped her. Eli's men had fixed her vehicle. She had to remind herself that wasn't news to be happy about.

She cancelled her taxi and started driving. Half a mile from work, her good mood bottomed out. The Ford had reappeared. For the next mile, she glanced every few seconds, and there it was, always at least three cars back. So intense was her scrutiny that she was late spotting a traffic light turn red. And the cars ahead stopping.

'Shit,' she yelled as she slammed on the brakes. But too late. Her car slowed, but not in time, and she was jolted forward by a mediocre bump against the vehicle in front.

The crash barely made a noise and didn't seem to cause damage, but it incensed the driver in front. He leaped out of his vehicle and threw his arms up in exasperation. He was young, pretty big, and wore a T-shirt bearing the slogan I FUCKED THE HORSE YOU RODE IN ON.

'What the fuck, you silly bitch?'

He went to the back of his car to appraise the damage, and kicked her vehicle. The insult and the violence hit a nerve in her. She put her window down an inch. 'Don't be a twat. I'll give you my insurance. Calm down.'

His anger hit a fresh gear. He stormed to her door and tried to open it. Finding it locked enraged him further and he punched the window. 'Get the fuck out, you stupid whore.'

He suddenly forgot about her and looked to his left. She glanced back and saw that the bruisers, still three cars back, had exited their vehicle and were approaching. All three of them. The driver yelled over: 'Get lost, lads. Not your business.'

The bruisers clearly didn't agree. The trio grabbed him. He yelled and struggled, but they were bigger. Kenna watched the men march the driver to his car and roughly stuff him inside. She allowed herself a smile.

Which she quickly abandoned. That wasn't the end of it.

Two bruisers also got in the car. Through the back window, she saw flailing arms and realised punches were flying.

Seconds later, the car promptly cut out of the queue, one of Eli's men at the wheel. It leaped through the red light and turned right at the junction. Gone. *My God. What are they going to do to him?*

Her attention was drawn by a rap at the window. The remaining henchman was standing right there, staring at her. She put the glass down another few inches. He poked something through. 'Take this. Keep it on you at all times.'

'What's going to happen to him? I don't want anyone hurt.'

'Schooling. Don't worry about it. Take this. We can't always be there to help. You're too important to be hurt. Keep it on you at all times.'

And then he was gone. He got back in his car, and just sat there. She looked at the item in her hand. It was a pink plastic device marked PEPPER SPRAY. It was still tricky to digest the last thirty seconds.

When she looked at the light, it was green. Everybody behind was waiting for her to shift, although none had dared honk a horn. She dumped the pepper spray in her door pocket and, with shaking hands, drove on.

When Ray returned home from work, Kenna was cooking. He hugged her from behind. Before he could ask about the men who'd followed her, she said, 'They fixed my car.'

'What do you mean?'

She told him the tale, including the event with the angry driver. When Ray discovered that the man with the Chinese tattoo had been present, he said, 'You could have bust his nose for me. Anyway, how did they know about the car?'

'I don't know. Heard the bad engine, I guess. But don't you think this is further proof they're trying to be nice?'

He sat at the table and she laid out cutlery and plates. He said, 'I'm not sure nice is the word. This is all part of some bizarre plan. They're not our friends, remember. Sorting out that driver was just insurance so you can do what they want.'

'But it's proof we're not in danger. They had no reason to fix the car. We're already planning to do what they said. I think their word is good.'

'They're criminals.'

Kenna took a cottage pie from the oven. 'Yes, but as long as we don't say no to them, I think we'll be fine. It explains why they have done things to help. They didn't need to. They could have stuck with the threats. I think they're happy with us because we've agreed to their plan and haven't gone to the police.'

'Happy with us? I'm not sure I like that. And happy for how long?'

His concern was not misplaced. 'Let's just not think about it for a while, please. Can we just eat?'

He agreed and she dished out the meal. But conversation on any other subject seemed pointless, and they ate in silence.

Halfway through the meal, they were interrupted by banging at the back door. The table would be visible if the door was open, so Kenna moved out of sight as Ray went to answer it.

'Is she in? We've got more business.'

That voice again. The slimy man called Alfie was back.

'Piss off, pal,' Ray said. 'We're having dinner. You people need to give us some space until this thing is ready to go down.'

'This is not good,' Alfie said. 'There are things to work out and I need her for it. You want me to go tell the boss you're both getting ready to trick us?'

'Go tell him we're doing what he wants and he needs to stop sending brainless goons here each night.'

'What the fuck are you saying, dickhead? You know who you're talking to?'

'Get lost. Don't come back here.'

Ray slammed and locked the door. There was a thud as Alfie booted it. Ray grabbed the handle, and she knew he'd go flying out there if Alfie kicked again. But that was the end of it. She peeked through the blinds over the window saw him walking down their back yard.

'He's going.'

Ray returned to the table to finish his meal. Kenna continued to watch Alfie. Strangely, he walked the entire length of their back yard and clambered over the fence at the end.

'Come eat,' Ray said.

'He might tell Eli. This might not be good.'

'All they care about is what happens Saturday. I'm sure Eli won't mind if one of his bozos gets sent packing. If they want to keep us sweet, like you say, then nothing will come of this.'

She hoped he was right.

ELEVEN

By eight that evening, two hours after dinner, Ray appeared to be right. Surely Eli knew about the scene with Alfie by now, yet nobody else had been to the house. Ray took it as proof that they'd seen the last of Alfie. But, when he came downstairs after a shower, Kenna unloaded a different theory.

'I don't think Alfie was sent here. I think he came on his own. I think he likes me. I reckon it's why he scuttled away across the back yard. Maybe he's worried about Eli finding out.'

'Possibly. At least he's got taste.'

'Don't joke, Ray. I don't like the idea of this man stalking me.'

'He won't. Next time we see one of their guys, we tell them to make sure Alfie never comes round again.'

'Good idea.' She looked him up and down, noting that he was smartly dressed in jeans and a blue shirt. 'Are you going somewhere?'

'Pub for an hour. You okay with that? I said I'd meet Joe for a pint. Didn't I mention?'

'No. But it's fine. I'm just worried about being alone if Alfie comes back. Or someone else.'

'I doubt it. But I can stay if you want.'

She thought about it, which was worrying. But in the end she shook her head. 'You go. I know you like to meet your rugby mates, and we shouldn't let this whole nastiness get in the way of our lives. I'll call if there's a problem.'

Ray kissed his wife and skipped out. He planned on having only a half pint, so he was good to drive. He knew of a pub about ten miles away where he could get what he needed. He stopped at an ATM en route and walked into the pub with a hundred in cash. He used his bank card to buy a half of cider, then stood near a fruit machine to watch the room.

There was a pool match in play and the place was busy. Seven guys were clogged together like outsiders, while seven others with cues seemed to be the centre of attraction. A league game, then, with the locals playing at home. When a frame ended and the crowd dispersed to the toilets and the bar and outside to smoke, Ray approached a couple of young men in sports gear and ball caps.

'I'm after weed if you know anyone?'

The two turned to him. One, who had teardrops tattooed on his cheek, said, 'You saying we look like druggies?'

'No, mate, you look like guys who know the area. Did I say weed? I meant a charging station for an electric car. Sorry for the interruption.'

He returned to his spot by the fruit machine. Soon, the next frame was in play and almost everyone was focused on the pool table. Almost. The two guys were giving Ray the eyeball. One sauntered over and jabbed a pound into the fruit machine. 'So you need your car charging, eh?'

'Yep. Can you help with that?'

'Hang fire a bit. Piece of shit robber.' Pound lost, the guy slapped the fruit machine and meandered back to his pal. He made a call on his mobile. Ray watched without making it obvious.

When the pool frame was done, Ray joined a group heading outside. At the front were the two young men. He walked to his car and waited there. When the smokers started to file back into the pub, the two guys saw Ray was hanging around and approached. Teardrops said, 'I know of someone. He'll only do a hundred.'

'I'll have a hundred.'

'Follow us, yeah?'

Ray nodded. The two guys got into a green hatchback, which he tailed for over a mile before it turned into an industrial estate. It was a single road, lined with businesses on both sides, and very dark. A fine place for a mugging, but also perfect for a drug deal.

At the end, the road curved before ending at a locked, disused gate leading to the overgrown grounds of a run-down building. It was very secluded, and it reminded Ray of the area where he and Kenna had been attacked on Friday night.

A car was already here. The hatchback pulled up behind it. Ray parked at the hatchback's rear and got out. Nobody got out of the hatchback so he went to the driver's window. Teardrops dropped it and said, 'Go see the guy up front.'

He got halfway. Both front doors opened and two young men jumped out. Behind him, the same scene with the hatchback. Four guys, boxing him in, and each holding a stick. Ray knew he'd taken a risk, and tonight it hadn't paid off. He pulled his wallet and tossed it on the ground. 'Guys, if I get out of here without a problem, no one will ever know. Take the hundred, call it a good night, and it's the last you'll hear of it.'

Something hard hit his lower back. His knees buckled and he dropped. Immediately, he curled into a ball on the cracked pavement, knowing he had to ride out what came next. His priority was to protect his head, so he wrapped both arms around it as punches and kicks fell like meteors. It left his torso wide open, but damage there might heal just fine.

What seemed like ages later, the blows stopped and hands grabbed him. He was hauled to his feet. Some of the heavy boot stomps against his arms had transferred energy to his head nonetheless and he felt dizzy. He wasn't quite sure what was happening until he was thrown into the back seat of a car. Two men were with him and they both forced him to bend forward over his own knees. One had a fist in his hair and another had a hand around the back of his neck. He heard doors slamming and within moments the car was moving.

'Just take the fucking money,' Ray yelled. He struggled to sit upright, but their downward force overwhelmed him.

'You fucked up now, pal. Say goodbye to everything.'

'I gave you the damn money you wanted.'

'An example has to be made, dickhead. You're gonna be it. Hope you wrote a fucking will, mate.'

They drove for what seemed like a long, long time. Ray's back was throbbing from being bent almost in half. He had stopped struggling some time back, but the hands remained on him. He had also stopped talking after every plea had elicited another threat.

He couldn't shake the notion that he was being driven to his final resting place. It seemed unreal that he'd be killed or seriously maimed, but if it was to happen, it wouldn't be in some other guy's car. So they would have to get him outside, and that would give him a single, final, shallow, risky but vital chance to flee.

Finally, the car stopped. Ray's breath became ragged. A

minute from now, he'd know his fate. Sixty seconds might determine the rest of his life.

The hands holding him let go. At first, Ray didn't dare move. Then he slowly sat up, and with every inch expected a whack. It didn't come. The driver was watching him in the rear-view mirror. The two guys with him in the rear were grinning. All three were men he didn't recognise. They weren't the fuckers from the drug deal.

He looked out the window. It took a few seconds for him to recognise the house they'd parked outside.

His own.

'What's going on?'

As he watched, a car passed the vehicle and parked outside his house. His own car. A guy got out and came over. He took the empty passenger seat and held out Ray's keys. This bastard was grinning like the others.

'Very funny, guys,' Ray said. 'So you've been following me as well as my wife.'

The driver said, 'And lucky for you.'

'What happened to the guys who tried to rob me?'

The driver handed Ray his wallet. 'They'll be giving that hobby up for a while. Now listen up. I like my word searches. You interrupted that. So do me a favour, right? No more drugs trips. Stay indoors with the missus. Have sex, watch TV. After Saturday you can go skydiving or alligator wrestling or whatever you want. Now get out.'

Ray didn't move. In fact, he sat back and even nudged aside one of the brutes by his side to make room. 'I think that drug deal would have gone just fine if you hadn't interrupted. Now I need some weed. I'm sure your boss deals. Call and ask.'

The driver laughed. 'You're misjudging your place here, Ray. We need your missus, not you. You're nobody. She needs to be kept sweet, and that's the only reason you're six feet above six feet under. Out you get before we lob you out.'

'I'm not moving. You throw me out, my nosey neighbours see. Someone's going to call the police about that. This car's registration is probably already on five CCTV cameras. Call your boss.'

Ray had pegged him as the leader of this trio, but the guy in the passenger seat, who'd brought Ray's car home, instructed him to head around the block. On another street, the driver was ordered to stop and call Eli. He got out to do so.

The passenger turned the rear-view mirror so he could see Ray. It allowed Ray to see his own face, and he was pleased to see no damage from the beating. Only his arms throbbed from protecting his head. He said, 'Seriously, though, many thanks for saving me from those drug dealers. I don't mean to be a pain.'

The guy gave no reply and stopped staring. The driver came back moments later, got in, and handed his phone to Ray.

'Nobody barks orders at me, Ray,' Eli said. He was sitting up in Sherrie's bed. 'Not a second time, anyway. Don't think your wife is some kind of forcefield protecting you.'

'I apologise,' Ray said. 'I'm not barking orders. I just want help. You guys can get weed. You're powerful.'

Sherrie, one of his whores, was right behind him, massaging his shoulders. She had heard Ray's voice because she whispered, 'Yes you are, big man. Powerful.'

'Aw shucks, I'm going to blush,' Eli told Ray. 'As goodwill for what your wife is doing for us, I'll get you some weed. I don't mind that at all. You could have asked anytime. But don't take it to mean I owe you anything, and don't push your luck, okay?'

'Don't mean to. I'm just trying to stay calm. This is quite

hard for us. Especially for Kenna. I just want to help her through it. Which reminds me. There's a guy, Alfie I think, who's been coming round and freaking my wife out. It would be great if he could stop.'

'I'll look into that. And I get what you're saying about Kenna. She can't deal with this problem and have you as an enemy. So I'll get you some weed, and you'll chill the hell out. You'll have it tomorrow. Hey, Ray, you know what else I can do for you?'

'What?' Given Ray's tone, Eli knew he must be expecting a threat, perhaps even a sarcastic joke.

'A second opinion about your head.'

A pause. That had the guy's brain in turmoil. 'What do you know about my head?'

'I have contacts. I know about your early-onset dementia. I also have access to a neurologist up in Manchester. Thrown a few quid, this guy might be able to reverse your diagnosis. A nice piece of paper saying that, wafted under your rugby manager's nose, could put a ball back in your hands.'

'And why would you do that?' He sounded suspicious.

'You're both doing a big favour for me. I'm grateful for you keeping your wife thinking straight.'

And with that he hung up. Sherrie said, 'That's not like you.'

He turned to look at her. 'What's that mean?'

'Complimenting that guy. You sounded like you owed him.'

Eli wanted to laugh. Instead, he pushed her hands off his shoulders and got up. 'I say nice thing to you, too. Means nothing.'

'That's not true. I'm your best girl. I know I'm the only one you fuck.'

'Yeah, but my sister's dog shit is the only one I'll pick up.'

She looked hurt, which was good. It wouldn't do to have people think he sympathised. They might take the piss.

Upset, Sherrie walked, naked, to the bathroom. She was a pretty thing, but stupid. He'd told her to tell none of the girls they were sleeping together. Why hadn't she realised he might have – and had – said the same to others?

He wasn't yet sexually satisfied, but he no longer wanted Sherrie. She was getting too clingy. He got dressed and, without a word, slipped out of the flat.

Ray passed the phone back to its owner. The car started moving again.

When they dropped him off, Ray strode towards the house without a look back. He paused at the door to watch the car leave, and to think. Eli had been very smart with his words. He'd called the Saturday thing a 'favour'. And he'd hinted that 'favours' could be directed right back at Ray... if he worked with them to make sure Kenna did what they wanted.

He tried to clear his mind and stepped into the house. Kenna was in the kitchen, reading by the radio at the table. She put her book away and smiled at him. 'Good evening? Nothing happened here. No one came to the door.'

She had a genuine smile for the first time in a while, and he really hated having to ruin it. 'We're being watched.'

'What?'

He told her his theory: Eli had men watching the house, ready to follow them if they left. He said he'd spotted the tail as he drove to the pub. Unwilling to expose his friend to them, he'd then turned away and led the tail car on a merry jaunt just to make sure, before returning home.

'My God. I mean, it makes sense,' she said. 'Does this mean they don't trust us?'

'It means they're making sure we don't do a runner. Not that we are. We'll get this Saturday thing done, then forget all about it and get on with our lives.'

Kenna was about to speak when he held a finger to his lips. He beckoned her to the bathroom, where he put the shower on full. For noise.

'What's going on?' she said.

'I think they've planted a bug. A listening device.'

'What? When? How? How do you know?'

'Maybe when they came in to fix the back door. I realised after Eli said something. He repeated something you said. *...I can't deal with this problem and have you as an enemy.*'

He immediately realised his mistake. Kenna would ask when Eli had repeated this line to him. He would have to admit he'd called their enemy. And admit why.

But she missed it, thankfully. 'I said that? Are you sure?'

'There are some things my brain keeps hold of, Kenna.'

'No, I didn't mean that. But even if I did say that, it doesn't mean anything. It could be coincidence.'

'I don't think so. And you said that in this house. So I think they've bugged it.'

'Let's assume they have. The bug could be anywhere. In all the rooms, maybe. Even this one. What do we do?'

'We just act normal. They've heard all sorts of stuff by now. We just make sure we don't mention the police or try to back out of this. I also got the boss to get Alfie off our backs.'

'That's something, at least.'

TWELVE

Half an hour after Kenna had gone to bed, Ray was in the living room with the TV. In the daytime he could deal with worries and headaches, but late nights were when he stressed over life's problems and the various paths through them. The best counter to this was comedy. He liked to watch YouTube videos of funny animals and fails. The current complication was a biggie, but he managed to forget it for a while. Until one video made him laugh so hard that his healing lip split again. He suddenly didn't fancy the cheese on toast he was eating.

He got up and looked around the room. For a while he'd also forgotten that the house might be bugged. Right now he hoped it was. He paused the TV.

'Hey, you guys listening? You hear me? I know you can. Maybe you've got my phone number as well. Here it is in case not.' He checked his phone for his own number and spoke it to the room. A notepad message stored on the phone held Eli's name. 'Eli, I've just had a great idea. I reckon it would be fun for your people. So call me right now.'

Kenna could sleep through Ray's loud and late TV binges, but something in her was attuned to his voice. Even though it was far quieter than whatever he was watching, it woke her. She had only been out half an hour, so there was no grogginess. She sat up, worried. She couldn't make out individual words, but Ray was definitely talking down in the living room. He never conversed with the TV, so had someone come into the house? Perhaps by invite?

Or was he talking to the hidden bugs? If so, and he was venting anger, she had to stop him. She got up, grabbed a dressing gown, and crept out of the room. If he heard her, he would stop. She needed to know what he was saying so she could do damage control.

By the time she'd got halfway down the stairs, she was able to make out words. She heard the tail-end of a sentence: '... yeah... half an hour, okay?'

She opened the living room door quickly, which made Ray jump. He had his phone in his hand. Nobody else was here. He saw her look down at it. 'Did you hear me talking?' he said.

'Yes. Who were you talking to?'

'A mate from the rugby club called me.'

She relaxed a little, realising she had misjudged the scene. Now she felt foolish for thinking he'd been talking to the listening devices. But her suspicions bloated again when he told her he had to go out. She asked where he could possibly be heading at almost midnight.

'My mate, who I was on the phone to. He needs to borrow my boots.'

A rugby mate suddenly didn't have rugby boots? 'You need to do that now?'

'He's got to set off early tomorrow for a game in Manchester. I can't sleep, so I said I'd take them round. That okay?'

While a little strange, that would have been fine. Except his story reeked. But, just in case, she refused to challenge him. Ray headed upstairs to get changed, then came down for his shoes and coat and car keys. When he was ready, he unlocked the front door and bid her goodnight.

'The boots?' she said.

He slapped his own forehead. 'I'm stupid. I forgot. You know what I'm like.'

Sure. Except this time she knew he'd overlooked the boots because said boots were bullshit.

As a proclamation of the end of his rugby days, Ray had put his old kit in the attic. He'd even jokingly held a funeral service. She watched as he entered the space and retrieved the boots. They were still caked in old, dried mud. He bagged them and headed for the door. The whole charade was bothersome. How stupid did he think she was?

And where the hell was he really going?

Once he'd gone, Kenna rushed to the dark bedroom to lurk by the curtains and watch him leave. Ray got in his car and started using his phone. He then put it in the suction cradle on his window, which he only used when employing his phone as a satnav. His memory could sometimes lose common routes, but here she doubted that was the case. No, his destination was a place he didn't know the way to, and that meant he wasn't heading to see a friend. He had used his phone to arrange a secret midnight meet.

But with who? Did he have another woman?

———

It was past 2am when Ray returned. She was dropping off when she heard the double blip of his car locking. For the entirety of his absence, she'd been determined to confront him the moment he walked in the door. Now, she chose to wait and see what he did next.

He came upstairs. He walked through the dark room slowly, careful not to wake her, and entered the bathroom. If he ran the shower, it was proof that he had a mistress whose scent – and god knew what else – he planned to sluice away.

She heard the light switch. But not the shower. Even in the gloom of the bedroom, she'd noticed an unsteadiness to his gait, and all thoughts of other women were pushed aside for a new theory: weed. Ray must have gone to smoke with someone, perhaps whoever provided his secret stash. Maybe that was a woman.

Well, she'd feign ignorance no more. She opened the door. Ray was standing before the mirror, dabbing his face with a wet cloth. When he turned, she let out a shocked wheeze.

'Jesus Christ, what happened to you?'

His face was a mess. On top of the original injuries he now had bruising on his forehead, scratches on a cheek, and one ear was bloody. She grabbed his head and turned it this way and that for a detailed examination. She sat him on the toilet so she could work on him with the cloth.

'I know you smoke that bloody dope, Ray. Is that where you went? To some drug den? Did they mug you?'

If he'd been shocked that he'd been caught, he was downright flabbergasted by her knowledge that he still smoked weed. 'How did you know about that?'

'Because I know you, and we live together. You've been smoking even more since you quit rugby. I know the shed is your little vice den.'

He wasn't that surprised, actually. 'There were some near

misses, like that time you came in the shed and I could still see smoke in the air. I kind of knew it would be impossible not to smell it. Why didn't you pull me on it?'

'You feel you need it.'

'Well, not anymore. I'm quitting. I've seen up close what criminals are like. I'm not going to play a part any more in making money for them. I'll have paracetamol for my headaches.'

'But what about tonight? Is that why you want to quit? Because you got mugged?'

He couldn't meet her eyes. He didn't want to talk.

'Ray, you have scratches on your neck. If it's not about dope, then what? They don't half look like some woman put up a struggle. You want me to assume you just molested someone? Start talking.'

She wasn't sure if she had cracked a joke or tried to trick him. Regardless, it worked. He started talking.

'Are you wearing sexy underwear?'

The telling moment, which was perhaps the biggest part of the thrill. She would play along, or she would end it right now.

'Freak,' the woman said, her voice full of sleep. There was a click and the line went dead. Eli took the mobile apart and lobbed it out of the window, into the grass alongside the hard shoulder of the M1, where he was parked. Bitch.

Freak? She had hardly delivered breaking news. But his fantasy, which he knew from research was called telephone scatologia, was shared by many. The strangest part for Eli was that when he was a kid, many of his friends used to make obscene phone calls to girls, yet he'd always frowned upon it. What a turnaround.

Well, he hadn't driven all the way out here in the dead of night just to give up after one fail, so he consulted his notepad and selected another number. They were all women who'd had a car serviced at his garage over the years. At least 200 numbers, and he'd burned through well over half. Three women had played along and eventually agreed to meet for sex, but he'd never partaken. First, it could be a trap. But more important: that wasn't what he wanted. He liked the disembodied voices.

Before he could call the number, his main phone for the evening rang. It was a guy known only as Ears: his surveillance man. Ex-Security Service, dapper, but a goddamn hypochondriac.

Ears said, 'Sir, Ray Barker just spoke to the living room in his house. I think he knows about the microphones. He gave you a strange message. I'll quote. "Eli, I've just had a great idea. I reckon it would be fun for your people. So call me right now". He also gave a phone number. Hey, boss, any chance you could ask that doctor from Almond street to–'

Eli hung up on Ears. He already had Ray's number and called it from a burner. He was intrigued. As soon as Ray answered, Eli said, 'By making this call, I just confirmed that we've got your house bugged. Bad move. Except I'm very interested in this thing you say will be fun.'

'The ape with the Chinese tattoo from the other night. The one who thought he was the bee's knees, but needed a guy to hold me while he threw lazy-ass punches.'

'What about him? You think I'll fire him for you? Are you forgetting what I said about your worth to me?'

'No, I know full well that I mean nothing and I'm lucky to be alive and all that crap. What I'm hoping is you're a man who likes things fair. Fair would be me versus tattoo coward freak boy.'

Eli laughed. 'His mum opted for the name Louis at the last

minute.'

'Right now. Give him a call. If he's a man, he'll come.'

'Mano a mano, a big balls competition. Something to prove to the ego, Ray?'

'No, just a fan of the idea of punching that sod's lights out. Give me a location.'

Eli paused. 'You for real?'

'Location.'

Eli laughed again. 'Wow. Okay. I'll call you back.' He hung up and called one of his fixers. All he said was, 'Get the arena ready.' Then he called Ray back with a postcode. 'Write it down, Ray, because that brain of yours will lose it in about five seconds. Go now.' He then hung up.

Eli drove to South Park. He parked where he could and entered the grounds and made his way to the tennis courts.

The fixer was here and he had worked quickly. Inside the tennis court was the brute Ray had asked for. He wore a tracksuit and a beanie cap, and he was shadow boxing. Four portable lamps had been placed around the edges of one half of the court, firing their light inwards to illuminate the battle arena. The fixer had even brought Eli a coffee, although he wasn't going to consume caffeine this late.

The fixer got a radio call three minutes later, which he relayed to Eli. 'Mr Barker is here.'

Escorted by another man, Ray entered the area from a tree-lined path a minute after that. He took a long look at his opponent, still boxing away in the tennis court, and then approached Eli. The escort and the fixer got nicely placed to intervene in case Ray tried something silly.

'Very cinematic,' Ray said.

Eli nodded. 'I love a good fight. If my guys have disputes with each other, this is how I have them sort it out.'

That was bullshit. Disputes were settled by Eli. The arena

was used when he captured enemies or caught a traitorous one of his own. A chance for that man to save himself, although usually Eli stacked the odds in his favour by pitting the condemned against two or even three opponents. 'You really ready for this?'

'Did you warn Alfie off yet?'

'All in good time. So, you ready?'

Ray nodded. Eli said, 'Okay, So, let's run over a few things. This ends with a knockout or a verbal tap out.'

'Fine.'

'If you're too tough for your own good, the guy standing nearby will play referee and save you. Same for Louis.'

'As long as he doesn't jump in too early.'

Eli loved it. 'Louis is a street fighter and they don't do rules, but he's willing to arrange a few with you once you get in there.'

'Cool.'

'Let's be serious here now. I need Kenna, not you. Even if you are lying in a hospital bed, the plan for Saturday still goes ahead. You sure about this?'

'I'm happy as long as nobody interferes. And you don't hold it against me if I beat your ape.'

'I won't. Afterwards, it's done and we forget about it. One more thing, Ray. The most important. That's a concrete tennis court and big guys like you two can fall hard. I had a guy go down for a one-punch kill. That sort of shit can come right out of nowhere. If Louis dies, I'll get rid of the body and cover the crime. You'll get away with murder.'

Ray said nothing. Did the warning even compute in the guy's misfiring brain? Or was he too enwrapped by anger to think of the consequences of his actions tonight? 'But there's a flip side, Ray, and I'll say it outright. If you die in there, you're gone. No body. No funeral. In Kenna's eyes, you walked out of the house and were never seen again.'

'Are we ready now?' Ray said. Eli laughed and nodded. Ray opened the gate into the tennis court. The bruiser was on the far side of the net, so Ray approached it. Louis turned to him and walked closer. They stood ten feet apart, separated only by that net.

'I'm all good for this,' Louis said. 'But just so you know, that other thing was business.'

'So is this.'

'Rules?'

'No biting. No eye gouging. No kicks on the ground.'

'Okay. But you say that now. Might be a different tale when I'm half-killing you.'

'And vice versa,' Ray said, and stepped over the net.

Eli settled down for a show.

———

Ray had supplied a full account to Kenna so far, but regarding the fight itself said only, 'I had to tap out. He got me in the liver, and that just shut my body down. But I broke his nose.'

Kenna wasn't impressed. She looked angry. 'That was a very bad idea, Ray. You could have been seriously hurt. Or killed.'

'We had rules. The guy was friendly afterwards. We actually shook hands. He's got a kid and he's a carer for his mum.'

She didn't care. 'You can't keep taking damage like this. I'm not going to rehash what doctors have already told you. I'm just going to say I'm very disappointed.'

'I'm sorry. I don't know what came over me.'

Of course he did. Kenna knew he'd had a few fights in the early years of their relationship. The pub attached to his rugby club had a sign above the bar saying REMEMBER THIS IS A RUGBY CLUB. It was supposed to ward off troublemakers, but sometimes it had drawn in thugs who fancied their chances. Nothing beat a good scrap as a painkiller following a loss at rugby, and Ray had always been game. Kenna didn't know half of what he'd got up to as an ego-fuelled twentysomething.

Ray thought he'd gotten past that wild phase of life, but the loss of rugby had created an adrenaline void and tonight's rumble had provided a sweet dose.

'Let's get you in the shower,' she said. She put it on, but when Ray got up to undress, she pushed him back down onto the toilet seat. He understood: the shower was just noise to mask what came next.

'What you did tonight was a bad idea,' she whispered. 'But not just the risk to your brain. You wanted revenge. You asked Eli for a favour. Now you owe him. Now he might think he can just come and ask you for whatever he wants.'

'I'll just say no. They're forcing us to do this Saturday thing, so I can't imagine he thinks he needs permission for anything.'

'He also knows we know about the surveillance on the house. He might suspect we're watching what we say. Before this, we had him convinced we're not going to say anything to the police. Now he probably isn't so sure.'

Ray hadn't considered that. He felt stupid. He was also a little ashamed of his childish search for revenge now that the buzz had faded.

She wasn't yet done making him feel like crap. 'I don't want to deal with these people unless we have to. We try to ignore them until we can't. No more contacting them for favours. For anything, I just want to get this whole episode over with and get these monsters out of our lives. I want to move on. I hope what you did tonight doesn't make that harder.'

He apologised again. He wished he'd never demanded the fight.

It had felt good, though.

THIRTEEN

R ay fucking Barker.

Alfie cursed the man's name all the way back home, which was in South Woodford. He parked his old Mondeo in the woodland road lay-by as usual and walked through the trees, along a trail of broken undergrowth created by his myriad trips. He took from his pocket the single rose, now bent and busted, and lobbed it away. The sky was starting to get dark.

He and Kenna had got along very well on their first date. There had been no kiss, but tonight might have been different, especially if he'd given her the rose. But his life had been filled with people trying to mess up his plans, and now there was a new enemy in town. Her own bloody husband. The knobhead knew Alfie was a threat, which was why he'd refused to bring Kenna to the door. Alfie cursed not having called out loudly for her. She didn't even know he'd visited the house. If not for Ray fucking Barker, they could be at the pub right now, cuddling.

He exited the woods, onto the edge of old Packer's land, where his small campervan sat. He could see Packer's big house from here and the library light was on. Good.

He got a key from behind a wheel and went inside the

camper, where he grabbed a beer from under his bed and sat at the tiny kitchen table. He pulled his notepad and dictionary close and started to write.

> *Dear Mum. I'm writing again to tell you that things are getting worse. My son's prosthetic is broken, so he's been kicked from the climbing team. It's a temporary thing, though, so if he can get a new prosthetic within a few days, they will take him back. Ben's been very sad and suicidal. A seven-year-old should not be thinking of killing himself. I don't know what to do because I cannot afford a new arm for him. Anyway, I hope all is well and if I can get my passport soon, hopefully I can come and visit. Take care.*
>
> *Oh, remember the golden rule not to tell anyone you've heard from me. Spain has just changed its laws and now it's the death penalty for faking your own death.*

Alfie signed the letter, finished his beer, and left the camper. He crossed the field and approached the back door of Maureen Packer's house. The key he'd had made was, as always, under the doormat. Once inside her kitchen, he called out her name. A bell rang, signalling that she'd heard. Her ears were good, but her voice was going.

Before heading to the old lady, Alfie checked the fridge and gnawed away a quarter of a block of cheese. He found her in her usual spot in the library, beside a table that held her drink and snacks. Yet again she was staring at a large, framed picture of a sunny beach and cove. It was called Maracaletta or something like that. Some hotspot in Menorca where Maureen and her husband had tied the knot a million years ago. Still she pined, even though he'd died twenty years back. It was one of the few things from her past she properly remembered. When she got into these staring and reminiscing moods, she could sit there for hours.

Seeing Alfie, the old lady raised a gnarly hand and gave him a thumbs-up, which he'd taught her. In her wheezy voice, she said, 'Alfie, boy. Hello. Did you hear from Michael?'

Alfie held up the letter he'd written. 'Got this this afternoon. Here you go.'

While she read, he scanned the books again. Every time he came here, he tried to pick one to read, but nothing ever took his fancy. Books were pointless. Reading the titles beat reading the books themselves.

He ignored Maureen as she put down the letter and wiped her eyes. He knew what was coming next, for it was the same bullshit as always. She would ask how Michael had looked and sounded, and Alfie would have to remind her that the letter had been posted to him, not personally handed over. He would repeat that he and Michael hadn't talked in years, since law school, and that her son had picked Alfie as his go-between because he could be trusted to keep quiet.

'The quiet part is important, isn't it?' he said after this common conversation. 'He can get in trouble. So we have to keep this secret, remember?'

She agreed. It was about all she remembered, daft beach wedding aside. Oh, and the death of Michael. On the day Alfie had chosen her land to park in, some six months ago, she had popped out to have a word. Alfie was used to being moved on, but on this occasion that hadn't happened. Maureen had told him he was welcome to stay if he did some gardening. He had agreed and that very day had mown some grass out front of the house. While he'd worked, she'd told him all about her son.

Michael, ever the thrill-seeker, had gone missing nine years ago while backpacking and rock climbing in the Julian Alps in Slovenia. No contact from him since. Cops and search teams got involved, but they found zip. Two years ago she had had him officially declared dead. A few weeks after their first meeting, and aware that her mind was rotting, Alfie had hatched his plan.

Suddenly, Michael was back. He had a new identity and a home in Spain, Maureen's favourite country. He was happily married and had a seven-year-old boy who'd acquired his father's love of climbing. He had decided to get back in touch with his beloved mother, but only her. But she had to promise to keep his secret. Nobody could know that he wasn't dead except her and Alfie, his old friend and go-between. Letter number one told all this. Letter number two begged for help. Prosthetics, medicines and operations were not cheap.

The trick worked again tonight. While Alfie tidied her bedroom, and pocketed whatever loose coins he found, Maureen got her bank cards. Alfie would hit cash machines to get Michael's important funds. When he took them, she asked him to let her come along to see Michael. Her old brain could never remember that they'd had this same conversation many times.

'No, I don't have access to him,' Alfie said. 'Remember? I just leave the money in a secret spot. He's got another man who collects it for him. I don't know who that man is.'

The same end-of-the-world look, followed by: 'Will you pass a letter along?'

Sure, he said. Again. And he fetched pen and paper so she could write to her dead son. This part was annoying because she took so long to scratch out her letter. Although it was kind of fascinating to see her take immense care with something so pointless.

If only his own mother had had a fraction of such love for him. The bitch.

When he left Maureen, Alfie paused in the kitchen to eat again. He read the letter, laughed at the silliness that came from her mind, tore the paper into bits, dumped it in the bin, grabbed some cutlery so he didn't have to wash the stuff in the camper, and got out of there.

He drove to a cash machine and used all three cards, for a haul of £750. That was the withdrawal limit, but come the morning he'd head out again for a repeat before returning the cards. He'd give it a week or so before scamming her again, just to make sure she hadn't opened her mouth to one of her carers or bingo buddies.

Ray fucking Barker.

The scam had taken his mind off Kenna and their future together, but once he got back home it was hard to think of anything else. He could have been kissing her right now, if not for that meddling husband of hers.

He picked up a cushion, pretended it was Ray's face, and punched it across the room.

———

Much later, after Alfie had eaten a pizza bought with a naïve old lady's money, an unknown number rang his mobile. Alfie had just been drifting off to sleep.

It was Dom. He said, 'Eli wants to see you. Down at the garage.'

Then he hung up. They were good pals, and Dom's cold approach told Alfie that Eli was annoyed. At least the meeting was at the garage, which was Eli's safe haven and no spot he'd ever spill blood in. Just a telling-off, then. Alfie had a pretty good guess why.

The garage was open 24/7 so nothing would be suspicious about people coming and going in the dead of night. Mechanics were working as Alfie left his car and entered reception. Dom was on the chair before the till, playing on his phone. He nodded at the back office.

Inside, Eli, wearing coveralls, was behind the desk. He killed a phone call when he saw Alfie and got straight to business. 'Kenna Barker's house. You went there earlier?'

No lies. Never lies. Eli knew more than he ever let on. 'Yes. I went to check up on Kenna. She's quite nice looking.'

'My guys out front never saw you. You been sneaking there round the back?'

'Yes. I'm sorry. That was more for the neighbours, not to avoid your men. I'm very sorry. She's so nice looking.'

Eli took a moment to think about this. 'No problem. I know, she's a pretty one. So you'll have to stop, if you don't mind. Her bloke's no fan of you.'

And there it was. Ray fucking Barker had grassed like a snotty teacher's pet. 'Of course. I didn't realise. I apologise again.'

'It's just that we need to keep this pair sweet.'

'Of course. Anything else I can do while I'm here?'

'No. On you go.'

'Let me make it up, Eli. Help out here tonight. I've got nothing on.'

Eli leaned back in his chair. 'I've got a valet on. That Skoda out back. It'll free up Johnny. You mind?'

'Minding isn't possible, boss. I'd be dead in a gutter if not for you.'

Eli gave a barely registered tut. He could tell ass-kissing when he saw it, but no one ever got fired doing such a thing.

Valeting a car was no fun, but it got Alfie time to hang around until Eli left, which was fifteen minutes after their chat.

He finished cleaning the Skoda and went into the office to leave the keys. And to steal a key.

It was in the lost property bowl. He knew which key because it was the shiniest one there. After all, the door it fit had only been installed at Kenna's house a couple of days ago.

Alfie knew it was called the witching hour, that period between 3am and 4am when demons and ghosts and, of course, witches were thought to roam the world. He didn't believe in all that crap, but he was well aware that the dead hours were the domain of even worse monsters. Two-legged ones. Hadn't his own mother called him a beast because he'd been lurking in a tree late at night, to watch a girl in her bedroom? Bitch.

He'd protested and he'd called her names, but she'd been right. She'd also pegged him as someone who'd get worse, do worse, and, well, mums knew their sons. The first time he'd busted into a girl's home, five years ago now, he'd considered it a one-off. Hell, to look at that sweet babe, anyone would have done the same. There had probably been a guy sneaking around her home the night before. And a guy who'd seen Alfie climb through the kitchen window and had opted to wait until tomorrow.

One more time, he'd promised himself. Then he'd cut that shit out. His biggest fear had always been that a girl would wake and alert her male partner, and hadn't it just gone right ahead and happened on his second foray? Luckily that chap had been weedy, easily bashed down, and since then Alfie had researched his girls. A couple of days watching a woman from afar was enough to know if she lived alone. Eight girls since, and nary a bloke in sight.

When Dom had recruited him into the Boys Firm, Alfie had

had to come clean about past infringes. It was imperative, Eli had said, that he knew of anything that could come back on him. At first, Alfie had been worried it was all a trick. He knew about those Mr Big investigation techniques the police had. Detectives trying to solve a crime would pretend to be a criminal gang, they'd recruit their suspect, toss him cash for tasks, and make him think he was part of a loyal family.

But true membership, and ultimate trust, meant the suspect had to unload his soul to the boss. The Mr Big would make a promise that the suspect's connection to whatever crime could go away, but only if he confessed every detail. Exactly what Eli had said. Alfie hadn't been convinced everything was legit, but then he discovered that Mr Big investigations were illegal in Britain. Besides, by then he'd witnessed the Boys Firm carry out crimes so bad that no police force would undertake them.

So, Alfie had had to tell Eli everything. The boss had used police contacts to determine that, yes, police had been called to the scene of Alfie's ten home invasions, and no, they didn't have any DNA or other biological evidence. He was in the clear, but he got a direct order to stop assaulting girls in their own homes.

He hadn't. Now he just travelled into other police territories so Eli wouldn't find out. So far so good. And there was no chance Ray would call the cops if Alfie got caught breaking into the Barker home. Hopefully, Kenna would be responsive and Ray would never find out.

The guys Eli had stationed on the Barkers' street would be settled down for the night, half-asleep and lazy, but coming from the front wasn't worth the risk. Alfie parked where he had last time, on a parallel street, and headed down someone's driveway, to the back fence they shared with the Barkers.

All lights were off in Kenna's house. He scuttled to the back door and jabbed his key into the lock. The key met resistance from another, but it hadn't been turned in the lock and he was able to push it out. He heard it plink onto the kitchen floor. Moments later, he was in.

According to Trevor, there was a listening device behind a picture on the living room wall. It was good enough to also pick up what was said in the kitchen, so Alfie walked slowly through the dark downstairs rooms.

In the front hallway, there was a bug behind the shoe rack for capturing any conversation that took place at the door. The third and final was in the main bedroom, whose doorway he stepped into thirty seconds after entering the house.

There she was, asleep under the covers with the bastard beside her, a good foot of space between them. He hoped that gap indicated a troubled marriage. But it was too dark to make out her features, so he crept across to the window and turned the blinds slightly. Strips of moonlight ran across the bed. He used a small plant on the windowsill to hold aside one of the blinds, so that the widened shaft of light illuminated Kenna's entire face.

Alfie approached her. She lay on her back, head tilted towards him slightly. Her hair framed her face perfectly, and there was a slight gap between her lips. He bent close, so their lips were only inches apart, and from there he could hear her breathing. It was such a shame that those mesmeric grey eyes were shut.

Next to her lay the bastard, and wasn't it also a shame that his eyes would open again at some point in the future.

Annoyed, Alfie looked to the rail holding the blinds, behind which lay the second listening device. Trevor had said that the audio was monitored in shifts, so somewhere a fresh, alert guy was listening hard. Officially for gossip, but maybe also for a bit of sex.

Could he wake her without rousing the bastard beside her? When she saw it was Alfie with her, she would remain quiet and they could sneak to another upstairs, bug-free room to kiss.

But the problem was that moment when she woke. She could moan, cough, or shift hard enough to wake her husband. Alfie didn't doubt he could handle the bozo, but it would create a mammoth problem. Eli had warned him against coming here. Chances were the chap on the end of the bug, suddenly hearing whacks and yells, could have the street surveillance guys in the house before Alfie and Kenna vacated it, especially if she insisted on dressing first.

He remembered the movie *Sleeping Beauty*, although not because he'd seen it. No, Carla, Eli's financial adviser, had mentioned refusing to let her kids watch it. Apparently it glorified sexual assault. For kissing a sleeping woman? Alfie found that laughable, especially since the woman in the story got with the prince afterwards. This was no different.

So, he bent close again and touched Kenna's lips with his own. In the movie, the woman opened her eyes and smiled at her beau. Not so romantic here: Kenna grunted, turned over, and unleashed a fart that he would have laughed at if he were not so annoyed.

Worse, her bastard husband moved, too. He grunted a word and rubbed his ear. Fearful that the fucker would wake, Alfie stood and backed quickly out of the room. Soon, all was still and silent again. He moved into the doorway once more.

He skimmed across the room and felt behind the blinds rail, for the bug. Surely Eli wouldn't suspect anything foul if it just... broke. With no one listening, Alfie could clamp a hand over Kenna's mouth and wake her that way, without a sound. He'd seen that in plenty of films. Then they could sneak out.

He gritted his teeth. The bug wasn't there. Trevor had learned the bug locations before the mission was carried out, so the planters must have changed their minds. There was no way Alfie could check the whole room.

He approached Kenna, stroked her hair, and then slipped out of the room. It was time to return the key, but not until he'd made a copy. If he could somehow find out where the bug was, he could return tomorrow night and enjoy more success.

FOURTEEN

On Tuesday morning, as Kenna and Ray were getting ready for work, there was a knock at the front door. Kenna looked out the bedroom window then called to Ray, who was shaving. She told him there was a salesman outside.

Ray wasn't so sure, even when he opened the door to see a middle-aged man in a suit beneath a long jacket and carrying a clipboard. 'What does Eli want now?'

The 'salesman' dumped his friendly smile. 'Invite me in.'

'You a vampire? Can't come in without an invite?'

The guy just stared. Ray backed out of the doorway. When they entered the living room, Kenna called down to ask if everything was all right.'

'Stay up there,' Ray yelled back. 'It's one of our stalkers.' Then, to the guy: 'The disguise is a bit overboard. You lot going to come as phone repairmen next time? What do you want?'

'It's what you want.' The man delved into a pocket and produced a ball of foil the size of a tennis ball. Ray took it, opened it enough to determine it was full of marijuana, and stuffed it into his own pocket.

'Free, right?'

'There's no fiscal payment, but is anything free in this world?'

'So your business is done. There's the door.'

The salesman reeled off a postcode. 'Have your wife there at 12pm. Today. You need to write it down? I hear your brain misfires.'

'Piss off,' Ray said. 'What's it for?'

'She'll see. Nothing bad.'

'This is all bad. She's going nowhere without knowing why.'

'Even I don't know why. You've played ball so far, and it would be a shame to ruin things now.'

'Then she goes nowhere without me. She's not going to some crack house or whatever alone. You've had your own ball game played so far, and it would be a shame to ruin things now.'

'What was the postcode again?'

Ray wanted to slap the smarmy sod. 'You write it down, or trust me to remember it. You just blurted it out one time. That's what I'll tell Eli if we get lost.'

The salesman got a pen. He wrote on the blank sheet of paper on his clipboard and tore it off. Ray pocketed it. 'Well, Mr cold caller, we have double glazing and satellite TV, and solar panels don't interest us. There's the door.'

The salesman went into another pocket. This time he held up a plastic bag, whose contents Ray could clearly see. A blood collection tube, syringe, and a small plastic pot. 'I need urine and blood from Mrs Barker.'

Ray stepped between him and the living room door, as if the man might just run upstairs to get what he wanted. 'Don't be a twat. What for?'

'No more games. I'm supposed to take the blood, but you can take this upstairs to your wife. I'll wait right here.'

Ray knew he'd pushed his luck many times, but the fake salesman's tone was deadly serious. This was something not up for debate. Ray grabbed the bag and headed out of the living room.

Kenna was waiting for him in the bedroom, and she'd heard everything. 'I think it's for a test,' she said. 'To see if I have a sexually transmitted infection.'

Ray had suspected as much. 'That means they definitely want you to sleep with this guy on Saturday.'

She took his arm. 'It's okay. Remember, I can say no, and I will. But let's do what they want. This test must be very important to them and I don't want to anger Eli.'

He didn't want to let go of the items and she had to prise them from his hands. She disappeared into the bathroom. A few minutes later, she brought back the bag, which now contained one red-filled tube and one clear filled tub. Ray held his hand out.

'No,' she said, 'let's both go down.'

The man was waiting patiently, standing exactly where Ray had left him. He took the bag and pocketed it. 'Sure you don't want solar panels?'

Without waiting for a response, he snickered and headed for the door. Ray went to the window to make sure the guy had left, then showed Kenna his phone. While waiting for her to bottle fluids, he had googled the postcode. 'It's a Tesco up near Stamford Bridge, the football ground. I have no idea what they want.'

'That's a busy store and it'll be in the middle of the afternoon. There can't be anything dangerous about that.'

'So we go? I'm worried they've picked a public place to trick us into thinking exactly that: it can't be dangerous.'

'We have to go, Ray. I still don't see what they earn from hurting us. We've done everything they want so far. I still think we can come out of this okay.'

Well, they would soon know.

Vicky had called in sick again, this time for the rest of the week. Kenna phoned her, but for the umpteenth time it rang off. Now she suspected Vicky was avoiding her. Perhaps because she wanted distance between them because of the threat hanging over Kenna. Kenna figured her best way forward was to give Vicky space, which would also keep her off Eli's radar. They could reconnect when this was all over.

Kenna told her boss she had a dentist's appointment at twelve, and he allowed her to leave an hour before. She called Ray as she was heading to her car, and was surprised to find he had not only skipped work early, but was already at the Tesco.

'I thought I'd check it out, see who came and went. Nothing doing. I'm in a corner near a key cutting stall. I took a taxi so we can just use your car.'

On the way to work, she'd checked for a tail and spotted nothing. Now, driving away, she again scanned her environment and saw no dodgy vehicles. It did little to convince her she wasn't being followed. She got to the Tesco with ten minutes to spare. She spotted the key cutting stall and headed over. Ray was sitting on a kerb bordering a grassy bank. He pointed to a free parking bay in the corner.

'Do we go inside?' she said when he got in the car.

'They know your car. Let's just wait right here. They can find us if they want us. We shouldn't have to look around.'

She had backed into the bay so they could see the entire car park and the entrance to the store. People came and went. Because they were seeking the approach of motor vehicles, neither spotted the kid on the BMX until he knocked on her window. He was about eighteen, handsome except for a healing split lip. She looked at Ray, who told her to wind the window down an inch.

As soon as she did, the kid blurted out a street name and 'Quick as you can,' and then got moving. He hopped the kerb, rode up the bank, and disappeared out of sight.

'Do we do it?' Ray asked. In answer, Kenna started the engine. Ray got on his phone and had the street map ready by the time they'd reached the car park exit. 'Baydon Road. It's a residential street to the northeast, off the A308. Half a mile away.'

'So we could be going to someone's house. That's okay.'

'Well, it beats a disused warehouse, but I don't trust these bastards. Let's be careful.'

The homes along each side of Baydon Road were terraced and sans gardens, so residents had lined the kerbs with their cars. It thinned the road enough to guarantee two cars couldn't pass without swapping paint. Kenna paused her car at the entrance.

'Do we just drive down?'

'Yeah, slow, so we can see what's what.'

No cars were oncoming, so the way ahead was clear. As her vehicle passed house after house, they stared at each door, each window, each resident on the pavements. Nothing stood out and nobody paid them any attention.

Halfway down, a car door suddenly opened right into Kenna's path and she had to slam on the brakes. A young man in double denim got out and glared at her. She was reminded of yesterday, when a trio of brutes had made a man regret his road rage. As denim dude came to her window, she wound it down, ready to warn him.

Ray had also sensed a threat and started to open his door. He had one leg out when denim dude reached Kenna's window and said, 'Court Four Avenue.'

And that was it. He returned to his car and shut the door. Ray shut his own and Kenna cruised past, onward.

'He was waiting for us,' Ray said. 'I think they're going to send us all around the city to make sure there's no police following us.'

'We didn't call them. They've got bugs in the house. They know we didn't call the police.'

'Maybe they don't know for sure. They can't hear what we say outside the house.'

'I don't like this.'

Ray rubbed her arm. 'It'll be fine. Like you said, we've done everything they want so far.'

She tried desperately to believe that.

Court Four Avenue almost three miles south, in Wandsworth. As they were crossing the Thames using Wandsworth Bridge, a rotund guy in a hard hat and hi-vis jacket was standing by the parapet. He chose a vital moment to decide to abruptly turn and step into the road, forcing Kenna on the brakes for a second time. The fat man slapped her bonnet and angrily came around to her window, but this time the charade didn't fool her.

'How much more of this run-around?' she said before he could utter a word. 'We didn't call the police. If this is to convince us that Eli has power, we get it.'

The guy did his job and nothing more. He spoke a postcode, said they should 'park in the car park', then he headed back to the pavement.

The car behind beeped. Kenna stared at it in the rear-view, in case the occupant was another envoy. He remained seated and laid on the horn again. Just a disgruntled driver, then. She drove on.

'So why cancel the Court Four thing?' she said to Ray, who was poring over Google Maps again.

'Maybe in case the police heard the instruction and are

winging their way there. Or just for fun. Who knows with these morons. The postcode is in Battersea.'

Specifically, Kassala Road, just off Prince of Wales Drive, which ran alongside Battersea Park. The address was another residential street, with a small block of flats at each end. The one on the south edge was their destination. The car park could hold only ten vehicles, but most bays were vacant.

The moment they parked, another BMX rider made his entrance. This one was no kid. He looked about fifty and his attire and bike competed for most shabby. He had the glassy eyes of someone high on drugs. From five feet away, as if he feared Kenna, he gave a postcode. 'Now wait here till I give a thumbs-up, man. Need proof I told you. Keep watching me, eh?'

He weaved away, pulled a wheelie, and skidded to a halt on the main road. He raised a phone and snapped a picture of Kenna and Ray staring at him through her open window. The promised thumbs-up came as he cycled away.

'I'm losing my nerves in favour of annoyance now,' Kenna said.

Ray had inputted the postcode into his phone. 'Back west again. Putney. We're rats in a maze and someone is laughing at us.'

She drove. They barely spoke during the journey. The destination was yet another residential road, but this time the houses on the left broke halfway along for a terraced row of five commercial joints. The centre one, a hairdresser's, had scaffolding outside and men working on the roof. There was another worker on the ground, inside the scaffolding like a caged animal. He saw their slow approach and wagged a finger. No subterfuge this time.

Kenna pulled up before him. Ray was kerbside so put his window down. The guy barely looked up from his phone. 'Park round back.'

Ray put his window up. To Kenna he said, 'This is it. No more run-around. Are you ready?'

Kenna nodded. 'Let's get this done and get home. I'm feeling sick.'

Neither of them knew they wouldn't be going home that day.

PART 2

FIFTEEN

R ound back of the terraced building was an open, unfenced parking lot for all five businesses. Outside the rear of the hairdresser's was an open-backed lorry and various building equipment and supplies, and four guys working. One of them, who wore jeans and a windbreaker instead of protective equipment, pointed to where he wanted Kenna to park.

Once done, Ray and Kenna got out of the car. The same man now pointed at the back door of the hairdresser's. The rotted wooden door was unlocked and led to a small kitchen. Another man was here, filling a kettle at the sink. On the far wall was a curtain hanging from a rail. By its size, Kenna guessed it covered a doorway. Against the left wall was a staircase heading upstairs.

'You want a tea?' the guy asked. Ray said no for them both.

'Fair enough. Go through the curtain.'

Sure enough, Ray slid aside the fabric to expose a doorless doorway. Beyond was the salon. It was clean, operational. And contained five people.

Two young women sat in chairs and chatted. Numbers

three and four were bruisers who stood around like security. But they weren't here to protect the shop or the hairdressers: the fifth individual was Eli. He wore a suit and sat on a sofa like a customer.

Five became eight as footsteps came down the kitchen stairs. A second pair of heavies appeared. They blocked the back door.

'Did we do something wrong?' Ray said.

Eli pointed at a couple of footstools, and the message was clear. Sit. The women had stopped talking and were watching. Ray and Kenna sat without word. One of the bruisers approached and demanded Kenna's car keys and both their phones. There was no objection, although Ray almost bristled with energy. The bruiser put their belongings beside Eli, who said, 'I couldn't risk you getting cold feet.'

'You want to keep us here? Till Saturday? We won't run or tell anyone.'

'You already did.'

There might have been a click in Kenna's head as it all felt into place. She would have never heard it over the rapid thudding of her heart. 'You mean Vicky, my friend. Have you done something? If you've hurt her, I won't–'

'She's fine,' Eli cut in. 'So remain calm. She got warned to stay away from you, that's all. Nice and politely. You brought her into this. You're lucky I didn't bury her. You're lucky she's the only one you blabbed to. But once this is over, I don't care who you gossip with. You can go see your friend and talk the night away about all of this.'

'So that's why you're going to hold us hostage for five days? Because you think we'll talk to people about you? There's no need, I promise.'

Eli shook his head. 'Like I said, I couldn't risk you getting cold feet. I did a little fibby-wibby.'

'What does that mean?' Ray said. He stood. The two

bruisers changed stances and Kenna knew they were ready to pounce if Ray made a move. She pulled him down onto his stool.

'You tricked us,' she said. 'It's tonight, isn't it?'

Eli nodded. 'Just a few hours from now, you will entertain my special friend.'

'I also kept this from ninety per cent of my people,' Eli said. He had taken off his suit jacket and pulled up a stool close to hers. Ray watched him with suspicion. 'So don't think you're alone. Tonight is very important. No obstacles. No interference. Nothing can go wrong. Only those who needed to know knew.'

Kenna said, 'You can't just spring this on us. I have to go back to work. Ray, too. We could have friends coming over. Or family waiting for a phone call. I'm not trying to threaten you. Please understand. It's just that people could notice if we suddenly seem to vanish.'

She wasn't making idle threats. Eli just didn't care. 'It's one night. One evening. It will all be over before midnight and you'll be free to go. I think unless you're part of the royal family, you can be absent for half a day without the cavalry being called in. Unless you have some kind of alarm system in place because you don't trust me?'

'What do you mean?' Ray asked.

'You know. Maybe you told someone to expect a phone call every two hours, and if you miss one, they call in the police.'

Eli caught a glance between the couple, and right then knew the pair had had the same idea. But he was certain they'd undertaken no such plan. She said, 'Eli, you've bugged our home, so you know we discussed that. But that means you also know what we decided.'

Actually, no. There were some dead zones in the house. He took a guess. 'You decided there was no way you could convince anyone to go along with it without making them scared and suspicious.'

Kenna nodded. He'd guessed correctly. 'So we always planned to do what you ordered. You gave us no choice. But just kidnapping us like this is risky. Again, I don't mean that as a threat.'

Kidnapped? He was mildly offended. 'Sequestered is a better word. Maybe accusing you of getting cold feet was wrong. You could have a car crash or fall down the stairs, and ruin that face my colleague is so interested in. I'm playing it safe. Besides, now you've got no notice and you don't have to spend the next few days worrying. Only the next few hours.'

'This place isn't a coincidence, is it?' Ray said. 'You want Kenna to have some work done.'

Eli pointed at the two women. 'Sally and Jemima. This is my place and they're my best girls. They'll have you looking like ten thousand pounds.'

Sally and Jemima gave a little wave and said hello. The girls didn't have a clue what was going on, but they did know not to ask and not to care. 'Oh, speaking of ten thousand pounds,' Eli added. He got up and lifted a plastic carrier bag from one of the hydraulic chairs arranged against the walls. The contents got tipped onto the floor. Loose notes, £10 denomination. A giant pile of money, right there. 'Not bad for one night's work. So let me show you that we're simply doing a business deal here. Make a choice.'

One of his men moved to the front door and unlocked it. Then he stepped away. Everybody waited. Door or money. Eli wasn't worried about the answer.

As he fully expected, Kenna and Ray bent down to scoop up the money and stuff it back into the bag. However, when it was done, Kenna held it out to Eli. 'I can't take this yet. The job isn't over. Give this back to us afterwards.'

Eli's world was inhabited by cutthroats, liars, deceivers, and he got by because of what he considered to be a criminal leader's best weapon: paranoia. He was instantly suspicious of Kenna. It stayed his hand long enough to give him away.

'I understand what's going on here,' Kenna said. 'We can't just say no and walk away from this. Our only chance is to do what you want and hope you hold up your end of the bargain afterwards. That's why I'm handing the bag back. If you choose to stuff us afterwards and keep the money, there's nothing we can do to stop you. I'm not saying I trust you. I'm saying I'm no fool and you have absolute control here.'

Ray didn't look surprised by this, and that told Eli the couple had discussed a moment like this. It changed nothing in the long run. She was willing to play ball and that was all that mattered. He took the bag from Kenna and dumped it on a chair. 'Okay, ladies and gentlemen, game on.'

SIXTEEN

Alfie got the key to old Ms Packer's back door and let himself in. First port of call, the fridge and more cheese. This time he took the block and nibbled as he headed to the library. But when he entered the hallway, he stopped. Voices. He recognised that of the lady called Simone, who was one of three carers who tended to Packer. But there was also a male voice.

Before he had chance to discern what they were talking about, the front door opened. Ten feet away, staring down the hall at him, was a woman. In uniform. Police uniform.

'Hello, sir. Just stop right there a moment. Can I ask who you are?'

Of course not. Alfie bought half a second's head start by lobbing the block of cheese, which hit her hip as she tried to avoid it. After that, he ran. Luckily, he'd left the back door wide open.

Halfway across the field, he looked back to see two officers in pursuit. A big male had joined the chase, but they were loaded with gear and unable to match his speed. Alfie blew past his campervan – that was now burned – and entered the woods. He thumped along the trail his own feet had made and blasted out the other side, into the lay-by where his car awaited. Luckily, he had his keys.

Seconds later he was on the move. No sign of the cops. Just before he made a turn fifty metres down the road, they appeared. In his rear-view, he saw them emerge into the lay-by, realise they'd been foiled, and haul their radios. That was his car burned, too.

Oh, and his cash cow. Old fart Packer had obviously decided she couldn't keep her spectacular news to herself. She must have told her carer about her son's faked death and the nice chap acting as a conduit between them, and she'd yanked in the cops.

Now he was in deep shit. The campervan wasn't in his name but the car was registered to him because Eli couldn't have his guys getting arrested at simple traffic stops. If the two cops had got the reg, their job would become a lot easier. Even if they had missed it, he'd been arrested twice by tyrants for auditing and his prints were on the system, so soon there would be a match to items in the campervan.

That was bad. He'd gone against Eli's wishes and had things in his mobile home that could connect him to organised crime. To Eli. That sort of infraction deserved a violent, perhaps lethal, punishment. But even if Eli was lenient, Alfie would be cut from the firm. Back to life on the streets for him. To shop roofs as a bed, days wandering superstores to keep warm, and alleyway muggings to buy food. Packer hadn't caused all this on purpose, but she had to pay. He'd torch her big house one day. And that carer, Simone, she would have to learn a hard lesson.

Later, of course. Right now Alfie had to lie low. Soon the car's identity would be out there for every ANPR camera to flag, and cops could descend on a given location within seconds. He needed another vehicle and Trevor was the man to help with that.

He called his friend, but a woman answered. It was Trevor's girlfriend. He could hear people in the background.

'Hi, Trevor is just on the toilet at the minute. We're out shopping at–'

'It's Alfie,' he cut in. 'Where is he? You got another number for him?'

'Alfie. Right. Er, no. He said he'll be back tonight.'

Shit. When a guy did a job for Eli, registered phones were outlawed because of cell site tracing. The trick was to let someone innocent take the device on a trip in order to create an alibi. Burners were instead used on jobs, but Trevor hadn't taken one. He would be out of reach until he resurfaced.

There was good news, though. Registered cars were never taken on jobs, so Trevor's would be at his home. He told the girlfriend, 'Eli's sending me to your house for something. There a spare key?'

'Yes. Under a patch of grass by the clothes pole. Are you allowed to go there?'

Another big no-no was visiting another firm members' house. If one guy was under secret police surveillance, suddenly two were. Alfie could hardly hurt Eli more than he already had by leaving a welter of criminal evidence in his motorhome. He told the girlfriend Eli had authorised it, then hung up.

Trevor's car was in the drive, as expected. Alfie parked outside and ran round to the back garden. There was a garden fork laying in a gravel boundary, so he used it to stab the ground in the vicinity of the clothing pole. On his third hit, it came away holding a neat square of lawn, and down in its nest was the spare back door key.

He entered the house and found the key hooks near the

front door. Jackpot: car keys. He searched the living room and found a clear vase with about £40. Even better, there was a packaged commemorative £100 coin in a picture frame above the fireplace. He took it.

He'd been whizzing around like a madman and needed a moment, so he grabbed cheese from Trevor's fridge and sat to let mind and body relax. Impossible. He was a fugitive. Every cop and soon every criminal would want him.

Eli's reach and power was vast, but it waned the further you got from London. So that was Alfie's play. Derbyshire he knew fairly well, despite leaving that place a decade ago. Eli would have very little clout up there and its police wouldn't give a shit about some fraudster wanted by a force down south. No one would come looking anyway because he had no friends or contacts in that area and hadn't spoken to his bitch mum in over a decade. No one from his old village would recognise the man he'd become.

He'd load up with petrol and leave, but not until he'd done one last thing. Perhaps he wouldn't be alone when he abandoned this place. Because there was a chance Kenna would say yes.

───────

Alfie pulled up at the petrol station and filled Trevor's car and a metal jerry can, for a total of £73. At the counter, he slapped down the £100 coin. The cashier gave it a puzzled look, picked it up, and said, 'Wow. Never seen one of these before.'

Commemorative were uncommon but still legal tender in the UK. If you tried to purchase goods from a shop, they could and mostly did refuse. Then again, they could refuse to take any legal tender; the goods would go back on the shelf and you'd leave empty-handed.

Not so with fuel. The petrol was in his car, now his property, and he owed the garage a debt. The law was different. If you visited a petrol station in the middle of the night and they insisted on card payments when you didn't have one, well, you'd be forced to return another day, and that just wasn't fair. So the law stated that any offer of payment of the correct amount in legal tender was suffice. A garage could refuse your cash, but they couldn't call it a drive-off if you departed, and they couldn't sue you for an alternative means of payment. Alfie knew his stuff and was ready for an argument.

'My missus would love this,' the cashier said. 'I'll put a ton in the till and keep this.'

And that was that. Truth be told, Alfie was a little annoyed it had gone down without hitch. But he had his fuel and now he could proceed with his plan.

He drove to Kenna's street. That bastard Ray's car was outside the house, but hers was missing. He checked the time and realised that she was probably at work. But why was the knobhead home?

He also didn't clock a car full of men, so nobody was watching the house. He wasn't sure why Eli would have pulled the surveillance, but it was good news. Alfie knocked on the Barkers' door and hid in the car, in case Ray answered. No one did.

Alfie drove to the parallel street and made his way over the back fence. The key was in the back door again and this time he couldn't get his in. No mind. He hardly cared what anyone thought from this point. So he smashed a window in the door and reached through to unlock it.

He grabbed a pizza from the freezer and stuck it in the oven. Then he turned the living room TV on. His plan: wait for someone to return. If Kenna was first, he'd ask her to run away with him. If he could convince her that staying here was dangerous, that Eli planned something bad, she might just do it. Hopefully, they could get away before her bastard husband returned. If that didn't happen, or if Ray returned home first, Alfie's job would be harder. But it wouldn't fail.

Kenna was his, and he wasn't leaving without her.

SEVENTEEN

Ray asked for a moment with his wife. Granted. But nobody was going to leave the room. He and Kenna shifted to a corner of the salon, put their faces close, and talked.

'What do we do?' he said.

'I don't feel comfortable taking dirty money.'

'We don't know if this thing tonight is illegal. Marshall might be a criminal, but it's not against the law to sit at a dinner table with him.'

'I didn't mean that. That ten thousand is dirty money. It's from drugs, prostitution, whatever.'

'There's another way to look at it. Maybe Eli got rich from those things, but if he got that cash from the bank, it's not dirty at all. It's not like he picked up the notes from the floor of a crime scene and had to wash blood and heroin off.'

She paused. 'Is this about more than money, Ray? You said Eli offered something else.'

She had an accusatory tone, and there was only one other offer Eli had made. 'The second opinion about my brain? You think I want to do this so I can play a game of rugby?'

'I don't want a dodgy doctor sending you back onto the field when it's not safe.'

'Neither do I, Kenna. I don't want that, either.'

She searched his eyes for the truth. Which was that he would have snapped up the offer if it was real. It wasn't just about rugby, though. Who wanted the crutch of an official diagnosis of early-onset dementia?

She didn't find that truth. 'Okay, I believe you. So back to the money. We can't carry that much around. Putting it in a bank would be suspicious.'

'We hide it. Spend bits here and there. Use different bank accounts.'

'Too much like laundering. And it might not be a real offer.'

'I agree. But what if it is? If we refuse, Eli might think we plan to go against him.'

Kenna glanced at Eli, waiting patiently and scanning his phone. Then at the bag of money. 'Charity. That's what we do if we take it.'

'If? I think we have to. We're in this far and we can't back out now.'

Kenna kissed his forehead. 'Then let's do this and get back to our lives. If possible.'

Once Kenna had said she was ready, the girls took her. Sally and Jemima literally grabbed and seated her, as if she was a VIP customer paying through the nose. Immediately, they started pointing out her hair, skin, eyes, everything, and working out what to do with her. They grabbed brushes and oils and all manner of other beauty paraphernalia. In any other situation, Ray would have found it amusing.

Eli took a seat and played on his phone. The bruisers also

relaxed. Ray was ignored and, weirdly, he felt like an intruder. He was certain Kenna was in no danger, so he said, 'Eli, can I have a walk around? Outside and stuff? Just in the back yard?'

Eli didn't look up, but raised a thumb. Ray pushed through the curtain and opened the back door. Nobody followed him. It seemed Eli trusted him not to run. How could he with his wife back there?

In the back yard, Ray sat on a box and watched two workmen cutting tiles with a machine. He returned their nods. A few minutes later, the guys halted their work and stepped aside to light up what Ray knew was a large spliff. He approached them.

'Care to share?'

The guy with the joint took a puff and held it out. Ray dragged deep and felt his head spin. Good stuff, and he said so. 'You guys work for Eli or independent?'

'We work for him. This is his place.'

'One of his legitimate businesses, I'm guessing. That's how guys like him operate. He has kosher businesses to present an image. And to launder money through.'

The guy who'd offered the spliff shrugged. His pal laughed.

Ray took another drag. 'Fair enough. We all have secrets. Just being nosey. You know why me and my wife are here?'

The guy who'd shrugged did it again. He held out his hand for the joint. Ray decided to do a test. Instead of returning the spliff, he returned to his box with it and smoked away. The two builders glared daggers, but didn't say a word. They rolled another joint.

It proved nothing. Yes, Ray and Kenna were important to Eli – but for how long?

The hairdressers washed, dried, trimmed and straightened wild portions of Kenna's hair. They threaded her eyebrows. Jemima worked on her face to give what she called the dewy glow look, while Sally performed a pedicure. Both girls massaged her hands and feet. Ray was in and out, growing progressively more bored. His attitude helped. While not exactly able to pretend this was a normal day getting made over, she found a measure of calm and even almost fell asleep.

At one point, Sally grabbed a packet of coloured false fingernails, but Eli said, 'No. leave the nails. I have someone else who'll fix them up. My girls wear black nails.'

Sally showed him Kenna's fingers. 'They're a bit rough. Just a file and some varn–'

'Leave the nails as they are.'

Sally looked gutted. He was interrupting her art.

An hour after they started fussing over her, the two girls announced that they were finished. Kenna stood up. 'Now what?' she asked.

'Clothing,' Eli said. He put his phone away and stood. 'Upstairs.'

The first floor contained two bedrooms and a bathroom. The sleeping quarters Kenna was taken to was fully furnished and clearly belonged to someone. On the bed was a low-necked sleeveless mini party dress with a lace fringe. She frowned.

Eli caught it. 'I believe your date likes the risqué.'

'Excellent choice,' she said, with no attempt to hide the sarcasm.

'Get dressed.'

Eli left the room. Ray said, 'Marsters is going to want to sleep with you in a dress like that.'

'Marshall,' she corrected him. 'And he'll go short.' She started to strip off her clothing. When she was in the new garment, she looked in the dressing table mirror. She hated what stared back.

'You're gorgeous,' Ray said. He sounded glum and it was obvious why. His wife was sexily dressed, but for another man.

They headed downstairs. The two hairdressers complimented her. Eli did the same then said it was time to go. Ray and Kenna followed him and the two bruisers followed them. A pair of cars had appeared in the yard. Eli opened a rear door.

'What about my car?' Kenna said.

'We'll get it back to you after,' Eli told her.

She got in, followed by Ray – or not. One of the heavies grabbed his arm. Eli said, 'Not you, big man. You go in the other car.'

Kenna felt her throat tighten. 'Why?'

'Because those three Goliaths will ruin my fuel economy. Or maybe it's because I want to talk to you alone. Don't worry, he'll be right behind us.'

They couldn't argue such a simple point at this stage. Kenna got in the back of Eli's car and Ray got in the other vehicle with the heavies.

When the gangster started driving, Kenna looked back to make sure Ray's car was right behind. It was. When she faced forward again, Eli was staring at her in the rear-view mirror.

'It's time you knew the plan. I'm taking you both to another house, where...'

...they would wait at the new destination until 7pm, at which point Kenna would be taken by car, east, into Mayfair and to The Mirage. A place Eli promised her she'd never seen the likes of.

Two bedrooms, a kitchen, a dining area and living space. The bedrooms each had emperor beds laid with Egyptian cotton and walk-in wardrobes. The dining room used similar silk to that in the *Titanic's* First Class Dining Room. The bathroom had underfloor heating and a six-person jacuzzi. The kitchen had a large pantry, dishwasher, tall fridge, although a chef and butler were on call so there was no need to cook and definitely none to wash up. The living area had a marble fireplace and home cinema. Throughout the suite was a European heritage aesthetic, including twelve-foot-high ceilings. And that didn't include the rooftop terrace.

Now memorise this map...

He handed her an A4 sheet of laminated paper showing a portion of a colour London map. It looked like a screenshot of a satellite image from Google Earth. The Mirage Hotel was circled and numbered two. A short distance west of it was a circled area marked one, and a clear route had been drawn between the two locations.

Kenna peered closely at circled area one. It was the Animals in War Memorial, located between the north and south carriageways of Park Lane. She was puzzled. 'I walk from number one? That means you're dropping me off in the middle of the street. Why am I not being taken directly to the hotel?'

'I can't have my people going close to the hotel. Unfortunately, tonight there's a member of some foreign royal family staying at The Mirage. They'll have their own security around and cops will be all over the place. Half the city council will be watching CCTV. Some of my people are wanted and I can't risk them being recognised anywhere near that place. So, you'll be dropped at the memorial. When the job is done, you leave the hotel and return there for pick-up. Then I'll have you brought to Ray and both taken home, ten grand richer.'

'What about when at the hotel? Will someone meet me? What do I say? To who?'

'Too much information for now. Just memorise that route. That'll be solid in your mind when we get to the next part.'

The route was easy enough, with just a single turn. Distance: half a kilometre or so. With nothing else to do or learn, she looked out the window and turned off.

A little later the car slowed down on a street with trees along the left side and expensive-looking detached homes on the right, each lurking behind high walls and ornate gates. Just as she wondered which house was their destination, the car cut a sharp left. Ray's car did the same.

Eli drove down a smooth dirt lane heading through the trees. When the greenery opened up, she saw a plot of land with a small lake and a brick two-storey house. The property looked a little out of place sitting alone. There was no fence or driveway and the track ran right up to the front door. The car parked directly outside the front window.

Eli was out first and ordered her to follow him. The front door seemed warped in the frame and he had to give it a shove to get it open. By this point the car bearing her husband pulled up next to Eli's vehicle. Ray and his pair of minders exited. Kenna rushed to his side.

Eli stepped back from the open door and directed the married couple to enter ahead of him. The five of them walked into a kitchen where three tough-looking guys sat on stools around an island. The room was suddenly very crowded. Eli had the rear and he locked the door behind him. Kenna didn't like that.

Her worries were justified. The two bruisers who'd accompanied Ray grabbed him. In the same instant, the three men on stools vacated them to assist. Eli snatched Kenna's arm.

'What's going on?' Kenna yelled as the four marched Ray towards an interior door. He struggled, but uselessly. 'Please. We did what you want. We're not planning to trick you.'

Someone opened the interior door and she saw a short hallway with another door. He then opened this door and the men holding Ray marched him through. From the bare plaster walls and the steps leading down, she knew it was a cellar.

Eli dragged her to a stool and sat her. She continued to beg for answers, while somewhere below Ray bellowed to be released. Eli refused to answer her questions. She was terrified. This betrayal made no sense after they had been so cooperative.

From the hallway another man appeared. Middle-aged, in jeans and a blue shirt, he was far from the enforcer type and looked more like an accountant.

Eli released her arm and stepped back. Kenna knew it was futile to try to run. She was trapped and helpless. But also a little emboldened by having no choice in what lay ahead. 'Explain this, Eli. There's something else going on here. We came willingly.'

'You and Ray will be kept apart until this is over. To guarantee that you do what I want. When you're dropped at the memorial, you'll be on your own. If you back out or call the police, your man down there is dead. You'll never see him again. Except his head. You'll get that in a parcel one day. Understand?'

'I always understood, right from the start. We said we'd do what you wanted. There's no need for this.'

Eli folded his arms and smiled. Before, he'd seemed professional, but now there was something cold about his demeanour. Especially that grin. 'Actually, there is. Because you're right. There's a very big twist to this tale.'

EIGHTEEN

Annoyingly, Alfie was ten minutes from the end of a movie when he saw a car pull up outside Kenna's house. He approached the window, bent low. His brow furrowed when he saw the person who exited the car and came up the drive. It wasn't Kenna. And it wasn't Ray.

When the man let himself into the home, Alfie was standing in the middle of the living room. His visitor got a shock.

'Alfie?' Trevor said. 'What the hell are you doing here?'

'How's Eli?'

'What? Fine. What are you doing in this house?'

No serious worry on Trevor's face. That meant Eli didn't yet know that Alfie had messed up and was on the run. Good. 'I came to see Kenna. We're friends. She must be at work.'

'Nah, man, it's on. Eli's got her. It's on tonight. I just heard. Since when were you and her friends?'

'What? The Magpie is in town already? Kenna is seeing him tonight?'

'So I hear. Magpie must be meeting Eli tomorrow, so maybe that's when we'll find out the score. Meaning if we still have jobs.'

Alfie's heart sank. Eli had either brought the meeting forward, or he'd lied to his grunts. That meant that tonight Kenna would be entertaining The Magpie, not driving away with Alfie. Fucking him instead of Alfie.

That changed things. If Alfie wanted Kenna, he would have to hang around in the snake pit for a while. 'I need your help. I need to see her before I go. You have to keep quiet about me being here. After that, I got to shoot off, Trevor. I have to go far away. I fucked up.'

Trevor asked how, and Alfie told it. Old Mrs Packer. The motorhome now in the hands of the cops. The key he liberated from Eli's office at the garage. The theft of Trevor's vehicle.

Trevor was aghast, but not because his pal had stolen his car. 'Eli's going to do something bad for this. Look, you know I should hand you in, right? But I can't do that to my mate. You need to run. I never saw you here.'

'I will. After. After she comes back.'

'You can't stay here and wait for her. That's mad. You don't even know if... you know.'

He knew. It was risky for Eli to leave a couple of normal folk hanging around with information about him and knowledge of The Magpie's British visit. He had tried not to think about what would happen to Kenna after she did her job. Now he was worried. 'What have you heard, Trev? Is Eli planning to off them afterwards?'

'I don't know. I have no info on that. I'm just a foot soldier, like you.'

'But you came here. You got sent. You got told about The Magpie coming down early. Someone confided in you. We're mates, so if you know the plan, Trev...'

'Dom told me to come collect the bugs, that's all. Honest. No one said a thing about The Magpie. I just heard a rumour and it makes sense if Eli wants the bugs removed. That's all. Listen, are you okay?'

Alfie realised he was breathing rapidly. He tried to relax and get his thoughts in line. Eli wouldn't need to kill Kenna and Ray. In fact, it was too risky to do so. He would probably pay them off and make sure they knew there would be payback for grassing. He'd done it before. Eli only had the most serious threats buried. So, Kenna would come home. To Alfie.

'You okay?' Trevor repeated.

Alfie had zoned out for a moment. 'I'm fine. Dude, I'm sorry about your car. Go on and do your job. Pretend I was never here. I think Kenna will be okay, and so I'm going to wait here.'

'Whatever you want, pal. I won't tell. Look, I'm gonna go get the bugs. That okay?'

Alfie nodded and Trevor got to work. He found and pocketed the bug here in the living room, then headed upstairs. Alfie sat down to watch the end of the movie — and got back to his feet. Something was wrong. Why would Eli remove the bugs? Surely he'd want Kenna and Ray spied on in the days after her date with The Magpie? He'd need to make sure she didn't call the police. There could be only one reason for cleansing the house.

Kenna was going to be killed after all.

He left the room and climbed the stairs, meaning to grill Trevor further. At the top of the stairs, he noticed the main bedroom's door was closed over. And he could hear Trevor talking on the phone. He moved closer, straining to hear.

'—sink all of us... don't know what's in that cesspit of his... sure... always was a dickhead, like I said... hold him as long as I can. Just make sure... what? Yeah. Just make sure they get here quick...'

Alfie said, 'Hey, Trev, did you know about the neighbour over there?' and opened the door.

Caught in the act, Trevor jammed his phone behind his back and tried not to look shifty. 'Alfie, Jesus. Scared me. I was just... what neighbour?'

Alfie stepped closer. 'Across the street.'

He pointed at the window. Trevor turned to look, which presented the back of his head for a moment. A moment was all the time in the world.

NINETEEN

The cellar was about as grim a place as imaginable. A peeling ceiling, dirty brick walls with patches of resilient plaster, and a wooden floor whose boards were stained, cracked, warped. It was dimly lit yellow by a single bulb on a grimy cable. Boxes of various sizes, some plain and some branded and most ruined by damp, were against one wall. Plastic chairs were stacked in five columns against another wall. By another was a heavy wooden workbench with a vice attached.

By the time the brute quartet had him marching down the steps, Ray had given up fighting. Wherever they wanted him, he wouldn't avoid it. And where they wanted him was bound to that bench. Two guys held his arm while another snapped a handcuff over his wrist, the other end of which went through a thick chain looped around one of the bench's legs. Everyone seemed to relax once he was in place. They all started heading for the door.

'At least explain this shit,' Ray yelled. 'We did what you wanted.'

The fat guy at the rear stopped at the foot of the stairs. His pals continued on their way. 'Don't try to escape. You're here so your bit of fluff does what she's told. You'll see her again if she does it.'

'She will. There was no need for this. You can take me back upstairs. Ask Eli. I won't fight.'

'Just sit tight. I'll get you some water. You've seen how we're in a field, so don't bother shouting for help. All you'll do is interrupt my TV. That happens and I'll show my gratitude by squashing your knees in that vice there. You won't be the first.'

Ray believed it and said nothing further. He didn't even complain when the fat guy flicked off the light before closing and locking the door. In a completely black world, Ray sat on the floor and prayed his wife was okay.

———

The man in the blue shirt led Kenna upstairs, with Eli at the rear. They entered a bedroom with an en suite bathroom and a large dressing table. Blue Shirt made her stand still in the middle of the room. Vulture-like, he did a full circle around her, staring. She kept trying to pull the hem down, but half an inch did nothing to quell the disgust she felt.

'Good. Short, tight, quick for a search and promotes openness.' He stopped and squatted. His face was just inches from her groin. She wanted to knee him right in the nose. 'How did you get that scar?'

'Bicycle accident. Years ago.'

The scar, on the front of her thigh, was white, curved and two inches long, thicker in the middle, like a crescent moon. It was one reason she didn't like showing her legs off. Blue Shirt touched it and she stepped back.

'Does it need covering?' Eli said.

Blue shirt stared. Thought. He checked his watch. 'Yes. Send someone for a garter. Same red as the dress.'

Eli got on the phone and made a call. While he did, Blue Shirt grabbed the chair from the vanity desk and moved it into the centre of the room. He told Kenna to sit. She did, and crossed her legs uncomfortably when he knelt just inches from her knees.

'Left hand on your left thigh, please. And keep very still while I do this.'

'This' was fake fingernails. From a clear plastic packet of them, he extracted one and took her thumb. Using thick glue from a bottle with no label, he bonded it in place. Kenna watched in such fascination that she barely registered wrists touching her thighs. The nail was painted black, an inch long, and heavier than she expected. After, he wrapped the nail and the top of her finger in tape so it could safely dry in place.

'What search are you talking about?' she said, just because the silence was deafening. Blue Shirt started on her second nail. He looked at her and she had to explain. 'You mentioned the dress being quick for a search.

Eli answered for him. 'When you get to the hotel, you'll be searched. For weapons. Nobody can go near The Magpie with weapons.'

'Okay.'

'Ah, you didn't ask who or what The Magpie is. I'm guessing you've done some research.'

'I did. You want me to date this man tonight. I wanted to know more. Which includes the plan. You said there was a twist. You want me to sleep with this man, is that it? To butter him up so you can do a business deal?'

'No, Kenna. I wouldn't need a masterful trick like this for a simple business deal. What you're going to do is something nobody has been able to.'

'And what does that mean?' she said, and she didn't dilute

the scorn in her tone. 'Am I supposed to rob his safe? Plant a bug? Photograph secret documents?'

Eli shook his head slowly. He picked up the bag of nails and extracted one. He held it up. 'The Magpie is paranoid and clever and powerful like you wouldn't believe. The man has security that would make the American president look like a sitting duck. He's escorted everywhere by his top guards, none of who get close and personal duty unless they've been with him for years. Except when he's with a woman. I mean, nobody wants to fuck a girl with his bodyguards all around. It will be just you and him in his plush penthouse suite.'

'What are you saying?'

Eli turned the nail in the air. 'This is fine titanium. It has a strength to weight ratio better than any other metal. Fixed in place with industrial glue.'

She got a sinking feeling.

Eli ran the point of the fake nail across the back of his hand. A fine red line of blood marked its path. 'What I want is The Magpie dead in that hotel room. His throat ripped out. And you're going to be his seductive assassin.'

TWENTY

'Dom. It's Alfie. I think I did something bad.'

Dom paused. Alfie could hear faint voices in the background of Dom's phone. 'What have you done? Where are you?'

'Not on the phone. I'll come to your house and tell you.'

'What? Hell no, Alfie. We don't do houses, remember. That's why we have meeting points. Where are you?'

'I just left Trevor at the Barker house. I had to hurt him. I was there. I killed him. He tried to stab me while he was on the phone to someone.'

'What? Jesus, Alfie, for real? Where are you?'

'I'm driving. I had to get away. But I want to come in. I want to explain to Eli what I've done. And it's something bad. I was hoping you could help. We're good friends, aren't we?'

'Sure, mate. I can help you with Eli. I helped you off the streets, remember?'

Alfie could hardly forget. On a cold afternoon, Dom's car had pulled up as Alfie was sitting in a recessed shop doorway and eating someone's binned food. He'd offered Alfie the chance to make some money. Alfie had never looked back.

He said, 'We look out for each other. I know you care, and I know you don't want Eli to whack me. But he'll want to when he finds out about how I've fucked up. I'm going to come to your house about four o'clock.'

'What? Hell no, Alfie. Never homes. My wife and kid will be there. Where are you?'

'This is bad, Dom. I'll be there at four.'

He hung up.

It was half two in the afternoon, and in about an hour Dom's fourteen-year-old kid would be back from school. Dom couldn't have the kid in the house if one of Eli's vicious foot soldiers planned to turn up, so someone would have to come get him.

His wife, Karen, was out somewhere with his official phone to alibi him in case things went wrong tonight. Dom wouldn't ever allow one of his gang near the place in case that guy was being watched by the police. Too risky to allow a neighbour inside because they might see something they shouldn't. No, despite how busy he was, the man would have to come for the boy himself.

His plan would be to meet his kid, who'd be back shortly, and pack him off somewhere before Alfie's arrival. There would be some heavies waiting to take Alfie, but they wouldn't be anywhere near the house. Dom would have to trick Alfie to get him to the ambush location. If Alfie's prognosis was correct, it meant Dom would be back very soon, and he'd be alone.

Spot on. Alfie saw Dom's Range Rover draw into the driveway with a solitary occupant. As the underboss walked into the living room, Alfie swung the man's own baseball bat and took out a knee. Dom was fat, unfit, far removed from the violent streets, and he went down instantly, screaming. But maybe old habits die hard, and this guy had begun his criminal career as an enforcer, so Alfie blasted the other knee.

He waited patiently while Dom got used to the pain and calmed his moaning. Agony turned into incomprehension. He demanded to know why he'd been attacked – by his own good friend.

'I saw right through your fake shock,' Alfie said. 'It was you on the phone to Trevor when I killed him, so my admission later wasn't breaking news. My guess is you sent some people to the Barker house. They probably missed me by seconds. I had to do it. You both betrayed me.'

'I'm on your side,' Dom said through gritted teeth. He smiled. The agony that had become incomprehension now morphed into fear. 'I wouldn't betray you. I came to help. We're friends. Please. I need to get my knees fixed. They hurt.'

'We used to be friends. And that friendship is why this hurts so bad now. You stabbed me in the back, and that's a lot more painful than your silly bloody knees. They'll heal, unlike my heart. So shut your whimpering mouth.'

Dom's agony turned incomprehension turned fear now transformed into rage. 'You fucked up, Alfie. So, yeah, you have to be punished. But I would have spoken in your favour to Eli. So what's all this crap, you dickhead? You killed Trevor, and now you do this to me? You're a damn idiot. You just fucking lost everyone who gives a shit about you. You're going back to the streets, but this time with a goddamn bullseye on your back.'

Alfie twirled the bat. 'Not everyone. I have Kenna. Me and her are in love, and we're going away together.'

Dom seemed to forget his pain, so vast was his surprise at this statement. He even managed a mild laugh at the absurdity of it. 'What? Since when? You're delusional. Is that why you were at her house? I don't know where she is, if that's why you're here.'

'It is. And you do. Talk while you still can.'

Dom tried to sit up, but he was too fat to do it without input from his legs or tweaking his shattered knees. He dropped onto his back with a moan. 'Alfie. Please. You've met Karen. You've seen pictures of my kid. Don't do this to them.'

'No, Dom, *you* don't do this to them. Tell me what I need to know, and you might live through this.'

'Alfie, listen. Please–'

'No time, Dom. You get in the way of me and Kenna, I get in the way of your family. Tell me or I'll bash in your skull and leave you here for your kid to find. He's back in about twenty minutes. That might be in time for him to see you take your last breath.'

'No, you wouldn't do that. You can't kill me. Think of my kid and what that would do to him. Please, Alfie. I know you and you can't be that cruel. It'll destroy him. You lost your dad around his age, so you know what that's like.'

Alfie gave a scornful flick of the hand. 'I turned out all right.'

TWENTY-ONE

Kenna put a fingernail on her thigh. Pushed the sharp point down into the skin. Dragged her finger an inch. Barely any pressure, but the titanium nail caused a scratch. It didn't bleed, but she felt the might of the weapon, and the solid connection to her finger. She knew her hands had the power to drive those nails deep into flesh.

But did her mind have the constitution to force those fingers to actually do it? To rip at a man's throat, spill his blood, and to watch him die?

The nails still felt alien. They were longer than she was used to, and heavy, and she didn't have her usual pinpoint dexterity. Like that time when Ray hired a van to collect a new fridge and she'd driven them home. She'd been clumsy on corners, and the elevated riding position had felt off. Did she even have the skill to perform the lethal task asked of her?

She would find out the answers to those questions, or she and Ray would die. She wiped tears from her eye.

'Stop. Don't smudge that make-up,' Blue Shirt said. He was by her side in the back of the car, while up front a man drove the darkening streets. She saw pedestrians zip by and she envied them. Sometimes, when she was feeling down, she'd see strangers and wonder what it would be like to swap lives. To bring up another woman's kids, work her job, deal with her problems.

It was a good mechanism for realising that her own life was pretty good, because who knew what heartaches other people faced? Well, today, now, it didn't matter what troubles blighted that woman in the hat or that lady carrying flowers – their lives had to be better than Kenna's.

She looked out of her window and saw they were on a wide road with trees to the left and buildings on the right. Beyond the trees on the left: Hyde Park. So, this was Park Lane. They were close.

The car pulled into a bus stop. Quickly, Blue Shirt got out and came around to open her door. He took her hand softly as she exited, as if he was her fine date for the night. As soon as he shut her door, the car returned to traffic and was gone.

They began walking towards a pedestrian crossing about thirty metres away. It was cold. Blue Shirt had put on a jacket, but she had nothing except her skimpy dress. It drew glances.

'I'm surprised we're walking the streets like this,' she said. 'People are looking at me. They might remember.'

Blue Shirt said nothing. They reached the crossing and he jabbed the walk button. They waited only seconds before a red light stopped traffic. Three lanes of it. Dozens of eyes. They started to cross. Kenna said, 'All these people watching. All of them will think about me and you when they hear about a murder in a hotel round here.'

Blue Shirt made no reply. They reached the central reservation. Other pedestrians continued ahead, to cross the southbound lane, while more passed them from that direction, all of them going about a business that didn't involve murder. Seven or eight people had stopped right here, which Kenna and

Blue Shirt mirrored. Because they had arrived at their destination.

The Animals in War Memorial had been constructed in 2004 at a cost of £2 million. It was a curved white stone wall with a gap in the middle. Approaching the gap were two bronze mules struggling under heavy backpacks. The left portion of the wall contained bas-relief images of animals, while on the right was an inscription. Blue Shirt stopped her close to one of the mules and took the other side, so they spoke across it.

'Are we meant to play the part of a loved-up couple enjoying London?' she said. 'Everyone is looking at my dress. And wondering what we see in each other because of the age gap.'

'This is London, highly covered by CCTV. In The Mirage Hotel, there are cameras, too. The Magpie will have a dozen security personnel check you out. By the time you get into the penthouse, your face will be well-known, well-recorded. Nobody will need one of these fools around us to pick you out of a line-up. We're here because it's close, yet beyond the perimeter patrolled by The Magpie's people.'

'What you're having me do is a crime. The worst kind. Cold-blooded murder. And you're taking no steps to guarantee my safety.'

'Of course we have. We went over your cover story, remember?'

She did, and the thought still made her shiver more than the cold did. Blue Shirt had drilled a fake story into her, involving a London gang called the Leery Lads. She knew they African criminals from Hounslow who liked to rob post offices and pedestrians. She knew where they were headquartered. She knew their Chain, which was the title of their top five officers.

Smaller gangs like these were no real threat to the big boys and often were left to tend to their little zones. Sometimes, though, psychos amongst their ranks got wild ideas about taking down Goliath. Two days ago, outside a library, she had been kidnapped by the Leery Boys and forced into this murderous job. They had sent her to Eli, who she had convinced to recruit her as a sex worker. He had no clue about the assassination plot.

'Will they believe that story?' she had asked.

If she was captured after the murder, The Marshalls would whisk her away to somewhere secret and a guy with serious interrogation skills would demand answers. There would be tools involved, and drugs, and it would be near-impossible for her to resist the torture.

'So the answer to your question,' Eli had said, 'is that they better damn well believe it. If you fold, Ray will be tortured and slaughtered. We'll see if your love of your husband beats your hate of pain.'

Eli would know if she'd succeeded when Leery Boys started appearing face-down in the River Thames.

'But what will happen to me?'

'If you're lucky, you won't be one of the floating faces.'

She stared at Blue Shirt over the bronze mule and said, 'You told me that there will be a power struggle in The Magpie's gang and after a few weeks they might just forget about who killed him.'

'Very true. Like in any business, once the snake's had its head cut off, another snake takes its place and the wheels continue to turn.'

'But Marshall's men aren't the only problem. I'm going to kill someone. The police might decide it's a good idea to find that person. They won't forget about the murder after a few weeks. No statute of limitations. Even ten years from now, when the case is cold, some newbie detective will be thrown the file and asked to see what he can do. They'll never stop hunting me. But nobody has told me what you plan to do to help in that regard.'

Blue Shirt didn't even have to think. 'Exactly nothing at all. If the police come for you, you're on your own.'

She searched his face for a lie, or a joke. None existed. This should have shocked her. It didn't. She knew why: she hadn't yet committed herself to carrying out this godawful plan, despite what she'd told these people. 'So why would I do it?'

'You're well aware. Your husband. Better he visits you in prison, rather than you talking to his gravestone. We've taken steps to guarantee that the police can do nothing to us, no matter what you tell them. Not our concern. You deal with the police if it comes to that. Would you prefer to be killed by The Magpie's men?'

'Of course not.'

'Then you escape the hotel after the job. That's your priority and you shouldn't even think about the police until you're safe. You don't escape, you don't live to regret it. We told you the escape plan. That's what's going to keep you alive. So talk me through it. And hurry because time is pressing.'

Kenna closed her eyes, remembering the plan as told to her by Blue Shirt back at the safe house.

The penthouse was accessed by a key card imprinted with the current code. There was only one card, so Kenna would have to get a temporary copy from reception. One of Marshall's men would take her to the desk, where a call would be made to Alan. If he consented to her visit, she'd get the key and ride the lift to the 'top' floor, seven. It wasn't exactly the top because the penthouse suite occupied a whole storey above it. The only way there was by a second key card lift, manned by a staff member. That lift could not be used unless the penthouse resident authorised it.

At this point she'd cut into the story. 'Wait. If he's dead, how can he authorise my trip back down.'

'He can't,' Blue Shirt had said. 'And you'd never be let out until his men had checked on him anyway.'

'Wait. I'll be trapped?'

No. Inside the kitchen was a secret door, beyond which were a stone staircase and another lift. These both led to a room on floor seven, for use by the penthouse guest's staff to send and receive items, and to a corridor under the hotel.

'A corridor?' she'd said. 'To where?'

'There's an underground bunker below the hotel. Churchill built it during World War Two. It's a vast complex where the government could reside as bombs fell.'

'Never heard of it. How am I supposed to walk around some bunker? Or get out again?'

'The corridor accesses the bunker, but it also goes directly alongside. I mentioned we'll be dropping you off at the Animals in War Memorial, right? Well, further along the central reservation is a grassy area with a hidden manhole cover. That's where you'll come out.'

Now, Kenna finished her recital of the escape plan with, 'Then I get picked up in a car and returned to Ray, and we go home and live happily ever after.'

Blue Shirt smiled. 'Don't sound so glum. This will work, and you'll be a lot richer.'

Kenna took a deep breath. Her eyes shifted to the memorial wall, and the inscription on the right-hand side.

This monument is dedicated to all the animals that served and died alongside British and Allied forces in wars and campaigns throughout time.

Blue Shirt noticed her shift of attention and said, 'Those

animals are like you. Doing a risky, but mammoth and important job, without even knowing it.'

Oh, she was like those poor animals in a far more relevant way. Beneath the inscription was another that read:

They had no choice.

TWENTY-TWO

The guy who opened the door was a kid of about Alfie's age, but he carried it better. He was Korean or Chinese – Alfie had never found out which and he found it hard to tell the Asian races apart. The kid had also come into the gang's orbit in a similar way, although he'd abandoned his family in order to date a white girl. Or something like that. Either way he'd been on the streets and now here he was. He was one of a bunch of psychos Eli kept around for looking after snatched people. Alfie had never been inside this house, but he knew it had a cellar for breaking hardnuts.

And that was where Ray would be.

'Hey, Alec,' Alfie said, 'Eli called Dom. Dom called me. Eli left, that right?'

There had been no calls. Alfie had been parked a short way down the road, watching the tree-shrouded entrance to the plot of land containing this house. Eli's car had left half an hour ago. He was off to his sister's birthday party to create an alibi for tonight.

Alec said, 'Yeah, short time back. Dom sent you?'

'Yeah. Dom. Look.'

Alfie pointed behind him, to where Dom's Range Rover sat about ten metres down the track. It was closing on dusk so the interior was dim, but Dom could be made out sitting in the passenger seat.

Alfie said, 'Dom's heading off soon, but he wants to show the prisoner the Spectacle.'

Alec's brow furrowed. 'What's that?'

'The Spectacle? Fuck knows. Dom's thing, top secret, whatever. You want to ask Dom about it, even though we're in a rush?'

Alec shook his head. He turned and walked into the house. For some reason the kitchen was at the front. Alfie followed. He could hear a loud TV in the living room and someone laughing at it. Alec entered the short hallway between the two rooms and slid a heavy deadbolt on the cellar door.

Just inside the door, on the wall at the top of the stairs, was a knife rack, from which Alec took the largest weapon. 'Don't need that,' Alfie said. He lifted his top and pulled out a snub-nosed revolver with a grip wrapped in white tape. 'Dom gave me this.'

'Better hope you don't need it.'

Alec flicked on the light and down they went. Alec led, which meant he trusted Alfie. Against the far wall was a workbench, and sitting before it, chained by one arm, was Ray. Alfie saw he'd been recognised and somehow the bitch's husband managed to find additional disgust to paint all over his face.

'Hey, dickwad,' Alfie said. 'Remember me?'

'Never forget something as ugly as that face. Where's my wife?'

'We're shifting you. Orders from on top. I volunteered, because I'm allowed to blow off one of your balls if you try anything. I so hope you do. So no tricks. You'll walk in front of me and get in the car, and then we'll take a drive.'

Ray said nothing. Alfie watched as Alec found a key in his pocket and unlocked the cuffs. Alfie trained the gun on Ray as the big man walked past and up the stairs. Alec offered to help escort the prisoner to the car, but Alfie was having none of it. 'Dom sees you help, he'll think I'm weak. Go back to your noodles or something.'

'Piss off. That a racist thing? We all eat noodles?'

'Piss off yourself. That a racist thing? We all think you eat noodles?'

Ray walked out of the door, and down the track, and stopped before the Range Rover. Alfie ordered him into the back seat, then climbed behind the wheel. The gun was just two feet from Ray's face, but the big guy's attention was elsewhere. He looked horrified.

'Did you do that? Who is he?'

'That's Dom,' Alfie said. 'He's coming with us.'

'Why did you kill him? Isn't he one of yours?'

'No, pal, he's not. Not anymore. He tricked us all, so that's why he's dead. His knees were fucked and it was hell to help him get in the car. That was before I put a knife in the back of his neck, so now he's a little less willing to help. That's where you come in. We need to dump the body and I can't lift it by myself.'

'Why would I help you do that?'

'You want your wife back, don't you? Well, it's your lucky day. I'm not on their team anymore, Ray. Now, I'm going to put this gun down so I can drive. Don't try anything. You need my help. I'm here offering it. Let's just drive out of here, dump this guy, and I'll tell you how you can get Kenna back. So just sit tight.'

'What about the police?'

'I would have already done that if it was a good idea. Eli has police in his pocket, as you well know. One of his cops hears the word, that's game over. Eli will cut his losses and have her killed. Instantly. We'd never find her in time.'

'So how are we supposed to? I have no idea where they took her. Do the people in that house know?'

'No, Eli doesn't tell the bottom rung what happens at the top, and especially in this case. But Dom told me everything and there's a guy who knows where Kenna is. Dom doesn't. So we'll get rid of his blubbery body and go see that guy. Are you in? Or you want to be a widower?'

Ray rubbed his face. He looked like he was about to cry. And then he slammed a fist into his seat, angry. Clearly the guy didn't know how to feel, or that wacky brain of his was misfiring. Finally, he nodded. 'I'm in. But I'm not touching that body.'

'We'll see. It wastes time if I have to do it on my own. Anyway, I'm putting the gun down. We drive, we dump, we rescue. That's the plan. Don't do something stupid and fuck this up. Here we go.'

This was the pivotal moment. He wasn't sure Ray believed him. Even if he did, he might think he'd be better off with police help. The moment that gun was out of the equation, Ray would have a chance to turn the tables. It was a gargantuan risk, but one Alfie had to take.

So, his eyes stayed on Ray, but his hand put the gun on the dashboard. Ray made no move. Alfie gave it a few seconds and turned away from the big man. He gripped the steering wheel hard and waited for a blow on the back of the head, or Ray's door to bang open.

Neither happened. Ray was on board. Alfie started the engine. 'Okay, big guy, let's go get Kenna back for you.'

'This is Putney,' Ray said, staring out the window. 'Are we going to the hairdresser's?'

'No. I know a guy who lives on a road down here.' Now that Alfie didn't need Dom's body to fool anyone at a distance, he'd forced the man down below the window and covered him with a blanket. As they crossed a busy junction on Putney High Street, he made sure the cover was in place properly. A short way across the junction, he took a left and drove down a residential street that ran alongside train tracks. An alleyway between two large, terraced buildings was his destination.

'Who lives here?' Ray asked when the car made the turn. 'How does he know where my wife is?'

'He doesn't. That's a different guy. This guy has a place we can dump the body.'

The alleyway ran past the houses and their back gardens and terminated at a fence shrouded in trees. Alfie stopped the car alongside a door in the high wooden fence of the garden on the left. He got out and opened the door, then called for Ray to help him shift Dom.

Ray got out. 'I can't.'

'We need speed. Anyone walking past this alley will be able to see if it takes too long. Just help me get him out of the car and through this gate. It'll take five seconds No one can see inside the garden except my mate, and he's never in.'

'I can't. Look, I don't want any part of this. I want my wife. I'm leaving.'

He tried to, but Alfie reached into the car, past Dom, and grabbed the gun. Without a care for who saw from the road, he aimed at Ray across the roof of the car. 'Listen to me, okay? I'm on your side. You asked me why I was doing this, and what I said was the truth. I want to do the right thing. But it's more than that. You know I like your wife. I know I can't have her, but that doesn't mean I want her to die. And she will if we don't do things my way.'

'I don't believe that. No way. Eli said all she has to do is–'

'Kill the guy.'

Ray gawped at him.

'Yeah, you heard me right, big man. This isn't about some fancy dinner date to butter a guy up. They want her to kill him. I got Dom to admit everything, Ray. And it's not the only thing they lied about. Trust me when I tell you that this is all a big trick, and unless you and I work to help her, she's gone forever.'

TWENTY-THREE

Blue Shirt took her arm to guide her across southbound Park Lane. As they found a break in traffic and stepped out, he said, 'Wouldn't do to have the plan ruined by a speeding car.'

On the other side, on the corner of Upper Brook Street and outside an Aston Martin showroom, he pulled an envelope from his pocket. 'Now take this. His people will need it.'

He didn't say she couldn't open it, so she did. Inside she found two printouts. Test results.

'How did you do this?' she asked.

'We have access to a biological scientist. She ran the tests. You're clean, you'll be happy to know.'

'I already knew that. I've only been with my husband for years.'

'Good to know you trust him so well. The blood we took was for a dual purpose. Some of it is waiting to be planted. I advise you not to do a runner. Or to go to the police at any time in the next fifty years.'

'What does that mean? Planted? At a crime scene? You're going to plant my DNA on a murder victim or something?'

'That's down to you.'

My God. 'So if I don't commit murder, you'll frame me for one?'

'Clever girl. Now go.' He abruptly turned and ran back across the road, to the memorial. She didn't like him, didn't want to be around him, but she suddenly felt alone. Across the roofs of passing cars, she shouted, 'What if the plan is ruined by a crack addict with a knife?'

'This is Mayfair,' he yelled back. 'You'll be fine.'

She tried to put that out of her mind and started walking. The air chilled her bare legs and exposed neckline, but stress was overheating her head. Either side of her were the sheer walls of four-storey buildings. Nominally such areas of London were a sight to behold, but now she felt claustrophobic. She kept her eyes down, ignoring all other pedestrians.

It was little more than a hundred metres to the first junction, where she'd turn left onto Park Street, but the journey was marred by the intrusion of three different men. One remarked that she could do with a coat. One called her a slut. One asked for sex. None got a reply.

Once on Park Street, it was another hundred or so metres to the next junction, where a right on Green Street awaited. Once there, she saw The Mirage Hotel at the end, where the road met North Audley Street. Another hundred metres.

She climbed a set of five steps to stand in a recessed doorway across from a small side street, so she could scan the area out front of the hotel. The drop-off area was large and the building sat twenty metres back from the road. There was activity as expensive cars circled a water feature to pick up or drop off guests. Two doormen under the long purple awning were greeting and waving off people.

Blue Shirt had informed her of what to say to the doormen, who would certainly accost her. But they would not be her first interaction. He'd promised her that Alan Marshall knew what she was wearing and that one of his men would meet her before she reached the hotel. She'd asked what 'meet' meant, but Blue Shirt had been vague: 'You'll see. Just don't get scared.'

It meant someone had to be watching her. Here, right now, for she was only a thirty-second walk from the hotel. She looked down the lines of parked cars, seeking a human shape within. But aside from those closest to her, every interior was too dark to penetrate. About fifteen metres away was a motorcycle parking bay, where a guy was fiddling with the engine of a scooter. He wasn't the only person out here, but she got a feeling he was...wrong.

And so it was. As she passed him, he said without even looking at her, 'Cross here. Do it now. Continue towards the hotel.'

The guy's engine was suddenly fine. Five seconds after his final word, he was on that scooter and riding away.

She crossed the road and continued towards the hotel. Two men twenty feet apart were heading towards her. The first didn't ring an alarm, but something about the second man... again, wrong.

And so it was. As he walked by, he said, 'Wave at the black van like you just saw an old friend.'

Like the biker, he exited her life a moment later. She didn't even turn to watch him go. Instead, she stared at a black van parked just ahead. It had rear doors and a sliding side door, and no windows in the back.

She gave it a wave. In the next instant, the sliding door was open and a woman had stepped out. About Kenna's age, she was dressed in trousers and a flowery blouse. She had a walkie-talkie clipped to her belt. She approached with a big smile and wide arms – like a good friend, Kenna realised.

The woman grabbed her in a hug and said, 'Get in the van.'

She then took Kenna's hand and led her to the van. The cargo bay was completely empty. There was no bulkhead separating the area from the cab and she saw a man behind the wheel. He didn't even look at her.

A push from the woman got her moving. She stepped in and sat on a wheel arch. As soon as the woman got in and slammed the door, the vehicle pulled away from the kerb. The woman took the envelope in Kenna's hand.

'What's going on?' Kenna said. 'I'm supposed to go to the hotel.'

Nobody said a word. The van drove past the hotel and turned a corner. Kenna was suddenly suspicious. And scared.

The van pulled in on the next street and the engine shut off. The woman had scanned the printouts in the envelope and now put them aside.

'Good. All clean. Now listen up, darling. You're going to be searched. It'll be invasive. Believe me, I'll hate it as much as you do.'

'No, I'll hate it more.'

'The man you're going to see is very important to us. We have to make sure there's nothing on you that could be dangerous to him. After the search, you can get out and head to the hotel. The doormen will ask your reason for coming in. That dress and the fact that you're alone might make them think you're a lady of the night—'

'Which I am,' Kenna cut in.

'Those doormen may ask you questions. You will say your name is Neela and you're here to see Mr Jacoby. That will be enough. Tonight you're his long-term girlfriend.'

'Get on with the search.'

'He likes girls with sweet attitudes. I hope this abrasive tone is just for my benefit.'

'Maybe I'll tell him you think his taste is atrocious.'

The woman didn't like that. There was genuine fear on her face. She told Kenna to stand up, which was tricky because of the roof of the van. Then the search began.

Including the invasive part, which the male driver shielded his eyes for. Not only were fingers placed into her knickers, but her shoes were analysed, her hair rifled through, and even her mouth searched. The woman looked at Kenna's lethal nails, but found nothing suspicious.

She even tested the strength of the garter Kenna had been given to cover the scar on her thigh. 'You can't keep this.'

Kenna didn't care. She knew why the item was outlawed: she could strangle Marshall with it. She'd even considered it as an alternative to clawing open his neck with her titanium nails. Not that she had decided yet what the hell she was going to do.

After the search, Kenna was more annoyed than scared. 'Can I go now?'

'One more thing. You're playing a role. Nobody inside knows Mr Jacoby and there should be no doubt that you and he are long-term lovers. However, if anyone should recognise you, you must let us know. There is a man inside who will approach you. He will take you to the lifts. You'll be searched again, but this time not so invasive.'

'There will be a slapped face if you're wrong.'

He ignored her threat. 'After Mr Jacoby is done with you, a man will escort you outside, to a vehicle. It will drop you anywhere you like. If Mr Jacoby is happy with your company, it's likely a cash sum will be handed to you as you leave that vehicle. He's been known to tip well.'

'Excellent. Now let me out of here.'

She hauled the door open. As she was about to step out of

the van, the woman said: 'Your employers didn't tell you anything about tonight's client, right?'

'No. He's just a client.'

'I'm puzzled as to why you haven't asked me. Given all this security, I would have imagined you'd be curious.'

Kenna almost called him Marshall, but stopped herself in time. 'Mr... Jacoby is just another trick in a long line. Perhaps not even my last tonight. In the bedroom, princes and paupers are all the same.'

The woman looked disgusted. 'And finally. The money you receive is actually a payment for silence. I'm sure the people who gave you this job have explained that whatever happens tonight needs to be kept secret?'

Like she needed to be told. She planned to take this night – this murder, if it came to that – to her grave.

TWENTY-FOUR

It wasn't a nightmare. It was real. The body before him, with a bloody hole in the base of the skull, was real. The degenerate with a gun was real. Dragging a fat man's corpse out of a car and into someone's dingy back yard was a memory his brain's hard drive would keep forever, no matter how wasted dementia made Ray in later years. It would be his only thought on his deathbed.

'Don't stop,' Alfie said. 'The bins there. Come on, before a neighbour gawps out the window.'

Alfie meant three wheelie bins by the back wall, standing in a sea of junk. A good place for a body to hide. But Ray had had enough. He dropped the dead man's leg and staggered back, fighting the urge to bring up everything in his stomach.

'You do it,' he said. 'I can't.'

Alfie still had the dead man's other leg. 'Ray, come on. We can't leave it here. Be a fucking man.'

No way. 'I want to know what you meant about my wife. You said they were tricking her.'

'Help and I'll tell you. Or fuck off and find her yourself.'

Ray's strength seemed to have departed. Otherwise, he would have shaken the truth out of Alfie, gun or no. Instead, he stepped up to retake the dead leg. The two men hauled the corpse another three metres across the concrete.

'She won't get away after she kills The Magpie,' Alfie said between heavy breaths. 'They told her there's an escape lift in the penthouse. Some bullshit about it leading to an underground bunker. No, man. It goes one floor down, to another room. The Magpie's people have that room. They use it to send him things so he won't be disturbed. There's no escape. She goes down that lift, it'll be right into their hands.'

'What are you saying? She's going to be captured? There's no way out?'

Alfie ordered Ray to shift the bins so they could lay Dom against the back wall. While Ray did this, Alfie said. 'Not captured. Killed.'

Ray grabbed him by the arm. 'What the hell do you mean?'

'Let's get this guy hid first.' He tried to pull his arm free, but Ray's grip was solid, and he demanded an answer. 'Look, Eli wants The Magpie out of the way, but his story has to hold up. He can't risk Kenna spilling the beans. Down in that room below the penthouse is a guy who works for The Magpie, but he's on Eli's payroll. He's new, so he can't get close enough to The Magpie to kill him. But he can get to Kenna when she comes down that lift.'

'He's going to kill her?'

'Shoot her dead, man. Without warning.'

Ray felt anger enrich him. He let go of Alfie and grabbed the body. He lifted it right off the ground, took three steps, and dumped it against the back wall. The two men then positioned the bins to block the corpse and kicked and stacked rubbish to completely hide visible parts.

'A fine job–' Alfie started. His next noise was a shriek as Ray grabbed him by the throat, forced him onto his back on the concrete, and knelt on his chest.

'Tell me everything you know, right now.'

Ray released his grip on Alfie's throat just enough to allow words. 'She has to kill him at 8pm. At five past, Eli's gonna ring and warn The Magpie's men about the assassination plot. Too late, of course, but it's going to look good. The story is that one of Eli's men was hanging around the lair of a gang called the Leery Lads. He spotted a man and woman in a car and took their photo. That's you two.'

Ray remembered the man on the pushbike outside the block of flats. The photo of them, purported to be proof of their interaction. 'That was a setup?'

'Yeah. The Leery Lads have said before they wanted to take out The Magpie. Eli's gonna claim he ran your number plate through his police contacts and got Kenna's name. When he realised she was one of his new girls, he sent people to get her. But she was already gone, so they got you.'

Ray could barely believe what he was hearing. He hadn't been captured to force Kenna to kill. 'And I told them everything, is that right?'

'Under torture, yeah. You told Eli that the Leery Lads paid you and Kenna to do the hit. Kenna went undercover as a whore.' Alfie grinned up at him. 'You're a tough bastard, Ray. You held out a long while. By the time you pissed your pants and told everything, The Magpie was already dead. Unfortunately, The Magpie's men can't chat with you because you died of your injuries.'

Ray released Alfie's neck, but remained kneeling on him. 'Jesus. So all along they planned to kill us? Right from the get-go?'

'Eli knows The Marshalls will suspect him, since he sent Kenna there. So you're his alibi. When The Marshalls raid the Leery Lads' hideout, they'll find a piece of paper with yours and Kenna's bank account details and names. To make it look like you were getting paid. That got planted this morning. There are some of Marshalls underbosses who'll be glad to see the back of The Magpie, so they'll accept it. Then Eli can start his takeover.'

Ray got off him. 'We need to go see this man you know. We have to get to Kenna before this all goes bad.'

Alfie got to his feet, dusted himself off, and held out the car keys. 'You drive.'

Ray took the keys and started walking. He got two steps before something occurred to him.

The dead man back there, under duress, had told Alfie everything. All the fine details. But not the name of the hotel where Kenna was? That was the most important piece of–

Ray was in mid-thought as he turned back to Alfie, and he was in the nick of time to catch him pulling back his arm. As Alfie struck the blow, Ray threw up an arm. A sharp edge of the gun in Alfie's hand dug deep into Ray's forearm, knocking it into his head.

'She's mine, fucker,' Alfie screamed, and raised the gun for another strike. Ray managed to backpedal out of reach, but Alfie came forward, ready to try again.

Instinct kicked in and Ray bent low and rushed forward. Shoulder to stomach, a takedown technique he'd honed from years of rugby. It would halt a charging behemoth, but Alfie was a skinny rake, and Ray barely felt resistance as he powered forward. He drove the smaller man hard into one of the wheelie bins. Alfie grunted under the impact and, winded, collapsed like a sack of potatoes.

Clearly, this had all been a trick: Alfie had brought Ray here in order to dump two bodies, so he could have Kenna to himself. He knew where she was carrying out her mission. He knew where she would be afterwards. And that was information Ray needed. A nice, threatening chat would give Ray what he wanted.

Unfortunately, anger and memory problems weren't the only symptom of Ray's brain damage. Another was rashness. He acted before he could fully understand that he needed Alfie in a position to talk. As the slimy degenerate tried to get up, Ray stepped forward again, this time driving a knee into his head. It bonged off the bin hard enough to slam it into the legs of the corpse behind. This time when Alfie collapsed, he stayed that way. Out cold.

'Fuck,' Ray yelled, well aware of his error. He tried to wake Alfie, but it was no use. The man might be out for just seconds, but it could be minutes, and Ray had no time to spare. There was no guarantee that Alfie would talk anyway, or tell the truth.

Ray grabbed the gun and fiddled with it until he pulled a little rod that opened the cylinder. Now he knew why Alfie hadn't used it: empty. It explained why Dom had been stabbed, not shot.

He checked Alfie's pockets and found his phone. He tapped the first nine of the emergency number and stopped. Eli had the police on his side. If one of them responded to the call or learned of it, Kenna would be in more danger. But even if the police did take serious action, time would be wasted mounting an investigation. Time Kenna didn't have. He needed another plan.

He put the gun in his pocket. He and Alfie were the only two men alive who knew the weapon was unloaded. Someone knew where Kenna was and Ray figured his best bet was the house where he'd been held captive. If someone there knew which hotel Kenna was at, he would make them give it up and then involve the authorities. It was a risky plan, but a workable one.

He had to hope he could get this done before Kenna made a murderous mistake.

TWENTY-FIVE

At least a dozen people were moving about outside the hotel, coming or going. At first relieved by this, Kenna quickly noticed that nobody was alone. There were women in dresses like hers, but they were beneath coats. She knew she would draw attention.

She waited for a sleek black BMW to vacate the kerb then crossed to the large double entrance doors. One of the suited doormen was conversing with an elderly lady and gent, but the other was free to step into her path. She instantly saw that his smile was bogus.

'Business here tonight, ma'am?'

'Meeting my boyfriend.'

She tried to step past. He said, 'Let me get the door for you,' and grabbed it. But did no more. 'May I ask who and which room?'

Now that the accusation had been made, albeit veiled, she felt no more shame. In fact, there was annoyance. 'I don't know yet. Whoever wants to pay the most for a girlfriend for the night.'

The doorman now stepped fully in front of the door. 'Not

tonight, ma'am. I would recommend another hotel. Here at The Mirage we don't–'

'Oh stop,' she said, louder than expected, which fielded more disapproving glances. 'Are short dresses for prostitutes only? Go and tell my boyfriend you turned me away because you think I'm a scatty whore. He's Mr Jacoby, in your penthouse suite. You'll be unemployed before I've even gotten out of the lift.'

The doorman turned bright pink and opened the door. He followed her with apologies almost halfway across the shiny checkerboard foyer floor, until she said, 'Leave it. I won't make a complaint. Go away.'

He promptly obeyed. She looked around the large, elegant foyer. Amongst a handful of guests moving here and there, she easily spotted a man in a black suit leaning against a pillar. Another in similar attire sat on a luxury occasional chair close to the lifts. A third and fourth were on stools at the bar. Numbers five and six occupied a sofa near the front window. They looked like fresh recruits from bodyguarding 101, but perhaps their appearance was meant to be obvious. Either a world leader was staying here, or these were Marshalls men.

She approached the desk, but before she could speak to the clerk, a voice behind her said, 'Mr Jacoby's partner, here to see him.'

It was the guard from the pillar. While the clerk printed a temporary penthouse key, she reminded herself that she was in no danger – yet. She was meant to be here. Marshall hired women all the time. For the next few hours, she was probably more important to him than any single one of his security detail.

Newly confident, she said, 'Calm down. No snipers around here. It's The Mirage. We're all safe.'

The guard was stiff and erect and scanning the foyer. 'Just doing my job, ma'am.'

'Relax a bit. Maybe you need a massage. Perhaps give me a nod when I'm done with your boss.'

That seemed to lighten him up him a little. 'I think if I did that, he'd kick my butt.'

'You're breathing heavy. A cold?'

'Just getting over it. Listen, it's nice to meet you and all, but now I have to get serious. When you take the key card, go over to the lifts.'

'Sure thing. Get some menthol crystals for that nose.'

When the card was ready, she headed for the lifts. The guard didn't follow and retook his place by the pillar. Obviously, Marshall's security team wasn't in place just to direct his date to the penthouse. They needed to be ready to spirit him away if the police raided the hotel, or a hit team from a rival gang blew in, guns blazing.

It was an anxiety-inducing reminder that the glitz and glamour was superficial. Above her was a man she was supposed to murder, and her life and Ray's depended on success.

Pillar guard might have shown a bit of the human, but lift guard was all cyborg. He took her key and opened the penthouse lift and said nothing as it rode up. It had a seat, which she took. The guard stood. He ignored her question about his health. He ignored her claim that he had a bit of food in his beard. She wasn't sure if he was playing Mr Professional or just hated sex workers. She nearly asked if his dad had left his mum for one.

When the doors opened, he held up a hand, meaning she should wait. Like a tag-team, he stepped out and a woman also dressed in black stepped in. She had a tight ponytail, which might have been designed to make her look tougher.

'I need to search you again.'

'Whatever.'

This examination was much lazier, possibly because the results of number one had been communicated upstairs. It was a cursory pat-down, nothing invasive, and over in seconds.

Kenna stepped out into another foyer, but much smaller. Ahead was a door painted gold. Either side of it was a large potted plant. There were cushioned benches against two other walls and here sat four men. One read a book, two played on their phones, and the fourth was doing standing press-ups against a wall. They looked a little bored and clearly it was because their job was to hang about in this small space.

Eli had been dead right about Marshall's security and the impossibility of getting a hitman anywhere near him. The scene reminded Kenna of her escape plan, which she wasn't yet sure she'd need. All the fear she'd been keeping at bay came flooding in and almost floored her.

The woman, her sole task completed, stepped into the lift with the guard and rode down. None of the others said anything. It seemed she had passed all tests and all that remained was to enter the penthouse. She raised a fist to knock, but the guy doing wall press-ups said, 'Just go in.'

Kenna opened the door, stepped inside, and shut it behind her. This was it. The endgame. The next few minutes would shape the rest of her life. However short it might be.

TWENTY-SIX

Remembering the route back to the house where he'd been held captive was out of the question, but technology was there to help. A quick check of Alfie's phone showed that he'd used Google Maps to find the house. It was just three kilometres south, on the eastern edge of a large green area between Putney Heath to the north and Cannizaro Park to the south. The All England Lawn Tennis and Croquet Club, where the Wimbledon grand slam was held annually, was less than a kilometre away.

Once there, Ray parked a short way past the entrance gateway in the woods. He had to assume the driveway could be watched by CCTV, so he threaded through the trees and came out on the far side of the lake. It was dark, which would help. Even better, he faced the left flank of the house and it had only a single window in each floor, both with shut curtains.

Jesus. Was he about to do this? Attack a house occupied by a number of criminals?

He was. Kenna's life might depend on it. He kept a distance as he circled the lake, so moonlight glinting off the water wouldn't expose him. Once house-side, he ran to the wall and paused. He waited for an alarm, or an exodus of armed men. Didn't happen. Nobody had seen him.

On the way here, he'd wondered if he could somehow trick the men inside, just as Alfie had. Now, he knew there was no chance. Alfie was one of them. Ray was a prisoner. So, he'd use brute force. Hopefully he'd get the same little Asian guy from before.

He turned a corner, approached the kitchen window, and carefully looked inside. Empty. He ducked, passed under it, and stopped at the back door. The small glass panes were pebbled, so nobody would know it was him standing outside. He knocked.

Soon, a shape appeared beyond the door and he heard a lock click. No backing out now. The door was a little jammed in the frame and the guy had trouble hauling it free. It flew wide open once released, which allowed Ray to step over the threshold and grab the guy by the collar of his T-shirt before he'd even registered the face of the caller. Ray's other hand stuck the gun in his face.

'Keep silent,' Ray whispered.

It was the Asian guy after all. He froze. His eyes went from gun to face and back to the gun. 'Just doing my job, pal. I'm guessing you're–'

He stopped talking as Ray pushed him backwards, into the kitchen, and shut the door behind them with a foot. It needed a kick to fully close. Ray could hear a loud TV from another room. Someone in there yelled: 'Alec, who's there?'

Ray put the barrel of the gun in Alec's ear. Alec responded to his colleague with, 'Your mum, wanting a bit of me.'

'Don't keep answering the door,' the other guy yelled. 'Who's there?'

'Sky TV salesman. Answer the door yourself next time if you're so interested.'

No response. To Ray, quietly, Alec said, 'He won't come out here, so you're safe. You're supposed to be just some guy. You killed Dom and Alfie?'

'And you'll be next if you don't tell me where my wife is.'

'I have no plans for Superman shit, my friend. But I honestly don't know. Hired help, me, that's all. Bondo, in the living room, he'll know.'

Alec looked scared, but that meant nothing. Perhaps he was more scared of Eli and a comeback for snitching. Ray had no way of knowing if the kid was telling the truth. 'Shout and ask him.'

'Just come out and ask him where your wife is? When I have no reason to know? Why would a guy with no gun in his face do that? It'll sound dodgy.'

'Call Eli.'

'My phone is in the living room. Don't remember Eli's number.'

Ray felt his composure starting to wane. He hadn't expected this kind of resistance. Now he didn't know what to do.

And then he did. He shifted his hand from Alec's collar to the hair on top of his head. 'Turn around.'

The kid's hair twisted in Ray's grip as Alec turned to face away. He jammed the gun into the back of Alec's neck. 'Walk slowly to the door. You're my human shield. You better hope that guy doesn't try anything.'

He pushed. Alec walked. They exited the kitchen and stopped in the hallway, between the cellar door on one side and on the other a staircase leading up. Three feet ahead was the living room door, wide open. The room was dark except for flashes of light from the TV. He pushed again and Alec moved.

The moment Alec entered the living room, he bolted forward, fast and hard. With his fist wrapped in the kid's hair, Ray was yanked forward. As he cleared the doorway, he became aware of a large Black man to his right. Lurking by the wall and wielding a goddamn cricket bat. Clearly Alec had alerted his comrade, possibly with the line about a Sky TV salesman.

Ray landed on top of Alec and immediately turned the gun towards the cricketer, who had now raised the bat for a strike. Seeing the gun made him give up his plan to behead Ray and instead dive for cover.

'Dom's empty gun!' Alec yelled.

Shit, they knew somehow. Ray pushed to his feet, using Alec's head, and leaped through the doorway. Although panicked, he remembered the stiff back door and knew he wouldn't get it open fast enough to avoid being knocked for six. But that same panic threw him a bad decision.

He had an unloaded gun, he was in a house with at least two men, one of them armed... and he ran up the stairs.

On the top landing was a wooden ladder to the attic trap, which was open. The attic? No way. As he passed the ladder and turned right, to use one of the bedrooms and escape by window, the door in front of him opened. The topless white guy who stood there looked sleepy, as if the commotion downstairs had woken him.

'Fuck's happening down–' He stopped, bewildered by the sight of a big guy running at him.

Ray lifted a foot and planted it in the guy's balls. He screamed and dropped to his knees, which unveiled the glorious window behind him.

And another enemy. As bad guy four – this time a naked woman – appeared, Ray forgot the window and opted for the attic after all. By the time he'd backtracked three steps to the ladder, Alec had reached the top of the stairs. The two men collided on the landing, and the lighter, precariously balanced one got the short end of the stick. Before hopping on the ladder, Ray saw something that on a YouTube fails video would have made him guffaw: Alec tumbling down the stairs and taking out the Black guy behind him. A slapstick jumble of limbs thudded at the bottom.

Ray threw himself into the attic. The ladder was held in place by hooks, so in one motion he yanked it free and threw it javelin-like over his head. It thumped somewhere in the dark.

Footsteps. Shouting. The trapdoor hung loose, but there was no way Ray was going to stick an arm down and offer it to someone. He stood up and prepared to stomp anyone who tried to enter.

He looked around and felt a lump in his chest. The open trap was the least of his worries. He had fled here in the hope of exiting through a skylight or window.

But there were none.

TWENTY-SEVEN

The penthouse suite stretched out before her and curved behind, in a U-shape, which explained the tiny dimensions of the outside foyer. She was in the living space, which was as big as the entire downstairs floor of her house. It was every bit as clean and elegant as Eli had made out. She could understand why it cost £4,000 a night. Jesus. And they said crime didn't pay.

'Make yourself at home,' a man called out from somewhere unseen. Marshall. Despite his years in France, his accent was Estuary English. 'Head into the living space. There's champagne free-flowing. Say "stereo" for the music. I like Elvis.'

The living room was through a wide doorway to the left. The upper half of one entire wall was a window giving a view of the lights of night-time London. There was a giant TV on one wall with a long sofa and a kissing chair before it. She wouldn't be touching that item. There was an armchair at an oak writing desk, so she sat there. The room was fabulous.

She remembered what he'd said. 'Stereo, play Elvis Presley.'

She couldn't see a stereo, but music oozed from speakers built into the walls. Amazing. Behind her on the writing desk was a bucket with a bottle of champagne. She needed a drink for what was to come, so opened it and poured a glass. Before even touching that, she glugged from the bottle.

There were three doors here, one wide open. A bedroom. She could see a four-poster bed with lace curtains, and it made her shiver. On any other day she would have gladly rolled about on such a bed. Read a book on it. Eaten on it. Tonight its presence was as ominous as a gallows.

One of the closed doors opened and steam billowed out. The bathroom. And the man she was here to kill appeared in the doorway.

He was tall, about fifty, with a full head of grey hair. His upper body was slim, toned, hairless apart from a line that went from his navel to the top of the only item of clothing he wore: a towel around his waist. His skin was wet.

He'd appeared just as she had the champagne bottle to her lips for the second time. It made him laugh. 'Eager for the good stuff, eh? Pour me a glass, please.'

She turned away to do that. As she turned back, intending to walk over to him, he'd covered the distance and was right there, two feet away. She jumped and sploshed champagne out of a glass and onto a large rug.

He laughed again. 'Forget the rug. Nobody dares complain about a penthouse guest.' He took the glass. 'Let me see those eyes.'

He leaned close. Real close, with his face just inches from hers. She looked past him and readied herself to receive a kiss. She smelled his cologne.

'Wow,' he said. 'Exactly as advertised. This is amazing. I'll meet you in the Haven in five minutes.'

With that, he disappeared back into the bathroom. He left the door open and she saw him sip champagne then move to a sink and begin rubbing a lotion onto his face.

Straight to business, eh? She poured a second glass of the good stuff and got up on shaky legs. She'd expected a man made overweight by the sort of excesses this place hinted at, but he was very fit and handsome.

She had to admonish herself for even thinking he was an attractive specimen. She wasn't here to sleep with this man. Even if that had been her only mission here, she was married, didn't know the guy, and he was a decade and a half older than her.

She took the two glasses and walked to the bedroom. Inside she found an armchair before a large vanity desk, so she sat there. One of the curtains across the bed was open, displaying plump pillows and fine sheets. She tried not to imagine herself lying there, submitting to him. Consensually or not. Perhaps, if he tried to rape her, murderous intent might not be beyond her.

She rapidly tried to think of her next move. Before, when her target had been faceless, the idea of killing him to save Ray had bobbed in dark waters at the back of her mind. Not truly considered, but not absolutely out of the question.

Now, having seen him in the flesh, a real, living man, there was no way she could leap on him and shed his blood. He was responsible for heartache, pain, death, but the only criminals she'd come across were the brash idiots controlled by Eli. It was hard to connect the man he was reputed to be with the one now oiling himself in a penthouse bathroom. He seemed more like a movie star. She just couldn't do it.

But what *would* she do? Ray's life was on the line, as well as hers. She couldn't tell Marshall the plan because she was part of it, had agreed to it, had come here with the intention of killing him. He would kill her for that, according to Blue Shirt. The only other option was the police, but while that might save her life, she would face charges. Conspiracy to murder. She and Ray would go to prison.

Her mind was spinning. She was caught in a trap. In a frying pan over a roaring fire. She–

'Daydreaming?' Marshall said from the doorway. He still wore that towel around his waist. She stiffened. This was it. It was going to happen. She wasn't sure she could bring herself to fight him off. She wondered if Ray would ever forgive her for cheating, if they got out of this alive.

'I'm sorry, I should have been clearer,' Marshall said as he stepped inside. 'The Haven is the rooftop terrace. Head up there while I get changed.'

She relaxed. A little confidence returned. 'Let me be honest. I know you ordered a girl for sex, but I'm really feeling ill and–'

'Stop,' he said. 'That's not why you're here. God no. It's true I was looking for a girl for the evening, but when I saw your picture... I continued the act, but that was just for everyone else's benefit. I wanted you here for another reason. I couldn't touch you sexually if I tried.'

Her head was spinning. 'But Eli said I reminded you of an old girlfriend. I thought...'

He shook his head, smiling. 'Everyone else's benefit, like I said. My man, who saw your picture, gave Eli that tale about an ex off the top of his head. A cover story. To hide the truth. Look, let's not do this here. Head up to the Haven and I'll explain everything.'

'What? Am I in danger?'

'No, not at all. Not from me. Head on up now.'

He waited for her to leave the room, then closed the door. Numb, in disbelief, she walked into the living room. She saw a glass door marked HAVEN, with stairs beyond that led up.

And a table with a mobile phone on it.

She moved to the table, staring at the mobile. She could call the police, right now, and end this nightmare. Perhaps they could find the house where Ray was being held before any harm came to him. She could then slip out of the penthouse using the secret escape route before Marshall had finished dressing.

Instead, she walked on, and opened the door to the Haven.

The terrace covered a raised section of the roof, so that the normal, ugly hardware on top of the building wasn't visible. It allowed a panoramic view of London, spoiled only by various taller buildings. The floor was tiled, with outdoor furniture, a heater, sun loungers, and even a TV in a waterproof clear plastic box. Again, the luxury made her own living room look like a dingy cellar. In summer this place would be a Shangri-La.

She stood at the barrier, which was waist-high toughened glass. She stared at the street far below. If a body smashed down there, the whole city would learn of it. The police would come. Marshall's people would come. Could she convince the good guys and the bad guys that Marshall had accidentally tripped and fallen?

'Shut up,' she said aloud. Even if she could bring herself to push him, there was a space of five feet between the barrier and the edge of the building. He was big, strong, and it was unlikely that she'd even get him over the glass, never mind far enough to plummet to his doom. It was a foolish plan latched upon by an anxious brain.

No, her best bet was to wait and see what he wanted from her. For sure it would be criminal, just like this mission, but she and Ray might be able to survive the night.

She heard footsteps. Marshall stepped onto the roof. He now wore black cargo pants and a long-sleeved polo shirt. It was a good look. In one hand he clutched his glass and the champagne bottle. In the other was a black book, like a diary. He stopped by her side, put the bottle on the floor.

'I looked into you and I know you're not a sex worker, Kenna. I know you were forced into this. I had to keep up the pretence to hide the truth, but I gave orders that you were not to be harmed. You were never in danger and absolutely are not now.'

He slipped something out of the book. She took it. It was a photograph.

It was a close-up of the top half of a girl at what looked like an airport. She wore a T-shirt and a backpack. Kenna was shocked. The girl looked like her. Remarkably like her. An ex-girlfriend after all? What was going on?

Marshall produced another photo. This one was a selfie taken by the girl in a mirror. A close-up of the girl's face, displaying lips painted like the American flag and half in shadow beneath a cowboy hat. But the lips didn't interest Kenna. The eyes did. They were bright grey, just like her own. She was speechless.

Marshall wasn't. He stared at her and he seemed... emotional. 'That's Lillian. My daughter. When my man saw your driver's licence, he was surprised. But when he found your Facebook profile and a picture that showed your eyes... Well, surprise became shock. The resemblance is truly uncanny.'

Thoughts raced in her head. Did Marshall want her to portray his daughter for some criminal act? Pretend to be her to bypass security somewhere?

'That photo of her at Heathrow, it was taken four years ago, when she was twenty-five. She went touring in Vietnam. Her tour bus was in an accident. She's dead. But now it almost looks like she's standing before me again.'

The champagne glass slipped from her hand and smashed on the tiles. Marshall took her arm and they carefully stepped aside. She looked up at him. 'Why am I here? I'm scared.'

'Don't be. Eli doesn't know what my daughter looked like. If he did, and he knew you resembled her, he might have... tried to use that to his advantage somehow. You might have been put in danger, possibly used as a bargaining tool. Plus, if I'm honest, my reason for wanting to see you might have seemed desperate. I wanted no one to know, hence the cover story about a former girlfriend.'

It was finally sinking in. Marshall hadn't brought her here for sex.

'You're in no danger. All I want from you is–' He stopped as a beeping noise cut through the air. He stepped back and snatched something off his belt. It was a pager. He pulled his phone from a pocket. 'Just a moment. Sorry.'

Whatever he'd been paged about, it was urgent. Marshall stuck his phone to his ear and jogged to the stairs. He vanished, leaving her alone on the terrace. Alone with her worries.

When she picked up the champagne bottle by the neck, her fake titanium fingernails dug into the bottom of her palm. There was no use now for them. She swigged from the bottle, put it down, and clamped her teeth over her thumbnail. She got a good grip and twisted. She pulled so hard her shoulder hurt, but finally her hand came away, sans nail. She spat the offending item onto the tiled floor.

There was pain, but her real fingernail hadn't been yanked right off along with its counterfeit partner. Strangely, the lethal weapon seemed help calm her a little, so she moved on to the next. Two minutes later, her hands were no longer deadly and ten plectrum-like implements lay about her feet.

She moved to a chair and sat, and drank. The minutes passed with no sign of Marshall's return. Soon, she began to worry. Why had he skipped out so quickly? Had he gotten wind of the police en route and fled with his band of ne'er-do-wells? If so, surely officers would have been here by now? It had been at least half an hour.

She waited about ten more minutes, but the tension became too much. She exited the terrace. Downstairs, she called out, 'I think I should be going home now. I really do feel ill.'

No answer. The claim of illness wasn't false. While waiting, she'd been turning over possible reasons why she was here. The sole theory she couldn't abandon was that Marshall wanted her to replace his lost daughter somehow. Did he plan to introduce her to the mother? Whisk her off to France, to keep her like a pet in his daughter's old room? Somehow try to communicate with the dead girl through Kenna?

No theory, even the supernatural, seemed out of the question. Kenna didn't want to hang around and see if she was right or wrong. For sure she wasn't going to like what he had planned, so it was time to leave.

She headed the kitchen to try to find the secret lift. It wasn't hard. On a blank interior wall were a pair of flush ring pull handles. Now she noticed the faint seams of a set of double doors. She rapped them. Thin wood, hollow beyond. She hauled them open.

Before her was a brick-lined space that contained a vertical concrete tube with another door in it. It dropped through the hotel and wrapped around it was a spiral staircase. The setup looked like a futuristic notion rendered by old technology.

But it made her heart leap. Blue Shirt hadn't lied. She had a way out, although it remained to be seen what lay at the bottom. The idea of a giant, secret air raid shelter and escape tunnel seemed preposterous.

Before she could do anything, the tube started to emit a rumbling noise. A lift, coming up. She stepped back, and watched in horror as the door opened. The occupant of the lift wasn't Marshall. At the same time, another man appeared at the top of the stairs.

Two of his security men faced her. And they didn't look happy with her. Something had gone badly wrong.

After the phone call to his wife, a man known as DD hung up and checked his watch. It was time. He entered the hotel. Hopefully he wouldn't be needed tonight and he could get home to the missus. They had birthday presents to wrap for their three-year-old.

He approached the lifts and stopped to admire a giant framed painting to one side. He was still there a minute later when a pretty woman in trousers and a blouse stopped before the closest lift and opened her purse. He didn't notice her until he heard coins spill all over the floor.

'Good gosh,' she said. DD immediately moved in to help. He didn't notice the lift two feet from him open.

'Thanks for this,' the woman said.

'No probs,' DD answered as he plucked coins from the floor. When he stood, the woman gave him a mighty shove. Only when he stumbled into the lift did he realise it contained two heavy-set men. They grabbed him as the doors shut.

When the time came, a car making circuits pulled into the cycle lane on Park Lane and stopped across from the Animals in War Memorial. The driver put the hazards on. There were two brothers inside. The car would wait five minutes and move on before some parking enforcement official could stick his nose in.

It would complete another circuit, return and repeat. It had made two already.

The driver counted the minutes, then moved on. The passenger was playing on his phone and hadn't stopped in half an hour.

On the fourth occasion that the car pulled in, something was different. A white van with no cargo windows was already in the cycle lane. The car stopped a metre behind.

'Dickhead,' the driver said.

'Piss off,' his brother replied.

The driver tapped his brother's shoulder and pointed out the windscreen. Seeing the van, the passenger said, 'Oh. Yeah, dickhead.'

'Make him less of one.'

The passenger glared at him. The driver tapped the steering wheel to remind him of their roles here: *I pilot the vehicle, you do the legwork.*

But before either man could move, something happened. The van's barn doors burst open and a big man in a black cap and a surgical face mask jumped out. Upon landing on the tarmac, he ducked, and that showed the men in the car a second, even larger individual inside the van.

In a fluid, pre-arranged move, the second man heaved out a long kerbstone. It sailed over his comrade's head and smashed through the windscreen. It hit the dash, broke the top of the steering wheel and dropped into the laps of the two men seated within.

The masked man stood tall and raised a gun.

TWENTY-EIGHT

As a builder, Ray had seen many attics, and many outlays, and he knew people kept all kinds of secrets in such places. This was a criminal safe house, so he'd expected drugs, guns, perhaps even bodies. But there was nothing. Literally nothing. No bag of clothes some kid had grown out of, no box of Christmas cards waiting for the end of the year. The floor was wooden panels, the ceiling bare rafters, and it all smelled of disuse. Why the ladder had been in place was a mystery, unless they'd been clearing the area out.

None of it mattered. Staying safe did. The floor panels were chipboard squares about three feet wide, laid across the floor joists. Ray grabbed one and was relieved to find it wasn't nailed in place. He slid it over the open trap. He laid three more on top for extra weight. Now nobody could poke a gun in and start firing.

But covering the trap had rendered the attic pitch black. The whole world seemed dead and silent. He knelt on a board a few feet from the trap – or where he thought it was – and listened for voices. The people below would be planning an attack, and he wanted to hear it. But there was nothing. He wished he'd brought Alfie's phone from the car.

A voice. He heard the lone female say something, but he couldn't make it out. It had been quiet, so not for his ears. Was she directly below, or in another room?

Next, pounding feet on the stairs. The noise grew fainter, and he wondered if they were leaving. He was still wondering when the footsteps returned. Shit.

He jumped at a loud bang. Right before his eyes, and right about where he thought the trap was, a shaft of light materialised between the floor and ceiling, like a laser beam.

He understood. Jesus. Someone had just fired a gun, believing he was weighing down the boards over the trap with his body.

'How will we know he's dead?' he clearly heard someone say.

'Shoot again to be sure,' the woman replied.

Ray froze as there was another loud crack and a second shaft of light appeared, this time two feet right of the first. He took deep breaths as his heart pounded. Whoever was shooting had picked a new spot.

He wanted to move, but didn't dare. He could create noise like a trail of breadcrumbs, or move to the next location chosen by the gunman. He considered his options. Remain silent and hope they thought him dead and... just left? But what if they tried to come in?

He absolutely didn't want that, so he called out. 'I just phoned the police! You better run.'

'Over there,' someone below said. Realising they'd marked his spot by his voice, Ray moved two metres to his left, slowly. A third shot was fired, but this time the resulting beam of light was even further away than the first two.

'You got lucky, dimwit,' the woman shouted. 'Come down now and you won't be hurt.'

'I just called the police,' Ray repeated. He shifted places again.

'Should have called an ambulance,' someone else said. And there was laughter, which said it all: they didn't believe him.

'Gun's empty.' This voice he recognised: Alec. It was quieter, not meant for him. But the woman decided he'd been able to hear it because she told the speaker he was a big-mouthed moron. Then she spoke to Ray. 'No cops are coming. If you come down, we'll go easy on you. I promise. Open the trapdoor now.'

'Or we burn this whole house down,' someone else added.

Ray thought they might just do that. Now he decided the attic was empty because Eli's people were leaving soon. It was a temporary base while Kenna did their vile business. Then again, would they really destroy an expensive house? It might belong to someone wealthy that they wouldn't want to annoy.

But he couldn't take the risk. He thought about the roof. He could easily tear through the insulation and roofing underlay and knock away the tiles. A jump to the ground might shatter his ankles, even on grass, so that option was out. However, once on the roof, he could yell for help. The street was only forty metres away. He might even be able to lob a tile to the main road, which would gain attention.

More feet on stairs, coming up. Two men cackled. Once again Ray jumped at a thudding noise accompanied the almost magical appearance of a shafts of light. Four neatly spaced ones this time. But not from four guns.

A garden fork, he realised.

'Bathroom this time.'

'You just told him, you fool.'

Ray panicked. The prongs of a garden fork would be long

enough to pass through the lower ceiling, the width of the joists and the chipboard flooring. Not by much, perhaps just an inch. But he didn't want that in his knees or ass. So Ray got up and stepped to a seam between boards, which put him on a joist and, hopefully, safe. He had to grab a roof timber above his head so he wouldn't overbalance. After that, all he could do was pray for luck.

Another thud. Four more lasers burned from floor to roof, over near a corner now. The bathroom. It happened again just a foot to the side. And again. Again. Faster. A couple of thuds resulted in no light, which probably meant the stabber had hit a joist.

'Did I get you?'

More laughter. He heard running feet and knew the guy with the fork was switching rooms. Ray thought about heading over to where the man had created a starry sky in the floor, because that room would now be free. He thought about hopping onto the four boards atop the trap because the fork wouldn't penetrate them all. He thought about how his wife would cope without him.

The next sound was completely different. Cars. Four or five, he thought. Racing fast and pulling up outside. Reinforcements. He was a dead man walking.

What happened next was a puzzling blur of noise and action. The unmistakable sound of a door being crashed open. Footsteps everywhere. Shouting. The police? Had the police raided the place?

No. Someone yelled, 'Jesus fuck, it's The Marshalls.'

The shock caused Ray's grip on the roof timber to slip, which overbalanced him. He landed hard on his front. He froze like that as gunshots rang out. A lot of them. Someone screamed. Someone bellowed a threat. After that, it seemed as if ten people were running and yelling. Below him was a slaughterhouse. He stuffed his hands over his ears to block the din.

He knew exactly why The Marshalls were here. Kenna had killed The Magpie, or she had tried and failed; either way, they knew everything, and they were on the warpath.

It meant Kenna was in big trouble, if not already dead.

For a few minutes after the gunfight ended, Ray heard men walking around and talking. He heard words like 'body' and 'blood' and figured The Marshalls, if indeed they were the intruders, were cleaning up the mess they'd made. He didn't dare move, determined to hope that somehow he wouldn't be found.

No such luck. He heard someone mention the holes in the ceiling, and after that nothing. No voices, no footsteps. He imagined men gathering below the trap. It was a good guess because suddenly the boards he'd stacked over the hole moved aside. A wedge of light pierced the dark.

'Don't shoot,' he yelled. 'I'm up here alone. I'm not one of their gang. They kidnapped me and my wife. They were trying to get me. My name is Ray.'

Silence for a moment. Then someone called for a 'J' and footsteps ran up the stairs. Ray heard whispering and figured this J was being appraised of the treasure found in the attic.

A French-accented male voice called out, 'Time is no luxury this evening. I need to know if you are part of a plot to kill The Magpie. I believe you are, so simply confirm or deny. Right now. Or we'll kill you.'

So they knew for certain not just about the plan, but also Kenna and Ray's involvement. 'Where is my wife? Is she okay?

This wasn't our fault. We were kidnapped. She didn't want to do it. It wasn't–'

'Just confirm or deny that your wife is the grey-eyed girl, Kenna Barker, and that tonight she intended to kill The Magpie.'

Ray bit back a lump in his throat. They knew everything. 'Yes. But Eli forced us. Please believe me. She didn't want to. Neither of us did. You haven't killed her, have you? Has she killed him?'

When the guy spoke next, Ray realised he was on the phone to someone else. 'We have the killer's husband. He confirms the plot. Go get her.'

Go get her? Ray's emotions blew up like fireworks. Kenna was still alive, but only because these people hadn't yet been certain of her culpability. Now they were.

Because of him. He had just signed his wife's death warrant.

TWENTY-NINE

The two men who came for Kenna took an arm each and led her down the spiral stairs. A full revolution of the lift shaft later, the steps terminated at a door on the floor below. That was when Kenna realised Blue Shirt had lied to her. The shaft provided access between a room on the seventh floor and the penthouse, and no more. There was no escape route into an underground bunker. She felt stupid for ever believing it.

When the door was opened, she saw a king hotel room that was full of Marshall's men. Eight at least. An armchair had been placed in the middle of the room and it was to this she was escorted. When the two men turned her around so she could sit, she saw Marshall. He was sitting cross-legged on another armchair beside the door to the shaft, which explained why she hadn't seen him upon entry.

Gone was his smile. He looked angry. She could imagine such a grimace as he ordered a beating or an arson attack or a murder, or whatever. The two men forced her into the chair and stood by each arm. They towered over her, making her feel tiny and vulnerable. But it was Marshall who produced all her fear.

'What's wrong, Mr Jacoby? Have I done something?'

'I think you know it's Mr Marshall. And yes, you have.'

It was pointless to lie. He knew. He knew it all. She said nothing.

'I have your husband. You could have had money and protection, but instead you chose to betray me.'

'No, no, I had no choice. I mean to come here. I was forced. Do you know about Eli?'

'I know everything. Forced or not, you came. You stood there while I bared my soul to you, and all the while you were looking for the moment to kill me.'

'No, I wasn't going to. Honestly. I just didn't know a way out of this. I had to come here or Eli would have killed my husband.'

'And now I get that task. Or maybe I give it to you. I still don't know whether or not to gouge those grey eyes out of your head for this. You don't deserve them.'

'Please.' She tried to stand, but foul hands pushed her back into the seat.

'Stop begging. You made your choice. You look like my daughter, but she was a blessing to this planet. You... you're a slight on it. You don't deserve to live.'

'That's right,' one of his men said. He was sitting on the bed, about six feet to her right.

'Be quiet,' Marshall snapped. He stood up. 'You could have told me the plan the moment you entered my penthouse.'

'I thought you would kill me for agreeing to do it. But I only agreed because I had no choice.'

She could tell he didn't believe this. He stood. 'Take this woman out of here. Throw her alive and bleeding on top of her dead husband and bury them bo–'

'No, she deserves to die here,' said the guy sitting on the bed. Another man approached him, perhaps to give a warning about speaking out. What happened next was quick. The man on the bed jumped up, reached into his jacket, and yanked out a black pistol. It was aimed at her face. The shock wasn't hers alone, as everyone reacted. Hands reached for him, but too late.

'Die you bitch,' the man said, and he fired. Kenna saw a white flash, felt searing pain, and then all became black and silent.

THIRTY

Ray had no choice. There was more than one gun down there. The Marshalls could turn the attic into a strobe light disco if they chose. He shifted aside the boards over the trap and peered down, hands up.

'I've got no weapon, so please don't shoot.'

'Be quick, sir,' one said. Very polite. Five hard-looking men in casual clothing and leather jackets crowded the landing.

'Where's my wife? Please don't hurt her. We didn't have a choice in–'

'Down you come, sir. Last chance.'

Last chance, yet he was called sir. It was all quite surreal. Ray grabbed the ladder, set it in place, and climbed down. He expected to be hauled right off, but nobody touched him. When his feet were on carpet, he said. 'Where's my wife. Please.'

Half a word in, they grabbed him. Not roughly, but firm. He was searched. They were not massive guys, but each one looked like he could snap Ray in half. Eli's mob seemed like maniacs pulled out of the gutter, while The Marshalls might have been recruited spy-style from universities. Yet they oozed menace. Ray had no illusion that he was in deep danger.

He remained silent during the search, staring at blood splattered at the bottom of a doorframe and pooling on the carpet. If there had been bodies lying around, these guys had moved them. Once the frisking was done, he was ordered downstairs at gunpoint.

He expected to be escorted out of the house, figuring that police might have been called about gunshots. Instead, back to the cellar he went. The handcuffs he'd worn earlier were still attached to the workbench, so he got introduced to them all over again.

The men cleared out, leaving him alone. They weren't so barbaric as to shut the light off. Seconds later, a new face entered. He was a tall black man in trousers and a shirt under a bomber jacket. When he spoke, Ray realised he was the French-accented man referred to as J. Some kind of boss, then.

A man who'd have the answers Ray needed. He demanded some immediately. 'Where is my wife? Did she kill your man? None of this is what we wanted. We were kidnapped by–'

'By the Boys Firm, run by Eli Anderson. I need to know what you know, Mr Barker. Tell me everything. Time is still no luxury, sir.'

'What's going to happen to me and my wife? Where is she?'

'I need to know exactly who you are. How you got involved. Everything. If necessary, I will obtain that by pain. I can bring vicious dogs right here. Start talking.'

The smart clothing and eloquent tone barely disguised a sleeping lion. This guy could set maniacal dogs on Ray, have his tattered body dumped, and go attend a kid's birthday party without anyone seeing a change in his demeanour.

'And what's going to happen to us after? Is my wife okay? We're sorry about this. Please don't hurt us. I just need to know my wife is all right. Her name is Kenna.'

'Such decisions are out of my control. I just need your story.

Someone else will take your wife's. After that, I don't know. To be honest, you might both have to die. But don't let it be in horrific ways. So, sir, start talking.'

Ray tugged at the cuffs. If freed, he would have fought like one of those aforementioned wild dogs to get out of here and get to Kenna. But the restraints held. 'I want to talk to her. Prove she's alive and I'll tell you everything.'

'Do you think you're in a position to demand anything? I have the authority to shoot you dead if you don't comply.'

Ray threw his fist at the bench. It stung and his knuckles started bleeding, but adrenaline washed away most of the pain. 'No. Fucking shoot me then. I'm saying nothing until I talk to my wife. Ask your damn boss, Masters, or whatever his name is.'

He saw the man's shoulders visibly slump. 'You can't talk to her, sir. I'm sorry. Truly. It's not that I won't let you. It's that you can't. It's physically not possible.'

Powerful. That was the word one of his whores, Sherrie, had used to describe him. She was right, but also wrong. Eli's power came from money. He had a gang of hard cases at his beck and call, but they had to be paid, right? Physically, alone, he wasn't up to much. If someone real tough came at him and he didn't have a forcefield, he was a dead man.

The threat faced by gangland bosses was massive. The public had a fanciful image of a man like him, living in a flash house, driving fine cars, commanding many, but they didn't understand what lay beneath the surface. For every madman and monster in his stable, ten more were lurking out there, eager to take what he had or revenge a slight. Eli's fine house needed a dozen men watching it round the clock while he slept. He required three cars full of gangsters to follow his vehicle everywhere. He couldn't even go to the corner shop for milk without a pair of bodyguards. He had a comfortable, sweet life, but it was only possible because of that forcefield.

Tonight he had no forcefield.

Eli paced the small room, fretting, waiting for the call. He couldn't relax, couldn't concentrate on the TV, couldn't drink or eat. The plan to murder Alan Marshall was the most dangerous he'd ever undertaken or even considered. It meant glory upon success, but anything short of that would mean his own demise, and he'd always known that. With every other endeavour, even other murders, the danger had always been the police. If they got his guys, nobody would dare sink Eli.

Not so here. The Marshalls had ways to make people talk, and if even one of Eli's gang got captured, it was all over. For that reason Eli had had to remove himself tonight. He sat alone in a dingy room in a B&B called The Imperial in Shoreditch, and not a single person on earth knew where he was.

Bizarrely, he likened himself to a man undergoing a heart transplant. Right now he was unconscious on an operating table and his heart was out of his chest. As good as dead, and by his own choice. If the surgery was a success, amplified life awaited. If not, he was a goner. He would wake as new man, or not at all. It all depended on one phone call.

Finally, it came. And it was bad news.

'The salon and the safe house have been attacked,' his guy said.

Eli hung up. He was numb. The safe house and the salon were established places he ran and anyone could have launched an attack on them. The timing suggested otherwise, but it was possible. He shouldn't panic yet.

He panicked a few minutes later, when his man called with more news. 'I've not heard from DD or the Carters.'

That one simple sentence told it all. Just in case Kenna

Barker somehow got out of the hotel, Eli had a guy called DD in the lobby to end her, right there. And if she somehow got past him and returned to the Animals in War Memorial, she would be finished off by a pair of brothers hovering around the area.

And now they were out of action. And that was no coincidence.

'Shall I send a car for you, boss?' his man asked.

Eli paused. The plan had always been to tell his man to send a car once the mission was over. But that was if everything had gone to plan and Alan Marshall was dead. It had failed and Eli had no way of knowing if any of his men had been compromised. Including the guy on the phone. The car that came could deliver him to an empty house, where bozos with bats awaited their new toy.

He made his choice. 'Yes. I'm at the Five Planets Hotel in Hackney. Come now.'

Eli hung up and smashed the phone against the wall. Then he grabbed his already packed bag and left the B&B. He was on his own now.

Game over.

PART 3

THIRTY-ONE

Stinging light, followed by loud sound. The former morphed into a room. The latter became a voice. It took a few moments for Kenna's waking brain to register what it saw and heard. The former, a room. The latter, Ray's voice.

'Okay, darling?' he said.

She was on a bed, staring up. Ray sat by her. Beyond him was a white ceiling with striplights. Not home. Not any place she recognised. Where was she?

She tried to sit up, but it felt as if a mammoth, invisible weight held her down. Ray added the weight of his hand. 'No, just lie there. Can you hear me okay?'

Now she could. The room had lost blurry edges, and his voice no longer had a shivering bass. Memories began to surface. The hotel room. Many people in black. Marshall, ordering her death. A man stepping up with a gun. A bullet fired at her face.

She threw up her hands to feel for damage. Thick bandages wrapped her head on the right side. 'God,' she said. 'My face.'

She tried to get up again. Ray's heavy hand again refused her. 'No, babe, stay. Your face is fine. The gun got nudged aside and the bullet... well, basically it scoured a groove across the side of your head. They had to stitch it, that's all. There's bruising. That's the reason for the bandages. A concussion as well. I'm not sure you could even call it getting shot. You're fine, though.'

'Hospital? So we're safe. Did the police come? How many days has it been?'

She didn't like his pause. He looked past the end of the bed. Her neck didn't have the strength to allow her to see what, or who, he was looking at. 'Not quite,' he said. 'They brought us to a doctor's surgery. It's closed. Some dodgy doctor on his payroll. And it's the same night. It happened about two hours ago.'

'Who? Who brought me here?'

'He's the one who knocked the gun away, so he saved your life.'

'Who?'

A man stepped into view, smiling down at her. The sight of him pumped grogginess through her brain again.

It was Alan Marshall.

After the 'dodgy doctor' had checked her over again and been happy with her recovery, Kenna asked for time alone with Ray. Marshall and the doctor left the room. Now her strength was fully back and she walked to the window, which overlooked a dark car park. She wore a long skirt and a pullover. Ray had told her they were garments left at the surgery by a staff member. He had been allowed to strip off her skimpy dress – blood-soaked – and redress her. While he did, she told him about Marshall's real reason for wanting her: the resemblance to his daughter. Now she wanted answers of her own.

'Tell me what happened,' she said.

'Marshall knows everything. I told him the truth about Eli's plan. The man who shot you was on Eli's team. We were both supposed to die, Kenna. It was all a trick. Eli had to sacrifice us so he could make out that he wasn't involved. He had a man planted in Marshall's gang. The man who shot you. Luckily, he failed.'

'Because Marshall saved me.' That was still hard to fathom since the crime lord had ordered her execution just seconds before. 'How did you know Eli's plan?'

'Alfie told me. I think he was told by someone else, who he then killed. And he tried to kill me afterwards. I think he wanted you all for himself.'

'How did Marshall find you? And why did you tell him about me?'

Ray looked hurt by a clear accusation. 'No, no, all I did was fill in some blanks. His men came to that house we were at and found me. But Marshall already knew most of it before he got to me.'

It was all still a little hard to get her head around. 'Marshall was about to kill me. Both of us. Why didn't he?'

Ray shrugged. 'Let's ask him.'

They got that chance a few minutes later, when the man himself called the couple to the surgery's waiting room. Seven or eight of his security sat around, as if awaiting appointments. Kenna and Ray sat on a sofa under a picture of an ocean paradise. Marshall dragged a chair close and sat before them.

'You were going to kill us,' she said. 'Because I came to kill you. Something changed.'

Marshall nodded. From his pocket he withdrew a number of small items, which he let rain onto the floor for dramatic effect. Ten of them. Her black titanium nails. 'You took these off. I found them shortly afterwards. I gather that meant you changed your mind. Was I wrong?'

'Yes. That suggests I planned to kill you. I never committed to it. I'm not like you people. I had no idea what to do.'

Ray touched her arm, as if to tell her to watch what she said. Marshall didn't mind her insult. 'Maybe. The end result is what matters.'

She said, 'When you got paged, that was about me, right? That's when you knew.'

'Yes. I was told about the house in Wimbledon. So I was kept safe while my people headed out to investigate. They found Ray, who admitted there was a plot for you to kill me.'

'At gunpoint,' Ray said. His words were for Kenna, and she knew he was defending himself. She stroked his cheek and told him it was okay. He'd done the right thing.

'That explains the long wait I had,' Kenna said to Marshall. 'You were verifying what you'd been told.'

'Yes. I hoped it was a lie. In which case I would have returned to continue our conversation.'

'If you knew everything, I'm guessing you were aware that a man had been planted in your team to kill me. Did you wait to see if he'd expose himself?'

Ray touched her arm disapprovingly again. She knew she'd adopted an accusatory tone she had no business with. She had been sent to kill Marshall and couldn't fault him for risking her life to find a traitor.

Not only was Marshall not offended, he seemed guilt-ridden. 'No, no, I had no idea about that. That man turned on you out of the blue. By that point my men had only just captured your husband. He'd told me nothing yet. We got lucky.'

'You, not we. Ray and I are still your prisoners. We still won't survive the night.'

Marshall seemed genuinely hurt by her indictment. 'I have no plans to hurt you. Not anymore. I can't. Seeing that man try to kill you horrified me.'

'You told your men to bury me alive on top of my husband's corpse.'

Ray stiffened beside her. He hadn't known of this scheme. Marshall said, 'I acted in anger. I'd just discovered a plan to have me assassinated, and by someone I felt close to. But I soon calmed down. I couldn't possibly harm you. It would be like killing my own daughter. You look like her and I want to keep it that way.'

She felt a throb in her head and massaged it softly through the bandages. 'Keep me, you mean? Like an exhibit.'

He laughed, as if she had said something preposterous. 'No. You can walk out of here. I have no plans to harm you, keep you, or stuff you like a big game kill. When we're done here, you can go back to your life.'

Ray and Kenna looked at each other. Each saw that the other didn't fully believe that. Yet. 'And you won't come looking for us?' Ray said. 'You won't want us to do something criminal in the future, like Eli did? You won't suddenly decide it's too risky to have us out in the world, knowing what we know?'

'You know nothing. All you could tell the police is that I was at The Mirage. I suppose they might have found out anyway. Regardless, they won't find me. They won't learn anything new about me from that hotel. So, yes, you will be left alone. No forced action, no blackmail, no death to keep your silence. I promise.'

Ray seemed to accept this. Kenna wasn't convinced. Even if she had been, there was another vital component to consider. 'Eli wants us dead for ruining his plan. So we're hardly safe.'

Marshall gave a derisive snort. 'Forget that foolish amateur. I was quite upset with him and broke a cardinal rule. I told the police a little story. Now Eli is wanted for the murder of a police officer a few days ago. He got out of the country. He's gone. He lost his crew, many of whom are now my fresh recruits.'

Ray said, 'Many but not all, right? People are dead I imagine. In fact, I was right there when at least four got taken out.'

'It's a dangerous business, Mr Barker. I should get out and sell flowers. But you two aren't part of that business. Not anymore. Eli and his bozos will not come after you. If you want to go to the police, feel free to tell them everything. Ray, you may even sing like a canary about how my men killed Eli's people in that safe house. I have a series of buffers and nothing will come back on me. I hate to blow my own trumpet, but I'm too big to touch. If you're scared about the police because there was a threat to frame you using your blood, well, let me inform you that I hear that was a bluff.'

'You really do know everything, don't you?' Kenna said. In a morbid way, it was impressive.

'People talk, even if they don't want to.'

She had no doubt he referred to torture. She already knew far more than was comfortable. Ray said, 'So we can just go? Right now?'

'Not yet,' Kenna jumped in. 'Mr Marshall hasn't finished yet. In his penthouse, he said he wanted me to do something. I'm guessing he still does.'

'Yes,' Marshall said after a pause. 'But not yet.'

'Not while I'm bandaged and injured, right? Because I need to look like your daughter again, don't I?'

Marshall stood. 'Unfortunately, yes. I hated seeing the way you looked after you were shot. I apologise for all the bandages. The wound isn't as bad as they suggest. I just wanted to make sure I didn't see the scar or the bruising. So, it means I do need still need something from you, but not yet. Not for at least a few weeks. So you'll hear from me. But don't sit on tenterhooks.'

That would be impossible. Kenna stood up. 'So let's see if you're telling the truth.' She took Ray's hand and they walked.

Marshall said nothing as they passed him. Nobody else made a move as they crossed the waiting room. At the glass exit doors, Kenna looked back. Everyone was watching. She still wasn't sure this was real. 'Swear on your daughter's grave that you don't mean us harm.'

She heard a whisper of surprise run around the room. Next to her, Ray sucked in a sharp breath. She might have just overstepped a line.

She hadn't. Marshall said, 'I swear on her grave that I mean you no harm. And I will make sure nobody else tries to seek revenge. Now go. And please don't worry about when someone will turn up on your doorstep for me.'

'One more thing. How did you know? I mean all of it. In the first instance. Who told you?'

'An anonymous caller, that's all I have. Someone with my interests at heart. I have a guardian angel, it seems. If he hadn't called in the nick of time, I might be dead, right?'

He grinned. Kenna didn't mirror it. The nick of time. How things might have turned out if not for that caller. 'I guess he is my guardian angel, too,' she said, and pushed open the door.

THIRTY-TWO

Alfie booted in the back door of his friend's house. He made sure no neighbours were watching from high windows, then he hauled Dom's body out from behind the bins. With three stops to catch his breath, he dragged the fat bastard's body into his pal's kitchen.

And left him right there. He found a pen and scribbled a note. *Alfie here. Soz about leaving this mess. Get rid of this body so no one finds it.* He had no idea if his pal could dispose of a corpse, but so what. It was his problem now. He then raided the fridge of a four-pint of milk and some corned beef and sat to fill his stomach.

Fucking Ray. Fucking Kenna. The guy could have the bitch. She wasn't worth the trouble. That bastard had stolen his gun, too. Alfie reached out to tip the rest of the milk all over fat Dom's head. Everyone knew the knobhead always kept his gun unloaded in case the police grabbed him – less time behind bars. If not for that, Ray would now be a corpse right beside him.

He left the house and walked down Putney High Street, still buzzing with rage. Across the road he spotted a petrol station, where an old guy was filling up a Kia Venga. Alfie walked up to the car and saw the keys in the ignition. Excellent.

He got in the car, started it, and drove. The owner was so shocked he didn't even pull the pump hose from his vehicle. It was yanked from his hands, still in place. In the wing mirror, Alfie watched the hose stretch tight, then tear from the handle and whip back. Comically, the torn end hit the old guy in the leg and floored him. It made Alfie forget his problems for all of ten seconds.

Once he was a few hundred metres clear, he stopped in the middle of the road to remove the pump handle. The car behind slowed and honked. Alfie tossed the handle at its windscreen, which was cause for another round of laughter.

A little later, Alfie pulled up behind a Peugeot 207 on a residential street and headed up to a house. The door was unlocked, as always. On the ground floor, a girl opened her bedroom door and gawped at him.

'Get back inside,' he told her. As he climbed the stairs, he passed another girl. 'What you looking at?' this one got asked. On the first floor, he opened the front door of a flat and walked in. He found sweet little Sherrie at her bedroom dressing table, where she was putting make-up on a bruised eye.

'What happened to you?'

'A horrible punter. I tried to call Dom about it. His phone is off.'

'It's busted up. Dom's gone. And I'm getting out of this city. Get your shoes.'

She stared at him. 'What do you mean?'

'You and me. Pack some clothing.'

Alfie helped. There was a rucksack in a corner, which he started to fill with clothing pulled out of drawers. Sherrie watched in puzzlement. 'What do you mean? I can't leave here.'

'We're going to be together now, babe. No more being on

the game. I'll save you from that shit. Come on, help me grab your stuff.'

'I don't understand. Please stop that.'

He didn't stop. 'We're going to be together. No more banging weirdos. Grab some stuff.'

'What? No. I'm not going to be your girlfriend.'

Alfie ignored her. He knew it was just shock talking. This girl had been servicing men for ten of her twenty-eight years and didn't know there was another world, another life out there. He moved to a wardrobe when the rucksack was full, and started hauling out jeans, tops, dresses. He even grabbed a nurse's uniform, which he'd never seen her in. Maybe she could wear that the first time they fuck–

'Stop,' she said. 'Just get out of my flat, Alfie.'

He didn't stop. 'I know you like me, and I like you. You were always the sweet one. I've got money. I mean I can get money. But we have to go quick.'

She laughed, and that stopped him dead. 'What's so funny?'

'You're serious, aren't you? Oh, Alfie, I could never leave with you.'

She sounded serious, too. He didn't understand. She liked him, and he could rescue her. They could have a nice life together. Marriage, even. Perhaps a baby. 'There's more than this place in the world, babe. I can show you. It'll just take time for you to adapt, that's all.'

She shook her head in disbelief. 'Alfie, even if I wanted to leave, it wouldn't be with you. I mean, why would I? You're a cretin.'

He looked down at his dirty clothing. 'I told you, I've got money. I've had a funny night. What's wrong?'

That normally sweet face of hers changed. Even her voice lost its cuteness. A demon seemed to have possessed her. 'Not a mess as in clothing. As in you're a sad little shit. Worthless. The one us girls say there's not enough diamonds in the world to sleep with. Understand? Now would you please fuck off and go sober up or whatever?'

He stood there with her nurse's outfit in his hands, numb, unsure if he'd heard correctly. Had someone poisoned her against him? He knew she liked him. 'But I want you.'

'No, what you want is someone about twenty years younger. A kid. That's what you're into, isn't it? Now fuck off, please. I've got a client due in—'

There was no client. Never again. There were only Alfie's hands, which closed around her neck. 'Shut your whore pie hole,' he screamed as he rag-dolled her to the ground and sat astride her. She fought, but fear didn't offer the strength of rage.

———

He found Sherrie's phone and money stash, and he found her car keys. He also took a pair of scissors she kept under her bed.

Before he left, he gave her corpse a kick in the head and said, 'I've heard that horseshit rumour. This didn't happen fucking yesterday. People seem to forget the passage of years. I was fourteen, you silly bitch. It ain't wrong for a fourteen year-old kid to like twelve-year-old girls. If you'd had half a brain to realise that, you'd still be breathing. But now look. Fucked up, didn't you?'

Another kick satisfied his anger. After that, he left and locked the door behind him, and he kept the key. Downstairs, he stopped at the door of the girl who'd poked her nosey head out when he entered the house.

He froze with his fingers on the handle as he heard two men's voices inside. Shit. The girl in there had a pair of blokes, so getting to her was out of the question. That meant there was no point hunting down the girl who'd passed him on the stairs, either. When Eli learned of Sherrie's murder, both bitches would blab that they'd seen Alfie in the house. Now he was in extra deep shit.

But it changed nothing. Eli could only kill him once. All along the plan had been to flee the city, and now he had extra cash and a car the cops weren't hunting. All was good.

Fucking Kenna. This was all her fault. For a few moments after he'd killed Sherrie, he'd reconsidered trying to take Kenna away. But then the old rage had returned. She had been too much hassle and now all he wanted was for her to suffer. He wanted to fuck her life up. But he couldn't get to her.

As he drove Sherrie's 207 off her street, he checked the time: 7.44pm. Kenna was sixteen minutes from tearing her nails into The Magpie's throat. He realised he still had a chance to ruin her, but he had to act now.

He pulled into the side of the road and opened Sherrie's clamshell phone. He'd have to dump it after this, which was a damn shame. That was also Kenna's fault. Well, soon she'd pay. He googled what he needed and got a phone number. It was answered on the third ring.

Alfie said, 'Look around the lobby. See those idiots who think they're Men in Black? Grab one to the phone. It's important.'

The clerk told Alfie to hang on. Fifteen seconds later, a new voice asked Alfie who he was.

'Santa Claus. So here's a present. Remember these places...' Alfie listed the addresses of the Wimbledon safe house, the hairdressers in Putney, and two more buildings.

'What are these places? And tell me who you are.'

'I'm someone helping your boss. Eli is planning to kill him. He's got someone on the inside.'

The bozo suddenly wasn't so dismissive. 'Who? When?

How do you know this? What's your name? You need to be very careful here, sir.'

'You think he's untouchable, but his dick's got him in trouble. She's upstairs with him right now, and she's going to rip his head off with her fake metal fingernails.'

Alfie hung up and drove. He lobbed Sherrie's phone when he passed over a bridge. Job done.

Now there was no obstacle between him and a new life up north. It was shame he couldn't be there to watch The Magpie's men interrogate, torture and feed Kenna to pigs. Hopefully, her last thought would be regret: if only she'd become Alfie's girl, she could have avoided a short life.

THIRTY-THREE

Marshall must have instructed one of his men to drive them home. After Ray and Kenna left the surgery, a man was waiting by an open car door. Ray wanted to scarper, not yet sure that there wasn't something amiss. But Kenna said, 'No, we have to take the ride. If Marshall is planning to trick us, there's nothing we can do. They'll just come another day.'

'I'd like that extra day.'

She took his hand. 'We'll know for sure if we get in that car. I don't want to spend any more time worrying about danger. Besides, I think we're fine now.'

Sold. They got in the back seat. Ray had sneaked a pen out of the surgery and he held it like a knife, prepared for action if the driver turned on them. He didn't. He drove them directly home. He didn't say a word on the journey, or when he pulled up, or after his passengers had disembarked. He was gone seconds later.

Still Ray had doubts and insisted on a hotel for the night, just in case. Kenna agreed. Kenna's keys had been confiscated, but not his. He entered the house and got money. Then they took his car and found a tacky hotel four miles away.

Kenna settled into bed and tried to pretend nothing was amiss. Ray sat by the window, in the dark, and watched the road for strange cars. When she woke in the morning, he was asleep in the chair with his head against the window. An hour later they checked out. Kenna asked the manager if anyone had enquired about them overnight. The answer was a stress-relieving no.

'Maybe it's over,' she said as they headed out to the car, which was undamaged and exactly where they'd left it.

'Hopefully.'

'Now we have a decision to make. Police or no police.'

They discussed it as they drove out to find breakfast at a place they'd never frequented. Perhaps, somehow, there was a crime the police could pin on them. If not, well, Marshall and Eli ran two of London's most notorious gangs, and all sorts of law enforcement agencies would be interested in what Kenna and Ray knew. They could be the subject of visits and interviews for months. They'd never get left alone. The media might even get wind and put their faces out there. Plus, Eli had come off badly in this snafu and he might have dangerous sympathisers.

'It sounds like you want to keep quiet,' Ray said as they pulled up in the car park of a Beefeater.

'We did nothing wrong. We're not criminals. What we know, about some of the places Eli took us to, might not help the police. And Marshall said there's nothing the police can learn from the hotel, except that he was in the country.'

Ray was unsure. He worried that the police had their faces and were now investigating. 'One day they could come knock the door.'

'If that happens, we'll tell them everything. But I don't think we should instigate anything. There's a chance we might not hear from any police or criminals ever again. I vote for silence and secrecy.'

'I vote that you know best.'

She kissed him. Decision made.

After a morning of wasting time, they finally decided it was time to go home and face whatever may come. As they approached the house, Kenna told Ray to stop. He pulled to the kerb and followed her pointing finger.

Her car was outside their garden. Someone had driven it here, but who? For which team did he work – good or bad? Was he inside the house?

Ray jogged the final fifty metres to find the answer. A few minutes later he appeared on the street and gave a thumbs-up. She drove his car and parked behind her own.

'Your keys got posted,' he said. 'Give me a minute.'

He opened her car, got in, and checked it over. Result: another thumbs-up. However, knowing someone had been to their home set fears running again. They decided to stay another night at a hotel.

They were checking in when Ray halted proceedings. 'I want to go home.'

They moved away from the desk for privacy. 'You sure?' she asked.

'We can't keep doing this. You said it yourself. We can't always be living in fear. How about I stay there and you go off somewhere for a little longer, just so we're sure?'

She didn't want to leave Ray alone to face trouble, if any was due, but he insisted. She chose to go see her friend, Vicky. Back home, Ray entered the house and Kenna got in her own car.

Vicky didn't answer the front door, so Kenna went round back and peeked in the window. She saw Vicky at the kitchen table. She knocked the window. From the shock on Vicky's face, Kenna knew her good friend had been hiding from her. Eli hadn't lied when he'd said Vicky had received a warning.

When the door was opened, Kenna said, 'It's over. I'm fine. I'm so sorry for what you went through.'

The two women hugged. The subject wasn't mentioned again until the women were seated at the kitchen table with tea before them. Vicky spoke first. She told a tale of a slimeball with dreadlocks accosting her in a car park. A threat to avoid Kenna for the rest of the week. Uncertain if she was being watched, Vicky had called in sick to work. Fortunately, the event in the car park was the sum of it. Nobody had contacted her since.

She was very sorry. 'I was thinking of both of us. I didn't want them to hurt me or you. But I felt bad. You were having a serious problem and people sometimes need friends. I should have been there for you.'

'You were, by not being there. You did the right thing.'

Vicky didn't look convinced and Kenna wasn't certain she believed her own statement. But what happened had happened. It would take more than that to fray their friendship.

Now it was Kenna's turn. 'If you want the whole story, I'll tell you.'

'Tell me what you're comfortable with.'

She would have been happy to impart everything, but one aspect could cause Vicky to worry: Marshall's plan to contact Kenna in the future. So she left it out. When the tale was told, Vicky needed half a minute to get her head around it.

'Murder,' she said, shaking her head. 'Imagine if...'

'I did. It was horrible. It won't happen again.'

'It doesn't make you bad, if you considered it. Did you?'

A question Kenna had asked herself many times. If

Marshall hadn't fled the rooftop terrace, would she have tried to kill him? She still didn't know.

'Is this something we should talk about again?' Vicky asked. 'If you want this "subject" consigned to the deep, we can do that.'

Kenna would love to lock away the whole sorry experience in a remote depth of her mind. Probably impossible, but it would help if she and Vicky could agree it was an absolute no-go area. So she nodded.

'After one final thing,' Kenna said. 'I want to use your laptop.'

Intrigued, Vicky raced upstairs to fetch it. Back at the table, she hovered over Kenna's shoulder as her friend jabbed away at keys. Kenna loaded Facebook and accessed her photos.

'You sure about this?' Vicky said. 'Brad Pitt will never see them. You could just make the profile private.'

Kenna deleted the photos without consideration.

Vicky sat and slapped the table. 'Done. How's Alexandra coping without me to bore her with nightclub stories?'

Kenna relaxed. They chatted about work, health, celebrity gossip, and by midnight she was able to smile again for the first time in ages.

The 'subject' was impossible to forget, though. Ray was up when she got home, watching out the bedroom window. He'd stayed up all night to make sure no bad guys paid a visit. On day two he did half the dead hours. Finally, on night three, he hit the sack when Kenna did, around midnight. They'd bought new locks, including deadbolts, and a burglar alarm. On night four he left everything unlocked and the alarm off. He was worried that vigilantes had tried the doors and been foiled, so this was a way of finding out if people were still after them.

'Really?' Kenna said. 'We'd find out the hard way.'

'I would, you mean. Go stay with Vicky tonight.'

He'd remembered her name even though it hadn't been mentioned for a while. She liked that. But not his plan. 'No. I can't leave you behind. We'll both do it.'

And they did. Ray put a piece of balled paper behind the front and back doors, which would be shifted if the doors opened. In the morning they found the balls in the same spots. Nobody had entered the house. The test result eroded a little more tension.

Kenna spent some time daily searching the news for mentions of two of London's biggest crime bosses. Marshall was mentioned just once and there was nothing about his sneaky intrusion into Britain. Eli had a lot of media coverage because he was wanted for the murder of a police officer. He was believed to be overseas. Possibly in Canada. Maybe in France. Or it could be Thailand. He had contacts in various countries, so who knew? His Boys Firm had been disbanded, according to one police source. There was speculation that its members had joined other gangs, including The Marshalls – which constituted the sole mention of the man known as The Magpie.

They had both phoned in sick to work for the rest of the week. On Monday, they returned to their jobs. Vicky was also back. As they'd promised, the girls didn't mention recent events, and found it surprisingly easy. Kenna managed to do her job without a hitch. That same night was the first that Ray and Kenna managed to avoid discussing what had happened.

Finally, everything felt normal again. However, her debt to Marshall was a bad penny. She could go long periods without thinking about it, but always the questions would arise, and always when she was alone. On Tuesday evening, while she soaked in the bath, it happened again.

When would he come for it? Tomorrow or a year from now? Would he ask for something criminal, something she just couldn't do? Would he just want her to pose as his daughter for a photograph, or sing one of her songs, or visit his home in France?

When would he want it? Tomorrow, or a year from now?

She knew she wasn't out of the woods yet.

Terrible proof of this would come that night.

THIRTY-FOUR

'One noise and you're dead.'

Kenna was wide awake within moments, and fully aware of the danger. Even in the gloom of the dark bedroom, she recognised the face above her. Alfie. He held something to her neck. Given that he used one hand – his other was fisted in her hair – but she felt a sharp object on either side of her throat, her guess was scissors.

'If he wakes, you go to sleep forever. Understand?'

She gave a slight nod. There was new pain in her head and she realised he was pulling her hair, to get her to rise. She got up, naked. For a moment they stood facing each other, a foot apart, and she considered kneeing him in the balls. But his reaction could be to close the scissors on her throat, even involuntarily.

He backed out of the bedroom, leading her. She glanced at Ray, who was still asleep. She considered shouting to wake him, but he would be groggy and probably no match for Alfie. To save him, she remained quiet.

The upstairs landing light was still on and she had to shut her eyes against the brightness. Here they paused and Alfie knew he was appraising her naked body. Squinting, she saw his eyes run her up and down. He had no free hand to touch her with, thankfully. Done with his analysis, which had put a smile on his face, he repositioned himself behind her, with the scissors now at the side of her neck. He led her to the stairs.

'Why are you here?' she asked as they reached the bottom, where the hallway light was also on. They always were these days.

'Living room. Go.'

They entered. He ordered her to turn the light on, which she did. She noticed that the coffee table had been moved off the rug in front of the fire. Now clear, that rug stood out as a place where she could lie. She knew that was his intention before he said it.

He guided her down, onto her front, then told her to flip over. He didn't let go of her hair and kept the scissors at her neck. Her skin grated against the blades as she turned onto her back.

Now, with her eyes adjusted to the light, she got her first proper look at him. He was skinnier than she recalled, his dreadlocks even grimier, skin greasier, eyes more bloodshot. He'd looked a mess before, but now it was worse. She got the feeling he'd been living rough for the week and a half since everything had come to a heated finale.

He kicked her legs apart and knelt between them. He released her hair, which gave him a free hand to unzip his jeans. 'I'm going to have sex with you. Are you going to fight?'

'No.' She glanced down and saw he'd released his penis. It was soft and he began the work to become erect.

'And then I'm going to kill you. Are you going to fight?'

'Why would you do that? I thought you liked me.'

'You fucked all that up. We could have had a connection.

But now you're just a piece of meat. You haven't asked what will happen if you fight me.'

She knew full well he'd say something about also killing Ray. 'I don't need to know. I'm not going to fight. You're too big and strong. And I know you mean to kill me. I don't want that but you are in charge.'

He seemed to like that. 'That's right. And there's nothing you can do about it.'

'It just seems strange that you've changed against me. You wanted me. You loved these grey eyes. You called me a Ferrari.'

'There's other Ferraris.'

'I'm a special edition. Commemorative, a one-off.'

He paused his masturbation for a second, thinking about this. 'You were, baby. Now you're creaking. Fan belt gone. Bodywork scratched. Fit only for the scrapyard.'

He continued to work to harden himself, and he was halfway there. She didn't have long. 'Fix me up. Don't scrap an exclusive.'

He paused again. 'What does that mean?'

'It means I see how strong you are. I need a strong man like that. Ray, he's got brain damage. He can't think straight. He forgets. He's got arthritis all over and he's hardening up. Five years from now he'll be in a wheelchair and he won't remember my name. I can't have that.'

'What are you saying?'

'This Ferrari will need a new owner. And I literally mean an owner. Ray is too weak. He tries to please me. I don't want that. I want to do the pleasing. I want to be controlled. I want a strong man. I'm a follower. A sheep who needs a shepherd.'

The force of the scissors on her neck lightened a little. But Alfie's other hand began manipulating his penis with a new frenzy. 'I am that man. But you need to prove yourself by not fighting me. And you have to respond. You have to like having sex right now. That might prove it.'

'Here? On a hard floor, with Ray above us? I can't make noise. I always moan so loudly during sex.'

'Then I kill him. He won't—'

'No. Ray is no good for me, but I've known him a long time. He has parents and friends. He can't die because they'd be upset and I like these people. Also, the police would hunt me. He might not have a great life ahead, but I want him to live it.'

Still Alfie worked himself. Now he was breathing heavy. 'What are you saying?'

'We go somewhere else. Your place. Or a hotel. Somewhere remote and quiet. And I'll show you that this one-off Ferrari is the best machine ever engineered.'

'You think I believe you?'

'I don't know. But I'll come willingly. No fighting. If you feel the same way after we've had sex, we'll be somewhere away from people, and you can kill me and my screams won't wake anyone. But you won't want to kill me. You're going to mend this Ferrari and drive it as fast as you like, as often as you like. And it will never break down.'

His masturbation stalled again. She saw his eyes, and she knew he was calculating his options. He would rape her right here and kill her... or he wouldn't.

She lifted a hand, slowly. He stiffened, but didn't react. She stroked his coarse, disgusting beard. The gesture became a feather added to evenly balanced heavy weights. Computation done. Her future had been decided.

Alfie stuffed his semi-erect penis back into his trousers.

He wasn't fully hypnotised, however. When he led her to the hallway, he kept the scissors on her neck. 'I broke the seal on the kitchen window to get in, so we'll go out the front door. Take the keys and open it. Try to stab me with them and I'll cut your spinal cord. And while you're paralysed, I'll go kill your husband.'

'I won't.' She took her keys from the hook on the wall. She unlocked but didn't open the front door. 'I can't go out here naked.'

On the other side from the key hooks were more for coats. He told her to grab one and she selected a long black garment that dropped to just above her knees. He kept the scissors in place as she put it on and zipped it up. She then stepped into slip-on shoes. As she opened the door, she removed the keys without him seeing.

They stepped outside. It was the dead of night and nothing moved. The moon was lost behind clouds. Aside from the streetlamps, a handful of bedroom windows provided the street's only illumination.

She thought he might try to camouflage his threat, perhaps by putting an arm around her, but theatrics weren't his style. He walked behind her, scissors at the back of her neck. She wondered if an insomniac neighbour was watching. She wondered if she could dart away before he could close the scissors on her flesh.

He seemed to read her mind: 'Make a break for freedom, and when you return, hubby dear will have bled out.'

'I won't run. I'm going to give this relationship a chance.'

He made no response. At the end of the garden path, he told her to go to the blue car off to the right. She saw it, a battered piece of junk. Instead, she held up her keys. 'I thought we were taking mine. If not then I need to put these back in the house so Ray doesn't suspect anything.'

He thought. 'No, we'll take yours.' She held the keys over her shoulder for him to take. Instead, he laughed. 'I don't think so. You drive.'

He made her get in through the passenger side and climb over the centre console, and he held on to the back of her coat while she did so. When they were seated, he reapplied his weapon to her neck. He put his seat belt on without taking his eyes off her.

'Where are we going?' she asked once the car was moving.

'I'll tell you before each turn. Like now. Go left at the end.'

Lefts, rights. For ten minutes they drove in silence apart from his directions. Then, as they rode down Fulham Palace Road, with shops arranged along the left and a fenced allotment on the right, he said, 'Gate coming up. There. Turn in.'

The gate led into the allotments. She made the turn. A wide, flattened earth track ran straight through the area. The place was as black as prehistoric times. The track seemed to vanish into nothing ahead, while either side she saw only the vague lumps of sheds and the lines of paths separating land parcels. She drove slowly.

'Why are we here?' she said. 'Do you live here?'

'I don't. You do. Forever. Until they find your body.'

She kept her eyes on the track. 'You plan to kill me? I thought we were going to be together.'

'I'm no fool. I know you were just playing me. You wanted me out of the house to save your pig-head husband. And I was playing you, you stupid bitch. I got you out without hassle. You ain't the only good actor.'

'I'm not playing.'

'It doesn't matter. I went off Ferraris, ever since you messed me about. But I'll kill you quick, since I've warmed to you. Stop here and turn the engine off. Leave the key in the ignition.'

She did. With the scissors at her neck, he got out of his side and dragged her with him, but not before she managed to dip a hand into her door pocket. He got behind her, weapon against flesh, a hand grabbing her coat.

'Now listen, bitchface. You die. Deal with it and don't fight. If you play nice, I'll be on my way and Ray can wake up in the morning. If you kick up a stink, I'll go back to your house and stab him in the balls. You going to fight?'

'No.'

'Good girl. So let's do it.' After kicking the door shut to kill the interior light, he walked her deeper into the darkness, to her death.

Some thirty metres from the main track, Alfie led her behind a rickety, large shed, to an area of wasteland littered with small debris. There was a hole in the ground, ten feet across and ringed by a foot-high packed soil fringe, into which an orange plastic mesh fence had been staked. Also in the earth were solar lights, which allowed her to see the contents of the chasm: blackened rubbish and the soot-stained metal remains of furniture, like beds and sofas and god knew what else. It was a burn pit.

She stopped. 'Are you going to burn me? Is that your plan?'

'My plan? I have no plan. Why would I? I don't know you, never met you. I have no idea why you drove here in the middle of the night and blindly tripped into that hole. God knows why it wasn't lit up to warn people. Turn around.'

Before she did, she again looked at the sharp, jagged metal in the pit. A fall from this height would impale her on something. If the piercings didn't kill her, serious bleeding all night would certainly do so. If Alfie removed the solar lights, as

249

he'd hinted at doing, the police might well believe it was a tragic accident.

When she turned to face him, he put the scissors against her throat and a hand on her chest. One push would do it. Her first step back would catch the earth fringe and trip her. The thin mesh fence wouldn't save her from falling. 'Why, Alfie? You wanted me for yourself and now you're not interested, but do I have to die? Is this some kind of "if I can't have you, no one can thing?"'

'No, this is a gone-off-you sort of thing. You had your chance.' He laughed. 'Come on, woman. Surely you didn't think I bought your bullshit? Did you really think I was going to believe that you would be with me forever and ever amen?'

'Of course not,' Kenna said, and that was when she yanked her hand out of her pocket.

Her fist came up, and squeezed, and a jet of fluid erupted from the spout of the pepper spray, coating Alfie's eyes, nose, mouth. Before he could react, she punched him in the face, to create a nanosecond when he didn't have her throat in pincers. She took full advantage of it and ducked aside. But when she tried to scramble away, her feet slipped and she landed hard on her stomach.

The pepper spray began its work. Alfie turned to where she'd fallen, but already he was blinking hard. He got one step towards her before his face creased. He threw his hands to his eyes. 'Ah, you damn bitch. The fuck?'

Unable to see, he kicked at where she'd been. The blow hit her thigh as she was rising and actually helped propel her to her feet. She backed away from him. Blind, and fighting the pain, Alfie swiped at nothing with the scissors.

She backed off to one side as he thrashed, screaming at her. Ten feet from him, her foot hit a brick, and even over his own voice, Alfie heard it. Analysed it. Sharp as a striking snake, he covered the distance in a flash and swung the scissors. She felt the blow hit her coat as she dodged.

'Where the fuck are you? I'll kill your entire family for this.'

She moved slowly, wondering if she could get around him. Her car was behind him and she didn't want to go deeper into the allotments. His eyes wouldn't be blinded forever.

There was a crack as her foot came down on a discarded piece of broken glass. The sound whipped Alfie's head towards her. Again, he judged the distance, covered it in half a second, and swiped at her. Luckily, she'd been ducking and the blades blitzed over her head.

The momentum of the strike caused one of Alfie's feet to skid, sending him to his ass. He roared like a stabbed bear. Kenna backed away, picked up a fragment of a house brick, and launched it at him.

The missile missed, but its impact two metres behind him got his attention. For a third time, he was there and trying to slice her open. She grabbed another rock and threw it, this time hitting the shed. As Alfie ran in that direction, she looked to her right, towards the track. Now the way was clear for her to run to her car.

But she didn't move that way. Alfie's eyes would heal. He would come back, possibly tonight but certainly another day. There would be no peace, ever.

Alfie swiped and hit the shed, which enraged him further. She lobbed another brick, this time over the pit. When it thudded on the far side, Alfie pounced, swiping, stabbing, yelling. 'I'll fucking gut you.'

He swished the blades all around, front and back, as if fearful she was creeping up on him. As he twirled and jerked, tears from his savaged eyes and spit flew in all directions. She stood tall and approached the mesh fence. Standing just two feet from it, and barely two metres from Alfie, she leaned forward and whispered, 'You couldn't kill a fly, you pathetic peeping Tom.'

Predictably, he turned to the sound, and launched himself forward. Towards the pit separating them. His second step hit the earth fringe and he toppled forward. The mesh fence barely slowed him. He flattened it and somersaulted over. And down. Kenna shut her eyes, but her ears were open.

She barely heard his landing, but the screams that followed wrenched through the night air.

———————

She had to know, so she peered over the edge of the pit. Slowly. The jumbled, jagged mass of lethal metal revealed itself slowly. Then she saw a foot. There she stopped, unwilling to see more. She watched that foot for movement. One minute. Two. It remained frozen. The world was silent. She didn't need to see more. Alfie was dead.

She felt guilt and relief at the same time. He would never come back, never threaten her again. But only because she had caused his death. She had fretted over whether or not to kill Marshall, but here she'd acted after just a moment's consideration. Was it her fault, though? If she hadn't called to him, he wouldn't have charged into the death pit. But he had been drawn by a desire to murder her.

She dropped to her knees on the hard soil. Something sharp dug into her flesh, but she ignored it. She might be undecided, but a court of law could decide that she was a murderer. And for sure the courts would be involved, because Alfie's body would be found. She couldn't possibly hide it. She could run, but Alfie's car was near her home and CCTV would have captured her vehicle around this area in the dead of night.

Even if she got off on involuntary manslaughter, for she had attempted only to save herself, she would be branded. Prison time or not, she would officially be a murderer. That would haunt her. People would judge her long after a court had.

Am I bad? she wondered. Here she was by a man she'd killed, yet her concern was society's opinion of her. Even worse, she had just considered trying to conceal her involvement in the crime.

She knelt there for a long time, trying to calm her panic and think ahead. And then two vehicles raced into the allotment.

The van drove in with its headlights off and stopped on the track. Behind it came a motorbike, which parked on the grass beside it. Two men exited the van and all three walked towards her. They did so lacking the haste with which they'd arrived.

Kenna wanted to run, but fear glued her in place. Police? The men wore black. They wore gloves. The two from the van had balaclavas and the biker was in a crash helmet. Not police, she decided. She suddenly feared that they were Alfie's friends, and they would finish the task he set himself.

The three men ignored her and approached the burn pit. After looking in, they removed the plastic mesh fence and carefully walked down the steep sides. She saw them bend over and work their arms, and knew they were freeing Alfie's body. Which they then carried from the pit. She looked away and kept her eyes diverted until their footsteps faded.

When she looked, the men were by their van. One opened the rear doors and all three slid the body inside. The two who'd arrived in the vehicle returned to the cab. While the van reversed out of the allotments, the biker came her way.

By now she'd got over her shock and rose on weak legs. She now had a good idea who these people were.

The biker stopped before her and held out a mobile phone. She took it. The screen was lit and she saw the word UNKNOWN. An active call.

She put the phone to her ear. 'I thought you were going to leave me alone.'

'I lied,' Alan Marshall said. 'By that I mean about knowing you'd be safe. Eli is in no position to send thugs after you, but I can't control every degenerate sympathiser lurking in the shadows.'

'So you had people outside my house all this time?'

'No. Someone found a receiver for a tracker. And a man willing to explain all about it. You were given pepper spray.'

She hadn't realised it was still in her hand. She remembered being told to keep it on her at all times. Maybe safety had been part of the reason, but only part. She dropped it. The biker picked it up and held it out. She put it in her pocket.

Marshall said, 'I apologise for coming late. Your car was tracked leaving your home at a suspicious time, but it took a while to get to you. You overcame your problem without us, though. Who was he?'

It didn't matter. 'What will happen to the body?'

'I can tell you what *won't* happen to it. A police investigation. Concern yourself with it no more. Unless you want to know?'

She thought. 'No. I guess this means you think I owe you, doesn't it?'

'Actually, Mrs Barker, you don't. I gave it some thought. Eli sent a girl to kill me. Anyone but you would have tried. You have a clean soul, and it was this that saved my life.'

'I nearly lost my own tonight, Mr Marshall. In no way do I blame you for that, but it happened because of this whole mess. Which all started because I look like your daughter. I'm probably being silly, but I think that might qualify me for an explanation.'

Marshall paused. She wondered if she'd upset him by pushing this matter. Which made it a system shock when he said, 'You're right. So here it is, front and centre. I want you to sing.'

Of all the bizarre scenarios that had whirled through her head, singing hadn't been one of them.

'My daughter, Lillian, was a country singer,' he continued. 'Just starting out, unsigned, but she was good and I was wealthy enough to pay for her to travel the world and perform small shows. She was in Vietnam for a show when she was killed. She had a specific look. Cowboy hat, shorts, and a denim shirt, with her lips painted like the flag of whichever country she was playing in.'

Kenna remembered the photo she'd seen. Now it had context. 'You want me to put on music shows dressed as—'

'Not quite,' Mashall interrupted. 'Just one song. Now, this is where the story becomes a little morbid...'

He explained that he planned a surprise for Lillian's mother, Emily. They had divorced a year after the death, but remained close friends.

'Maybe friends is the wrong term. She took the death hard. It changed something integral inside her. She still hasn't gotten over it...'

Emily had kept every single item owned by their daughter. Some parents keep a bedroom untouched, like a shrine. Emily had preserved Lillian's entire house and garden. Nothing had been touched, right down to the car parked in the driveway. At his wife's behest, Marshall had even bought the homes of the neighbours either side, so he could demolish them and install a wall encircling Lillian's house.

'It sounds like a nice touch,' Kenna said. 'Not morbid at all.'

But his wife had soon wanted more. She purchased a life-sized 3D photo crystal that depicted Lillian with a microphone. When that failed to satisfy her, she employed a reborner to create a full-length doll, which still sits on a chair in a room in Emily's home. And, scariest of all, she recently started researching plastination.

'Don't ask me what that is,' Marshall said. 'I wish I'd never heard of such a thing.'

'I'm sorry. This must be hard for you. I don't know what to say. But I have to ask what it is you want from me.'

'A gift to my ex-wife, that is all. I don't know if it will help her, or make things worse. I sought opinions and my people are split. But it seems like a nice touch. She celebrates Lillian's birthday each year with a fancy party. My vision is to have my daughter's mirror image stand on stage, with her guitar, dressed in her outfit, and sing a single song.'

Kenna gulped air. 'Me? I don't sing... I... guitar... I...'

'One night, three months from now, which is plenty of time to learn the song and the instrument.'

'I... I mean... do I have to?'

'You're forced into nothing, Kenna. Go confer with your husband. When he asks where, say it's Corsica, France, where I'll put you up for a week in a villa, all expenses paid. When he asks if there's a fee, tell him it's £100,000. If the answer is yes, give me a sign within the next thirty days. Let's see...' He laughed, then added, 'How about you go out in cowboy hat one day?'

Was that a joke? Kenna needed a few seconds to digest everything. The money was certainly hypnotic, but Marshall was an infamous criminal. A killer. It all seemed like a waking dream. Or was it a nightmare? She couldn't tell because her brain seemed to jerk and skip like a scratched record.

'But all of that is for another time, Kenna,' Marshall said. 'It's late. Now, go home and try to forget.'

She gave a dry laugh. 'Impossible. Partly because I know your people are watching me.'

'You won't see anyone, Mrs Barker. You won't hear from anyone. Think of cookies on a computer.'

'That doesn't make me feel better. Cookies spy.'

'Then think of an invisible forcefield. I'm not about to watch someone with my daughter's face come to harm. Now, please, it's late. France is an hour ahead of the UK. I need you to say goodbye. For my man to know the conversation is over.'

'Goodbye,' Kenna said, and the line immediately went dead. The biker took the phone from her ear and made it vanish. He followed suit moments later.

Five minutes after that, Kenna played copycat.

THE END

A NOTE FROM THE PUBLISHER

Thank you for reading this book. If you enjoyed it please do consider leaving a review on Amazon to help others find it too.

We hate typos. All of our books have been rigorously edited and proofread, but sometimes mistakes do slip through. If you have spotted a typo, please do let us know and we can get it amended within hours.

info@bloodhoundbooks.com

Printed in Great Britain
by Amazon